# Red

# Red

# Wine

## IAIN CAMERON

i

# DEDICATION

For Mum and Dad, I owe them so much

# ONE

The air in the rear saloon was heavy with the fug of sweat and beer, overlaid with the acidic reek of vomit. This surprised Chris Fletcher as he had taken the ferry between the UK and France many times before and didn't think the seas were rough tonight. Whatever the reason, this crossing didn't agree with some people and he decided to get out of their way for a bit and take some air on deck.

According to a leaflet he'd read in the past, most likely the time when his e-reader had run out of juice and his back-up paperback lay somewhere at the bottom of his rucksack, this ferry had been refurbished three years ago. By the look of the rust on the structure, the narrow walkways and the marked and scarred walls, the refurb didn't do much good as the old tub was past its best.

He wasn't a fan of ferries and looked back with affection on the days of Hoverspeed, a time when he and his father would often go to France so Dad could buy wines for the company he worked for then. To his juvenile eyes, travel had been an adventure; to walk up to that giant machine, its rear fans idling with malevolent intent and its rubber skirt slapping in and out of the waves impatiently.

When the mighty turbines started to turn, the

hovercraft would rise majestically on a curtain of air and skim across the water faster than any ferry. Inside, the noise could halt conversations, the smell of fumes could make the anxious traveller sick and the bang it made when it hit some of the larger waves would scare many children older than him; but he didn't care, he loved it.

He walked to a railing, close to the stern of the ship and gazed at the lights of Dieppe, small white dots retreating into the distance. Breathing in lungfuls of salt-encased air, thick with the moisture of the fast cooling day and tinged with a hint of funnel smoke and diesel, he stood there unmoving for five, ten minutes. The sound of movement behind him broke his reverie.

'Hello Chris.'

He turned. Two men faced him. It was dark with no deck lights nearby, so he couldn't see their faces, but he could tell that one was of average height and stocky, and the other tall and thin.

'Can I help you? How do you know my name?'

'You've been blabbing your mouth off, mate,' the tall one said. He sounded young but sure of himself. The accent was London but he couldn't say where.

'What? What are you on about?'

'Don't come the fucking innocent with us,' the stocky guy said. 'We know you've been talking to people. You were seen yakking to the American investigator who's been sniffing around Château Osanne, the place where you work. Or should I say, used to work. Ha, ha.'

'How do you know? Who are you?'

'What did you tell the American?'

'I didn't tell him anything.'

'But you did speak to him?'

'What is this? Yeah, I spoke to him, but it wasn't anything–.'

'Like, you were just passing the time of day, was you?'

'No, I...I...'

Something whacked him on the back of the head and before he could catch a grip of the hand rail, his knees turned to jelly and he slumped down on the deck, warm blood dribbling down his cheek. He blacked out for a second, and when conscious again, he felt weightless, as if flying.

Chris struck the freezing water with a thump. The shock sucked all the wind out of his lungs, leaving him breathless. He clawed for air, his clothes and boots hindering his movements as they filled with water. Damn! Why couldn't he wear trainers like everybody else?

He swam and swam but still couldn't find air or relief from the dull ache building up in his lungs. He tried to swim harder, desperate for oxygen but realised only too late; his strokes were taking him down, not up.

# TWO

Detective Inspector Angus Henderson, Surrey and Sussex Police Major Crime Team, signed the overtime report and added it to his groaning out-tray, the result of a decidedly productive afternoon session. He could never fathom how in the days just before he went on holiday, he sailed through admin like a hot knife through butter, while at other times it felt like walking through treacle.

Perhaps it had also something to do with him moving into a house following three years in a flat, something he hadn't done since leaving his former wife, Laura, in Scotland and relocating to Sussex. He hadn't made this move on his own, though, as his girlfriend Rachel Jones had also sold her apartment in Hove and they'd pitched in together to buy the house in College Place, so called as it was located down the hill from Brighton College in Kemptown

Rachel worked as a journalist at Brighton's main newspaper, *The Argus,* and while his job interfered more often with their social life, the start of summer was a busy time for her, with a diary choc-full of country fairs, agricultural shows and village festivals. For Angus, it was the time of the year when he looked forward to spending some weekends aboard his boat, as the winter had been dreary with rain, high winds and the occasional Atlantic storm.

An hour later, he'd finished all his admin but rather than rest and admire the heaped out-tray, he left the office and walked into the Detectives' Room. It was nearing the end of a long day for many, evidenced by drooping shoulders and bins filled to overflowing with brown plastic coffee cups and screwed up paper; so much for the Force's attempts at encouraging recycling.

DS Carol Walters looked happier than some, which meant she had either got shot of a tiresome boyfriend or had just met a new one. Henderson had been there too many times before, putting his foot in it by asking, so he said nothing. She would tell him in her own time.

'Afternoon, gov.'

'Hi Carol. How's it going with the coastguard?'

She reached across her desk for a paper buried under an untidy pile. 'It seems the coastguard, customs, the lifeboat service and everybody else who has anything to do with our part of the English Channel, are either out looking for a missing swimmer, or are tied up sorting out the freighter that ran aground near Shoreham a few days back.'

'Bloody hell,' Henderson said.

'It's not my fault, I'm only the messenger. It means I don't think anyone will be free to look at our case until the middle of next week.'

'I don't believe it,' he said banging his fist on the desk in frustration. 'They could be landing the guns tonight for all we know and the coastguard and all the rest of that shower are too busy worrying about some idiot who's probably sitting in a cafe drinking a mug of hot cocoa. How long is it since we spotted the van?'

She searched through some papers. 'The report we got from the guy at the weighbridge is dated two weeks ago.'

'Damn. We'd be in a better place if we hadn't let them get away.'

'They did crash through a closed level crossing barrier and miss getting smacked by a train by only a few feet. I'm sure you'd rather that than two dead cops.'

'Yeah, but it doesn't stop me wanting a more favourable outcome.'

'You're a tough man to please.'

'So people tell me. Is there anyone else we could use on land?'

'I don't think so, as we don't know the exact location where they'll dock. It could be anywhere along the coast, which is why we need the assistance of our sea people.'

Henderson was about to let off steam when his mobile rang.

'Yes?'

'Hello Angus, who's been pulling your chain? Don't answer that. It's the front desk here, in case you didn't know. I've got a Mr Fletcher here to see you.'

'Fletcher? I haven't got any meetings booked for the rest of the day.'

'All I know is he came in and asked to speak to a senior detective. He says it's about something important, so I thought of you.'

'Steve, you're all heart, or are you still sore over the

fifty I took off you at poker the other night?'

'I'm a big boy, Inspector, I'm over it but don't think I won't win it back.'

'No chance, the way you play. Give me a few minutes and I'll come down and talk to him.'

Henderson put the phone back in his pocket and looked at Walters. 'So, there's nothing we can progress until next week?'

'Nope.'

'Right, first thing Monday, get straight on the phone and make sure they're working on this. You never know, the smugglers might be delayed. Don't forget,' he said as he started to walk away, 'the Highlands may be backward in some ways, but we get a decent phone service in Fort William and I'll be checking up to make sure something's going on.'

'Trust me gov, I'm a detective.'

'She says, as the shit hits the fan.'

Henderson walked downstairs to Reception. He pushed through the double doors at the bottom of the stairs and glanced over at Sergeant Steve Travis behind the desk. He nodded in the direction of a fifty-plus man sitting in a short row of institutional chairs, head down, looking at his hands and not at his phone as the others either side of him were doing.

Henderson walked towards him. 'Mr Fletcher? I'm Detective Inspector Angus Henderson, Major Crime Team.'

The man looked up, stood and offered his hand. 'Pleased to meet you, Inspector. I'm Dennis Fletcher.'

'Is it something quick we can discuss here, or would you like the privacy of an interview room?'

'An interview room, please.'

Henderson turned and looked over at Travis. 'Steve, are any rooms free?'

'Yep, use three. One's busy and two's being cleaned after a druggie threw up.'

'They must have been given a coffee from the machine. Thanks Steve.'

Using his pass to open the security doors, he led Dennis Fletcher into the interview room and closed the door. He decided not to have a corroborating officer present and didn't switch on the recording machines, but he could change his mind depending on what his visitor had come to tell him.

'Would you like something to drink? I recommend the water.'

'No, I'm fine.'

Dennis Fletcher had greying brown hair and sallow skin, giving the impression he didn't get out much or kept away from the sun. He looked tall, an inch or so under six foot, and thin but stooped as if carrying a heavy weight, and by the look of his craggy features, the effects of his burden were etched there.

'So, Mr Fletcher, what did you want to talk to me about?'

'Call me Dennis, please. I'm just trying to think where to start.'

Henderson said nothing. He'd drummed into junior officers the importance of controlled silences when interviewing subjects, and if one of them had been sitting beside him now, he would have made sure they didn't say a word.

Fletcher let out a long sigh. 'I reported my son,

Chris, missing last week.'

'I see. How old is he?'

'Twenty-seven.'

'Ok.'

'Yesterday, I had a visit from a police lady who said a body washed up on the shore near Newhaven at the weekend was identified as him, and could I come over and confirm.'

He bent his head and sobbed.

After a few minutes, Henderson said, 'Did you identify him?'

'Yes, I did. It was him; it was my son.'

'I'm sorry for your loss, Dennis. It can't be easy losing a child. Is there someone at home you can talk to; are you married?'

'I was, my wife died two years ago.'

'I'm sorry to hear that. Did Chris have any siblings?'

He shook his head. 'He was an only one.'

'Would you like me to arrange for someone to call round to your house to talk to you?'

'That's kind of you but it's not the reason why I'm here.'

'No, what then?'

'I'm not happy with what your people are telling me about how my son died.'

Henderson remembered the 'floater,' the term used by police to describe bodies washed up on the beach, when the incident had popped up on the serials, a computerised system that listed crimes committed overnight in the region, a day or so ago. 'Floater' was a blanket description for a whole variety of deaths, ranging from those who fell off boats when drunk or in a storm, to those who got into trouble while swimming. In rarer cases, deliberate acts such as suicide, or criminals trying to dispose of a body.

This particular 'floater,' a young male, aged between twenty and thirty, had displayed all the signs of drowning and enquiries by local police in Newhaven traced his last movements to a cross-Channel ferry. The case hadn't landed on Henderson's desk as the investigating officers didn't consider it to be a crime, but as a keen sailor, Henderson took an interest in anything occurring in the waters off Sussex.

'Dennis, why do you say you weren't happy with the explanation you received about your son's death?'

'Let me explain. I'm in the wine business. I own three shops: Camberley, Bracknell and Wokingham, and Chris, when he was younger, would help me out with deliveries and serving in the shop. At the time, I thought he was doing it just to earn some pocket money, but it turned out he was really interested in wine. When he finished his A Levels, he signed up for a course in viniculture at Plumpton College, down here in your neck of the woods, and when the course ended he went over to France to work in a vineyard and learn the ropes. He hoped to open his own vineyard one day.'

'What sort of work did he do out there?'

'He said he wanted to understand the business from the ground up, so he went as a hired hand and did anything and everything, from picking grapes to cleaning out the vats, but he loved it.'

'Where did he last work?'

'At a place called Château Osanne; it's a few miles outside of Blaye, in Bordeaux.'

'Ok.'

'For the last few months he'd been telling me things didn't look right. He said lorries were coming and going in the middle of the night and people were turning up who didn't know anything about wine and looked more like gangsters.'

'I see.'

'He called me about a week ago and said he had discovered something big, something that would rock the world of wine, but he didn't want to say any more on the phone. He said he had some leave coming up in about three weeks' time and he would talk to me then. Two days before he died, Thursday of last week, he called. Short and sweet; he'd been fired for opening his mouth and he wanted to come home.'

'That was all he said?'

'Yes, it was our last chat together.'

'You don't have any idea what he discovered?'

'No, he didn't tell me.'

'So, you don't know if what he was talking about was a big deal, like adding anti-freeze to white wine, or something more trivial, like cheating on the declared alcohol levels on the label?'

'What you've got to realise about Chris, he is, was, a very serious boy and not prone to exaggeration in the slightest. If he said it looked like something big and important, I for one believe him.'

'Could you hazard a guess?'

'I've been racking my brain, I assure you, but no, nothing jumps out. I mean the château where he worked is a mid-level vineyard, modern in its methods and with a state of the art bottling facility, but not one of the big players by any means.'

'If we can return to your original statement. You said you didn't feel happy with the explanation you received about how he died. What did you mean by that?'

'The police officer I spoke to said he fell from the deck of a cross-Channel ferry.'

'It happens more often than you think, Dennis, especially if people are larking around and alcohol or drugs are involved.'

'He didn't do drugs and didn't drink much either, and he'd made the journey hundreds of times, as he accompanied me whenever I went to see suppliers and wholesalers. He knew the dangers of falling over the side, as I'd told him over and over, even from an early age. No, Chris didn't jump and he didn't fall, he was pushed. My son was murdered, Inspector Henderson. Murdered for what he knew.'

# THREE

Henderson threw his legs out of bed and sat there for a moment trying to clear his head. He couldn't do this in his old flat in Seven Dials, as the sash windows leaked air and his bedroom in the morning could be bitterly cold, even with the heating on. Dawdling, even with the impediment of the severest hangover, didn't come as an option.

'What time is it?' Rachel said from somewhere beneath the duvet. At least that was what he thought she said, as her voice sounded muffled and croaky.

'Six-thirty.'

'What day is it?'

'Oh, a harder question this time, Ms Jones. Thursday, I think.'

No response. He walked towards the en-suite bathroom, careful to avoid the assorted rubbish scattered over the floor, an aborted attempt at emptying packing cases last night that had ended when Rachel pulled the cork on a bottle of wine.

He switched on the shower, set it hot and stepped inside the steam-filled cubicle. Initially, he'd been reluctant to move in with Rachel, not because he didn't love her, he did, but being a DI in Major Crime meant at times he would be working a big case. When this happened, all his energies would be focused on the investigation and not her. It had buggered up his marriage to Laura, and he was damn sure he didn't want the same thing happening again.

What changed his mind was the house. They both liked the idea of living in Kemptown, and one day while out walking they'd seen the three-bedroom mews house in College Place in an estate agent's window. No way could he or Rachel have afforded it on their own, and while he wouldn't say it was the main reason they'd moved in together, without doubt it provided the spark that fired up his inertia.

He dressed and headed downstairs. More debris, packing cases, bubble wrap and lots of things he didn't recognise. He tried to ignore them all and made a pot of tea. He took a cup up to Rachel but all he received in return was a grunt emanating from a mass of untidy hair.

One of the joys of being in this new place was the garden. His old flat was on the top floor of an apartment building, and while it overlooked a communal grassy area, it didn't offer any privacy. The expanse of greenery at the back this house was small and wouldn't require giving up half of his weekend to mow and maintain, but big enough for a table and chairs and a few flowers around the edge. This being Brighton in early May, the sun was shining. He carried his bowl of granola, topped with muesli, and a mug of tea out to the table and sat down.

It was a beautiful spot, on an elevated position overlooking the tops of houses lower down the hill. From where he was sitting, he could smell the sea and hear the cawing of the chip-thieving seagulls that were always awake before him, almost drowning out the light chirping of blackbirds and sparrows in the trees and rooftops nearby.

He understood now why arty types liked to settle in this part of Brighton, as it was replete with twee shops, interesting pubs serving real ale, and a variety of good restaurants. To him, that all paled into insignificance against the pleasure of basking in the sun in your own space and listening to the sounds of the city as it stretched and rubbed its eyes from sleep.

He finished breakfast, sat back and shut his eyes. He didn't feel tired or hung-over, surprising after a late night, a few beers and half a bottle of wine. He was thinking about a question someone had asked him at a party a few nights back, did he think crime novels reflected reality, when he felt a tickle on his face that made him jump. Warm lips smelling of toothpaste enveloped his.

'Good morning, Detective,' Rachel said.

'Good morning to you too.'

She sat down on the chair opposite. With hair brushed and teeth cleaned, she looked her normal self, an inquiring, nosy journalist, eyes alert for the next story, if only the Pooh Bear pyjamas and fluffy pink dressing gown could be ignored.

'Now we've moved in together, can I expect a cup of tea in bed every morning?'

'Perhaps madam would like some bacon and eggs to go with it?'

'That would be nice.'

'Fat chance.'

'I thought so.'

'What have you got on today?'

'Let me think. Yes, I'm going to see the organisers of the Henfield Show. My boss has moved there and thinks the place could do with some publicity. What about you?'

He told her about his meeting the day before with Dennis Fletcher and his suspicion that his son's death may not have been an accident.

Rachel's face crumpled. 'It must be awful, losing an only child.'

'Horrible. Children are not meant to die before their parents.'

'So you think there must be something else to his story – otherwise we wouldn't be talking about it?'

'Now, now, put your pen and notepad away. I didn't say I found anything suspicious about his death, it was his father that said it.'

'Is it common, to have grieving parents disputing the cause of death?'

'No, not often. I've known many relatives unable to accept it when someone close to them is killed; maybe this is part of the same thing.'

'I hope you'll investigate his claims. You wouldn't want to leave the poor man heartbroken and accusing you of not taking his allegations seriously.'

'Don't worry,' he said standing up and stretching, before leaning over and giving her a goodbye kiss. 'If I did, journalists like you would be on my case and I would never hear the end of it. See you later.'

In part, their justification in moving to Kemptown and taking on such a large mortgage was that they would be closer to Hollingbury where they both worked. At the time, Henderson was based at Sussex House, and a few streets away Rachel worked at *The Brighton Argus*. *The Argus* was still there, but Sussex House was now closed, a victim of budget cuts introduced by the Government to help meet their deficit targets. They could have pulled out of the move to Kemptown, but by then they both loved the house.

His team were now located in Malling House in Lewes, a myriad of buildings tucked behind a Grade 1 listed Queen Anne building that served as Sussex Police Headquarters. His people were in a refurbished area, a more spacious working environment than Sussex House, where peeling paintwork and damaged walls were starting to make it look its age. The downside of the move was it brought them closer to the top brass, as the Chief Constable and all his ACC's were based there.

This morning he headed along Lewes Road in the general direction of Malling House, but before getting there, turned into Woodvale Crematorium, the home of Brighton and Hove City Mortuary. He parked the car at the rear of the Mortuary, a place exuding the air of a domestic bungalow, reinforced by the view over terraced houses in nearby Gladstone Place.

If the building looked normal, even suburban on the outside, what went on inside was far from it. Any death deemed violent, unnatural, occurring in state custody, or if the cause of death was unknown, ended up in here at the end of the pathologist's razor-sharp scalpel.

Most people who were regular viewers of police dramas and CSI-type television programmes were aware that one of a pathologist's jobs was to remove a victim's organs, examine and weigh them, but Henderson suspected few people knew why. It looked to be an academic exercise, the results published in dusty journals and only read by a few fellow scientists, but the truth was more prosaic.

The month before, Henderson was responsible for investigating the case of a woman strangled to death during a vigorous sex session with her boyfriend. He was questioned and after admitting his part in killing her, was arrested and charged with manslaughter. A few days later, an examination of the heart during the post-mortem, revealed a congenital defect and it was this that had killed her, not the scarf tightened around her neck by her boyfriend to increase her sexual pleasure. He was subsequently released and would face no further charges.

Henderson rang the bell and mortuary assistant Marie Starling let him inside. She was a small, intense woman with bright red hair and various metal piercings on her face. While Henderson had never seen her in normal clothes, he suspected her arms and legs would be covered in tattoos.

He donned a pair of clean overalls and hat and walked into the brightly lit area where the head pathologist, Grafton Rawlings, had his back to him, leaning over a bench and writing notes.

'Hello Angus,' he said, without turning round, 'I'll be with you in a jiffy.'

'No problem.'

Six metal tables were laid out, all scrubbed clean and sanitised, ready to receive the day's unfortunate visitors. Dotted around were whiteboards to note the findings of any post-mortem for all to see, but they too had been wiped. The expanse of grey metal, the white tiling on the walls, the pristine clean floor, gave it the look of a hospital operating theatre, but there could be no mistaking the smell; a variety of disinfectants trying without much success to mask the scent of death.

'Right Angus, I'm finished,' Rawlings said as he signed something with a flourish. The pathologist was thirty-eight with a mop of black hair hidden beneath his cap, a dark, tanned face from being called out in all weathers and being a keen sea angler, and the spiky growth of a man who would have to attack his face with a razor three times a day to look clean-shaven.

'How did the house move go?'

'Very well I have to say, nothing's broken. Mind you, it's not all unpacked.'

'My wife and I moved house four years ago, and there's stuff out in the garage, untouched and still in the mover's original boxes.'

'There's hope for me yet. When we're settled, you and Serena must come round for dinner.'

'I'd like that. Give me a shout when you're ready to receive visitors.'

'Sure.'

'You said on the phone you wanted to take a look at Chris Fletcher?'

'Yes. Have you completed the P-M?'

'I finished it last night. Do you want to see him?'

'If I could.'

Rawlings nodded at Marie, standing behind Henderson. She walked to the bank of four drawers lining the wall, looking like a giant's filing cabinet, and opened it. Inside, the corpse of Chris Fletcher. With a care and delicacy belying her rough looks, she transferred the body from the drawer to one of the scrubbed benches.

Dennis Fletcher had told the DI that his son was twenty-seven, and this was apparent from his trendy haircut, unblemished teeth and the pile of modern clothes, tagged with his name, lying to one side. The Police Constable who handled the case had found the lad's wallet in his jacket pocket, hence the speed of identification, a job made many times more difficult if he had spent longer in the water.

With the report in one hand and pencil in the other, Rawlings pointed out the key items of interest.

'Classic drowning scenario, would you say?' Henderson asked when the pathologist had finished speaking.

'I would. His lungs were filled with water, there was water in his pleural cavities, diatoms in his tissues. I have no doubt he drowned. I understand he was crossing from Dieppe to Newhaven and hearing this only confirms my belief that the victim must have fallen overboard.'

'The one question I have, is did he jump or was he pushed?'

'I wondered why you were taking such an interest in this particular one. Your question may be answered, or at least narrowed down, if your enquiries reveal the victim exhibited suicidal tendencies and eye witnesses saw him climbing a rail.'

'True. Is there anything else you've spotted that I should be aware of? I can tell you haven't told me everything.'

'I was saving the best for last,' Rawlings said, his face deadpan.

He tilted the dead boy's head and with his pencil parted his hair.

'How did he get that?' Henderson said, a strong element of surprise in his voice.

'He could have hit something on the side of the ship on the way down, but I think it unlikely as these sorts of vessels, to my knowledge, don't have much in the way of extraneous equipment.'

'You're right as it would affect streamlining and get knocked off the next time the ferry tried to dock.'

'I next surmised he might have struck something in the water, but when I analysed the wound I couldn't find traces of algae or any marine organism that might be expected to transfer from an object which had been in the water for some time.'

'Still, he could have smacked his head on a bulkhead and, feeling dazed, fell overboard, or maybe he had been in a fight.'

'Possibly, although not likely given the position of the wound at the back of the head and the depth of the indentation, but Angus, that's for you to decide. Take a look at this, it might help you make a decision.'

Rawlings reached down and lifted an arm, and there, faint against the alabaster-coloured skin, Henderson could see bruises, the shape indicative of a gripping hand. 'It's the same on the other arm,' the pathologist said.

Henderson drove to Malling House, deep in thought. The death of Chris Fletcher was bothering him. His purpose in coming to the Mortuary had been to tell Dennis Fletcher that his fears were unfounded; his son's death, no matter how tragic it might be, was an accident. However, what he saw of Chris's head injury and the bruises to his arms had convinced him otherwise. The difficulty now was persuading his boss to allow him to investigate.

# FOUR

The sprawl of greater Bordeaux receded into the background as Harvey Miller crossed the Dordogne River and headed towards the town of Blaye. It was perhaps too grand a term to call many of the houses he passed 'châteaux', as the French chose to do, since they were often no more than ordinary detached farmhouses with a vineyard, but it didn't stop him feeling envious.

Former journalist, now private investigator, Harvey Miller came from Philadelphia. While he admired the soaring skyscrapers of New York, Chicago and of his home town, there was something quaint about the simplicity of life here, as if he had been transported to a bygone age. Lying on the passenger seat of the Peugeot hire car, possessing an engine with less power than his ride-on lawn cutter at home, was a map of Bordeaux. Inside the glove box, copies of articles printed from the internet and from magazines about wine fraud.

His backer on this job, a Philly financier by the name of Robert Wilson, made a fortune trading bonds, and in his spare time focussed some of the passion he reserved for making money, on wine. He not only spent large amounts of money buying wine, he had converted the basement of his Washington

Square mansion into a gigantic wine cellar. With deep pockets and a willingness to spend, Wilson didn't drink wines from the local wine shop or cases he'd sourced on the internet, but only the finest wines around. Even for everyday consumption, he thought nothing of drinking bottles costing over one hundred bucks a throw. Harvey Miller hadn't even tasted a fifty-buck wine, but some of the stuff they served in the wine bars around Bordeaux wasn't bad at all.

About a year back, Wilson became suspicious that some of the wines in his collection, ranging from well-known French châteaux and venerated Italian producers to the new, coveted wines of California, didn't match the description on the label. Sure, Wilson told him, he expected some of the wines from sixty or seventy years ago to be corked or taste like old socks, as he didn't know how well they had been stored. But for them to taste like a ten-buck wine from the convenience store on the corner; no way.

Miller had been away from the States for over a month, first to the Barolo region of Italy and now to Bordeaux. He was armed with no more than rumours garnered from the web, law enforcement agencies and limited PI investigations about the likely sources of those fakes. They didn't go as far as to name particular producers, as nothing had been proved, but he knew now the areas he should concentrate his energies on.

He hadn't been making much progress with his tried and tested method of following vineyard workers into bars and engaging them in conversation, but a week back, persistence received its reward. A Brit called Chris Fletcher had told him about strange goings on at the place where he worked, and Miller was heading there right now.

He reached Château Osanne half an hour later, following a delightful drive past vineyard after vineyard with regimented lines of vines. The concentration of vineyard properties in this part of Aquitaine known as Cars reminded him of California, but here the properties were smaller and missing the marketing hype, openness and tasting opportunities so beloved of his compatriots.

He drove along the front of the property, marvelling at the opulence. He had never seen anything like it except at the very biggest châteaux, yet this minor league team had a high metal fence set atop a three-foot wall running all around the place. He stopped at the main entrance, further progress blocked by two locked ornate gates.

The two vineyards he had visited a few days back to try and find out something about the château where Chris Fletcher worked were both small, family affairs. Even though both were involved in the production of wine, their properties looked more like farms than vineyards, with geese and goats in the yard, and old tractors lying rusting in barns.

Château Osanne was on a different level. The house was large with an expanse of light-coloured gravel covering the area where a garden should have been. It had an impressive oak front door flanked by two Greek-style pillars, tall sash windows and high-ceilinged rooms with glittering chandeliers. To the left of the house, a triple wooden garage and to the right and behind an old stone well, the edge of a large warehouse. It reeked of money and in his business, following the money wasn't such a bad thing to do.

His exit from the small car was ungainly; he was a big guy. It wasn't a patch on the monster Jeep he drove back home with doors big enough even for him to alight with some level of dignity. He walked over to an entry phone cut into one of the stone gate pillars and pressed the large 'call' button.

'Hello?' a voice said in English a few seconds later.

'Hi there,' he said. 'I've been looking around for some wines and I heard you guys make some good ones. I was wondering if I could come in and take a look round; maybe do some tasting and buy some?'

'This is private property, we don't allow visitors.'

'Ah shoot, I wasn't aware.' He thought for a second. 'Is Chris Fletcher around? He told me I should check you out.'

'Wait a minute,' he said.

Miller could hear muffled voices in the background before the same voice came back on the line. 'Someone will come out to see you.' There was a static burst, then silence.

A few minutes later, footsteps approached. A man wearing blue overalls and carrying a shortwave radio walked towards him. He was a big man, a touch over six foot and well-built, large arm muscles much in evidence with both sleeves rolled up.

'G'day. You say you know Chris Fletcher?'

'Yeah.'

'You American?'

'Yes I am. You Australian?'

'What's your name?'

'Harvey Miller. What's yours?'

'Are you a journalist?'

'Nope.'

'How do you know Chris?'

'We met in a bar and started talking. He told me he worked here and what fine wines you produced. I came along to try some, if I like 'em, I'll buy some.'

'Chris no longer works here. He quit his job a couple of weeks back and went home to the UK. Where are you billeted?'

'I'm at the Hotel Gambetta in the centre of Bordeaux.'

'I know it. We're a private organisation here and don't normally offer tours, but if anything changes, we'll contact you at your hotel. How long are you staying in Bordeaux?'

'Until Friday,' he said, the first day that popped into his head.

'Goodbye, Mr Miller.' The big Aussie turned and headed back to the rear of the château.

As a thick-skinned investigator, he had experienced rejection many times before, but something about the man's abrupt manner and attitude riled him and set his suspicions racing. He returned to the car and stared at the château for several minutes, a plan forming in his mind. It was too early to accuse Château Osanne of any wrongdoing, but if they treated customers the same way they treated visitors, it made him wonder how they'd managed to pay for all this real estate.

\*\*

Around three in the afternoon, Harvey Miller drove into Blaye, the warm, spring sun straining the little car's puny air-con system. He parked the car in a space close to the dramatic walls built by Vauban to protect the town from sea attack, and searched for a bar. The Bar de Sports was just as it sounded, a bar dedicated to sports with memorabilia on the walls and football match on the television. A place where someone like him, who loved all sports, could spend a happy afternoon without looking once at his watch.

At four-thirty, fortified by several cold beers and a ham baguette, made with chunks of real ham and thickly-cut bread, he drove back to Château Osanne and parked in a lay-by with a decent view over the front gates. He had done stakeouts before, stalking criminals who claimed their innocence or politicians rumoured to be on the take, but he knew little about vineyards and how they operated. He had no idea if the people inside toiled on a regular nine to five, or started work when the sun rose and went home at sunset.

By six, the French radio stations with their strange brand of Euro pop, and the English-language rock stations that faded in and out as if broadcasting from Mars, annoyed and frustrated him in equal measure and forced him to turn the radio off. He could handle rock, but what sailed his boat was country music and he couldn't care if it was as old as Hank Williams or as young as Lauren Jenkins.

He closed his eyes, trying to still the voice in his head that was saying, 'Harvey, what the hell are you doing here,' when he heard the gates of the château whirr open. A large Citroen passed with a middle-aged man inside, wearing a shirt and tie and looking to the world like the accountant or the export manager; no good. He needed to meet another shop-floor worker like Chris.

A few minutes later, a battered Peugeot 206 drove out, making him sit up, but alas, it went the other way. He decided he would only follow a car if it was going towards Blaye. He'd done a fair amount of driving and map-reading in the area and there didn't appear to be many settlements in the direction the Peugeot was heading, and knowing his luck, he'd end up following the car up a dirt track to the family farmhouse.

His patience was rewarded minutes later when a Citroen Saxo approached the gate, and he could tell from the car's position on the driveway it was heading the way he wanted. When it passed, he started his car and followed. They were on the main road to the town of Blaye, a couple of miles away, and providing the Saxo didn't stop or turn off anywhere, he could afford to keep his distance.

The Saxo drove into the centre of Blaye with Miller's car close behind. They were travelling along the Cours Vauban, Miller glancing occasionally around at the great man's masterpiece, cold and grey in the overcast light but still dominating the town, when the target suddenly swung into an empty space between two parked cars. He realised it wasn't the Saxo driver's way of trying to shake off his tail, but simply the French way of driving and parking, as he'd seen it done several times before. Miller drove past and found a space further up the road, but by the time he reached the Saxo the driver was nowhere to be seen.

From here, several bars and shops lay in his line of vision and assuming the driver had parked close to the place where he intended to go, Miller walked over to the nearest bar. The guy wasn't there, easy to spot as he had been wearing a yellow top and his hair was gelled and spiked at the top. By the third bar, he struck lucky. He was sitting in the corner with three friends. Miller bought a beer and wandered over.

'Excuse me, monsieur. Do you speak English?' Miller asked him.

'Yes, I do.'

'Good. Can I have a word with you?'

The man smiled. It was the easy smile of someone comfortable in his own skin. He spread his arms wide.

'No problem, monsieur. Go ahead.'

'If I may, I would like to speak to you in private,' Miller said. He pointed to an empty table near the door. 'We could sit over there if you like.'

He shrugged. 'I don't see why not.'

The man edged around the table as his friends eyed the stranger with languid suspicion and continued to follow their movements over to the empty table. They both sat down.

'My name is Harvey Miller,' he said shaking the man's hand. 'And you are?'

'Pierre Lafrond. Are you a journalist or a private investigator?' He spoke excellent English with only the hint of a French accent, which was just as well as Miller's French was terrible.

'I'm a friend of Chris Fletcher. Do you know him?'

Lafrond leaned back in his chair as if considering a difficult question. 'Sure. He left the château a few weeks back to return home to England.'

A waiter began cleaning the table beside them. Miller turned to him. 'Excusez-moi, monsieur. Deux bières, s'il vous plait.'

'No problem.'

They made small talk until the drinks arrived. Miller took a long sip before leaning closer to the Frenchman.

'I was up at Château Osanne this afternoon and they told me the same as you: Chris left his job at the château and returned to England. Do you know anything more?'

Lafrond shrugged. 'There were rumours he was sacked but I do not know what for. You see, he also did some work in the office but I do not know what he did there.'

'What's it like working at the château? Are they good employers?'

Lafrond turned to look at his mates and gave them a thumbs-up sign. From the corner of his eye Miller watched to make sure it wasn't a prearranged signal for them to come over and hustle him. When they didn't make a move, he relaxed.

'What can I say? They are English and not so laid back as we French, always want it today; pressure, pressure.'

'Why the urgency? Everyone says the wine business is slow moving.'

'We are working on a big contract at the moment

and need to get the cases out.' He finished his drink and stood. 'I must get back to my friends, monsieur. It has been nice talking to you and thank you for the beer.'

Miller sat for a few minutes finishing his drink before rising up from his seat and leaving the bar. More on a whim than on any pre-conceived plan, he searched for bottles of wine from Château Osanne in a couple of wine shops, but couldn't find any.

He returned to his car and drove to Bordeaux and his hotel, his mind on a hot bath, his iPod playing some country music and his hand gripping a large scotch. He was unsure if it had been a successful day or not, or if it added to his sum knowledge of wine fraud, but Château Osanne was the only lead he had. Chris Fletcher had told him of his suspicions, but either because he was too scared, or was playing the American until he pulled out his wallet and handed over some of Robert Wilson's money, he hadn't said any more.

Chris Fletcher was gone and by the sound of it, he wasn't coming back. It was time to nurture some new contacts like Pierre Lafrond. It wouldn't meet with the approval of the big Aussie in blue overalls at the gate, but this was a bridge he would cross when he came to it.

# FIVE

Henderson flicked over the final page of the post-mortem report and sat there mulling over its implications.

'Morning gov.'

He looked up to see DS Walters standing there. 'Morning Carol, come in.'

DS Carol Walters took a seat in the visitor's chair facing Henderson's desk.

'How's the move going?' she asked.

'Not bad. I didn't have a lot of stuff, and where we had duplications, like toasters, we generally settled on Rachel's things as mine were a bit older than hers. I'm pleased to say the mover's big packing cases are now officially empty and ready to be returned.'

'Well done both of you.'

'We had to, as we've got nowhere to store them.'

'You should count yourself lucky you don't have a garage or a garden shed. I know loads of people who, when they move, put boxes and bags of things out there and when you look years later, they're still sitting there, unopened. What did you want to see me about?'

He picked up Chris Fletcher's post-mortem report and handed it to her. 'Take a butcher's at this.'

Like most detectives, she read the first page for a

summary of the pathologist's findings, and flicked past the detailed medical examination, photographs and exhaustive descriptions of injuries, and focussed on the conclusions at the back.

'Our cute pathologist doesn't mince his words,' she said after a few minutes.

'You think Grafton's attractive?'

'Not only me, Sally Graham thinks so too.'

'Doesn't the work he does, cutting up dead flesh, and his more traditional sense of style, put you off?'

'What, like the old Austin Healey and the tweed jackets he probably buys from the family tailor?'

'Yeah.'

'No, not at bit. I like a man with a unique identity, but I must say the casual way he writes and talks about serious injuries and organs is spooky. It wouldn't make for good after-dinner conversation.'

'What do you think about our victim?' he said.

'When I first saw it on the serials I thought, uh-oh, another drunken sod who thinks it's a good idea to try and walk along the hand rails, but–'

'Rawlings throws a spanner into the works with the head wound.'

'As a seafaring man yourself, don't you think he might have received it aboard the ship, or when he fell overboard?'

Henderson shook his head. 'I can't see it. If he jumped off a hand rail or accidentally tumbled over the side, there's nothing sticking out of a ship's hull to create a head wound like it.'

'He could have hit his head on something aboard the ship, felt disorientated and tipped over the side.'

'I'd thought of that one myself, but I just don't see it.'

'Which leaves, someone must have smacked him over the head and chucked him in the water.'

'Now that sounds a lot more plausible, and makes me think there's something going on here.' He took back the report and stood. 'I'll go up and see Edwards and find out if she'll give her approval for a murder investigation.'

Walters pushed her chair back. 'Does this mean we're going to France? You know I love the place; the wine, the food, the skinny men, but not necessarily in that order.'

'In this age of budget restraints? Don't forget, the only reason we moved here to Lewes is because they closed Sussex House to save money. She'll likely tell me I need to conduct interviews via Skype or email, but don't you worry, I'll be asking the question.'

His boss was in a meeting when he reached her office. Henderson took a seat outside and waited. In terms of a space-grab, Chief Inspector Lisa Edwards had done all right. Sussex Police Headquarters was located in an elevated position, overlooking the rooftops of the East Sussex town of Lewes.

With a population of 16,000, Lewes was not only the administrative centre for the county and the home of Sussex Police, but it also had its own Category B prison. For most towns, this would be sufficient fame, but Lewes was arguably more renowned for the bonfire celebrations that took place every 5th November. Guy Fawkes' failure to kill the protestant King James I with explosives hidden under the

Houses of Parliament was celebrated annually in the town, in a spectacular procession of banners, period dress, firebrands and a cacophony of noise attracting over 80,000 visitors.

The headquarters complex was fronted by the Queen-Anne styled Malling House, but tucked to the side and the back were a multitude of other buildings of various ages, sizes and shapes, many topped with a metallic forest of satellite dishes and aerials. The Major Crime Team were located in a large modern block at the rear, and Edwards, to her credit, had nabbed a corner office with an open aspect and plenty of room inside for holding meetings and berating the incompetent; just as she was doing now to two ladies from accounts.

The crestfallen bean counters trooped out minutes later and Henderson decided to wait a little longer and allow her to cool down. It was not to be, as seconds later the cry of, 'Angus, in here,' rang out, forcing him to rise from his comfortable seat on the leather settee.

'Morning boss.'

'Not a good bloody start is it, after these two prats messed up my expense claim. It's thrown me into overdraft.'

'I must admit, I'm reasonably savvy on financial matters, having emptied all my savings accounts and negotiated a new mortgage, but I can't help you there.'

Her mood softened. 'Did the move go well?'

'It did, we're in now and everything works, although we did have to manage without a phone or broadband connection for a couple of days.'

'How about Rachel, has she settled in?'

'Yes, but she hasn't had to live with me during a murder investigation yet; until now.'

'A neat dovetail, Angus. Why haven't I heard about this one already?'

'You might have seen something on the local news over the weekend about a floater recovered near Newhaven? They said he was a passenger from the Dieppe-Newhaven ferry.'

She nodded. 'I heard someone say something about a big stag party. I assumed it was one of them.'

Henderson reiterated the story told to him by Dennis Fletcher, and outlined the main findings of the post-mortem report which he laid out in front of her.

Five minutes later she looked up. 'Chris Fletcher's father thinks he was murdered as a result of something going on at the vineyard where he worked, and Rawlings comes out with one of those, 'on the balance of probabilities' verdicts. It's a licence for detectives to put two and two together to make five.'

'It's a bit more than a balance of probabilities, I think. Look at the head wound.'

She turned to look at the photograph. 'The tox report said he'd been drinking but not much?'

'Yeah.'

'You don't think he maybe got into a fight with the stag party boys, they shoved him against something solid and he bashed his head?'

'If so, he would have had more bruises on his face. One heavy smack to the back of the head suggests an attempt to debilitate him before someone chucked him over the side.'

'I'm forced to agree, when taken in conjunction with the bruises on his arm.' She slapped her hand down on the report. 'We need to investigate. I'm not saying we open a Murder Book and staff up, but I want you to conduct preliminary investigations. I'm still keeping an open mind, as the bruises may have happened hours before from something unrelated. Looked at separately, Fletcher's death looks innocent, put it together with his father's complaint and it looks like murder.'

He nodded. 'Fair enough.'

'See if you can find something concrete to corroborate what we have and if you do, I'll re-evaluate the situation, but not before.'

'Ok.'

'I assume some of the work has been done already as I imagine uniform have interviewed passengers and talked to the crew.'

'You would think so but I'll check.'

'Set up a small team, four or five, no more. Anything else?'

'The victim worked at a vineyard near Bordeaux. It would be helpful to go over there and speak to local police and the other employees.'

She shook her head, her expression tense. 'If I had a pound for every time the Chief Constable or ACC said, 'cost saving', I could retire.'

Henderson expected this but nevertheless felt disappointed. 'Surely we've achieved our target with all the civilians replacing officers, closing buildings like Sussex House, scrapping old pool cars, and all the rest?'

'The chief reckons it will take another two years for us to reach it. Until then, he says, we have to work more and ask for less, and this includes trips overseas.'

**

Henderson walked downstairs into the open plan area where the detectives were based. It was filled with light coloured desks, flat screen computers and a carpet still retaining that 'new carpet' smell. It didn't look as homely as Sussex House as there were no marks on the wall, no odd aromas emanating from the small kitchen and no continuous noises from squeaky and broken chairs, but he was sure it wouldn't take long.

He found DC Sally Graham, DS Walters and another new face, DC Deepak Sunderam, and called them into his office.

They settled around the meeting table, larger than the one he had in Sussex House, while he summarised the findings of the Chris Fletcher post-mortem report and re-iterated the Chief Inspector's warning about incurring unnecessary expense.

Henderson got up, walked to the whiteboard and picked up a pen. He wrote and underlined 'Chris Fletcher,' and turned to face them. 'We can't go to France and talk to local police or the people at Chris's former place of work, what else can we do?'

'Review the interviews done by uniform,' Sally Graham suggested.

Henderson wrote it on the board. 'I suspect they

talked to a few crew members and some of the passengers, but as the ferry didn't turn back or broadcast an alert, I don't expect anybody saw anything. We need to talk to them again, look at CCTV, ask staff if any aggro went down or if someone got drunk and started throwing their weight around.'

'We should call local police and talk to people at the vineyard,' Walters said.

'I agree,' Henderson replied.

'Hang on a bit though before you write it up, sir,' Deepak Sunderam said. 'If Chris Fletcher was killed because of something he found out at the vineyard, as his father thinks, if we call the vineyard it will alert them to our interest.'

Aged twenty-two, Deepak had come to the UK from India as a child, and had the blackest hair Henderson had ever seen. He came to them from Surrey Police, as the CID sections of both Surrey and Sussex had been merged to save money. It was part of the Home Secretary's attempt to make UK police forces more efficient, but just because it looked good on paper didn't mean it was acceptable at ground level, and it would take a few more appointments like this one to make it work.

'Whoever calls the vineyard,' Henderson said, 'needs to make them believe we're investigating a floater and trying to locate his family, and gauge if they sound concerned or are cagey about answering our questions.'

Henderson turned to the board and wrote, 'call vineyard' and below it, 'make contact with local police'. 'We need to find out if anything suspicious has been going on at this vineyard.' He stood back and looked at the sparse list. 'Any more?'

'Research the owners?' Sally Graham suggested.

'Yep,' Henderson said, writing it down.

'I need to find out more about wine,' Walters said, 'I know bugger all about it, except how to drink it.'

'Me too,' Sally Graham said, 'but forget the drinking part, I can't stand the taste.'

'C'mon people, concentrate,' Henderson said. 'Anything else?'

'I'm thinking,' Deepak said, 'if someone pushed Fletcher overboard, it has to be someone on-board the passenger ship. If so, their name will be on the passenger list.'

'It would,' Henderson said, 'but we're not talking here about a small hotel with thirty or forty people, these ships can hold five or six hundred people.'

'We can still use the list,' Walters said, 'to cross-refer any suspects we bring in. By rights, they have to be there.'

'I wouldn't place too much store by that,' Henderson said, 'until we know if the shipping company records every name accurately. I suspect they don't and if someone turns up with cash and say, an Italian ID card, they would let them travel.'

He turned and wrote something to that effect on the board.

He turned back to face them. 'Are we done?'

There were a few nods so he put the pen down and retook his seat. 'To tasks,' he said. 'Sally, you and Deepak take on the ship interviews. Read through whatever Newhaven have done and then go down to the port and talk to the crew of the cross-Channel ferry.'

They both nodded.

'Carol, as you speak French, I want you to take on the calls to the vineyard and the local police.'

'Mais oui, monsieur.'

'Since I've got the contact with Dennis Fletcher, I'll take on the role of building a profile of the victim. Deepak, I also want you to find out anything you can about the owners of the vineyard. Any questions?'

Henderson looked at each of them in turn but there were no takers. 'Great,' he said standing and collecting together his papers. 'Let's get started.'

# SIX

Late on Friday night Harvey Miller headed back to Château Osanne. He drove past the building and warehouse complex and parked in a lay-by about two hundred yards further on.

The day before, Miller had waited outside the château for most of the morning. At lunchtime, he'd followed two workers to a bench overlooking a beauty spot nearby. Both lads were English and they had been working at the château for several months. Unlike Pierre, they knew Chris Fletcher well.

On Chris's last day at the château, the boys had witnessed a stand-up row between Chris and the vineyard manager. What had alarmed them more was not what they were arguing about, Chris refusing to do something, but the attitude of three men known to be close to the château's owner. As soon as Chris walked away, they collared the vineyard manager and an animated discussion followed with much gesticulating and angry faces, and it was clear they were talking Chris.

These men did nothing in the way of wine making or moving boxes, but were only interested in making sure delivery vans were loaded and went out on time, and ensuring that the perimeter of the winery was secure. This was an odd concern in this part of the country, they said, as even the French guys could not recall the last time there had been a break-in or an assault on a vineyard worker, here, or anywhere else in the area.

A little of the jaundiced journalist still remained with Miller after twenty years of pounding the Philly crime scene, and he treated their sensationalist reports with the tiniest pinch of salt. They were painting the worst picture to explain away the hurt they felt about their friend for upping sticks and deserting them. He was no amateur psychologist, but he'd heard enough bullshit statements made under an adrenaline rush, the fog of booze or a cloud of resentment to think otherwise.

Like Chris, they hinted about something odd going on at the château, evidenced by the number of secret meetings taking place whenever the security people were in town, but admitted they didn't know what it might be. The boys gave him the names of everyone they knew at the vineyard and told him most of the strange activity took place at weekends, Friday and Saturday nights.

It didn't sound like much to go on but enough to keep his interest alive, and now, under the cover of darkness he hoped to have a look around the site and maybe get inside and find out what was going on. He set off from the lay-by and in the shadow of thick gorse bushes, he began to climb a small hill overlooking the château.

Despite wearing decent walking shoes, the light sweater and chinos were the warmest things in his suitcase, and were found wanting for a night-time hill climb in May. It didn't take long for the chilly night air to seep through, and by inadvertently walking into gorse bushes which were all around, his arms and legs were soon full of scratches.

At the top, he sat down for a few moments to catch his breath before moving to the edge to look down on the château. To his astonishment, the rear of the building was bathed in the bright sodium light from a number of large lamps fixed under the roof of the warehouse. It looked nothing like one of the sleepy wine businesses that dominated the local area, as this part of the château, which couldn't be seen from the road, was bustling with activity.

Two white vans were being loaded, and Miller could tell from the colour of the licence plates they both came from the UK. There was a logo on the side of the vans, but even though he was now more used to the artificial light, he still couldn't pick out the detail. He had to get closer. Taking care not to loosen the rocks or scree dotted around the hillside, he edged his way downhill and knelt behind a large rock.

From his new position, it was not only obvious they were loading boxes into the vans, he could now see they were cases of wine, each bearing the logo of the Café de Paris, a nationwide chain of French bistro-style restaurants in the UK. Printed above the logo, the silhouette of a leaping grey wolf, which he assumed to be the château's logo.

Plenty of people were working which put the bullet into his idea of getting inside the compound to snoop around. A couple of men were loading boxes into the vans while three other guys were leaning against the perimeter fence watching proceedings and having a smoke. On two fishing trips to Scotland he had visited two whisky distilleries, where lighting-up was strictly banned and enforced, as it was a bloody stupid thing to do with all the alcohol fumes around, but he wasn't so sure about a winery.

If fences could ever be interesting, this one was. It was at least three metres high and made from small-gap chain-link, with the top bent inwards and stretched between tall concrete posts. It ran all the way round the perimeter of the buildings and provided no discernible holds for a burglar or nosey private investigator to climb. It seemed to him a strange choice for a vineyard with nothing to steal but extremely heavy barrels of immature wine, and something more often found surrounding a cigarette warehouse or a depository of used bank notes.

In the twenty or so minutes he'd been there, the scene in front of him hadn't changed and while it didn't seem to be advancing his investigation one inch, his body temperature had dropped several degrees and now he was freezing his butt off. The call of the hotel beckoned, the comfy armchair at the back of the lounge beside the radiator and the lovely Nicole to serve him a steady supply of Jack Daniels. Fortified with some Tennessee whiskey, he would try and work out his next move, as it wasn't so obvious from where he was crouching at the moment.

In a final attempt to salvage something from an unproductive evening, he decided to note down the licence plates of the vans. He had a contact in the Metropolitan Police, and perhaps finding out who owned them would tell him something useful. To do this, he needed to move closer.

Peering out from behind a rock, he could see a row of bushes at the bottom of the hill. From there, he would be able to see the licence plates of the vans, but it was only half a metre from the fence and would greatly increase the risk of being seen. He waited a few moments until the two loaders were inside the van and the smokers were engrossed in conversation, and scrambled down the slope as quietly as he could.

The bushes were thinner than they looked from above, and if it wasn't for the presence of the van, he could be easily seen by the men at the fence. He quickly wrote down the licence plate numbers and looked for an escape route. There was an exposed gap of about five or six metres before reaching the shade of a building, where he would stop a few moments to catch his breath. From there to the road it was open ground and he had to hope that the bright lights would dazzle the vision of onlookers and give him the appearance of a black shadow.

He took a couple of deep gulps of cold night air and ran. He made it to the cover of the building without being seen. His heart was thumping from the exertion and his own fear, but now, standing out of sight, he relaxed. A few minutes later, he walked to the edge of the building's protective shadow, and after a quick look round, started to run.

Almost immediately, a shout went up. 'Intruder! There!' He looked behind him and although the detail of the faces was obscured by bright lights, everyone had stopped working and was looking his way. He tried to run faster, difficult as the ground was uneven and boggy, and further up the slope where it was less slippery, loose stones and big rocks made the going treacherous.

He could see the road up ahead and the closer it was, the more it diminished the effect of the bright security lights for his pursuers. He heard shouts, some in English, some in French, but there was no mistaking their anger or their intentions. He kept running.

By luck, the lay-by where he'd parked the car was on the northern side of the château, meaning he didn't need to run past the gates, important now as he could hear the sounds of car doors slamming and engines revving. The car lay directly ahead and with shaking hands he fumbled for the keys. He grabbed the door handle, yanked the door open and jumped into the driver's seat. Without buckling up or adjusting the heating and air-con controls as he habitually did, he started the engine and with a spin of wheels on the loose gravel, drove off.

With the château's lights receding from view and no cars on his tail yet, he decided to get off the road as he knew his little car could never outrun the big Shoguns and Range Rovers he'd noticed parked in the grounds of the château. The little car whined and rattled as it touched 100 kph and he almost missed the turn-off to the beauty spot where he had met the two lads yesterday. He stamped on the brakes and swung the car hard into the corner, almost losing the back end as a large metal signpost grew larger in his vision. Fifty metres or so further on, he entered a parking area, killed the lights and brought the car round in a half-circle to face the way he had come.

Twenty or thirty seconds later, two dark 4x4's raced past on the main road, their rear lights bouncing and weaving as they slowly faded into the distance. Once they were out of sight, he gunned the engine and drove back to the main road. Executing a turn a little less frantic than the one he did earlier, he headed off in the direction of Bordeaux.

As he sped past the open gates of Château Osanne, he glanced over to see all the lights blazing like a Christmas tree, but mercifully, no more 4x4's came rushing out from there to chase after him. Forty minutes or so later, he made it back into Bordeaux without incident.

He'd utilised the time spent driving to try and cool down and reduce the pounding in his chest, making him feel that his first cardiac arrest was but days away, as his daughter often warned. He also used it to try and understand what had just gone down. He had been chased from the château like a fox that was terrorising their chickens, but for what? Watching a couple of guys load some wine boxes into the back of a van?

The hotel didn't have its own parking, which wasn't surprising as it was located smack-bang within the pedestrianized area, so he drove into an underground car park close by. Bordeaux city centre was served by an electric tram service and he was surprised to find such a convenient car park as he would have expected a 'park and ride' space somewhere out in the suburbs, a scheme he'd noticed operating in many other European cities.

He exited the car park and walked across Place Gambetta. It was ten after midnight with little traffic, except a few taxis and buses. In daylight, he liked walking this way as he could gaze up at the beautiful stone archway which marked the start of the pedestrianized area, a relic of a bygone age standing alongside modern glass-fronted shops and cafes lining both sides of the street. Tonight, he passed underneath with barely a glance, his mind fixed on a large glass of JD.

The sign for his hotel glowed in the distance and he enjoyed the warm evening air, a welcome change from the chill of the hill. He crossed to the other side of the narrow street to take another look in a trendy clothes shop where a cream leather jacket had taken his fancy. It was expensive, but the hell with it, he thought, he would buy it in the morning.

On the point of crossing Rue de Ruat, only a few yards from the hotel, a young man appeared from nowhere and approached him. 'Excuse me mate, do you have a light?' he said in English.

Miller stopped as the man was standing in front of him, blocking his path. 'Sorry I don't–'

A hard blow struck him on the shoulder and his whole body turned to jelly. Before he could fall, strong hands grabbed him from behind and dragged him into the darkness of a side street. They threw him into the goods entrance at the back of one of the shops and two sets of fists and boots started laying into him.

Blows rained into his face and kicks were aimed at his legs and genitals. He was so busy protecting the remains of his good looks, he failed to anticipate a low one in the stomach, knocking the air out of his lungs, leaving him helpless and unable to protect himself.

Due to the rapidity of the attack, it took several moments to consider fighting back, as he was a pretty useful street fighter when the situation demanded it, but it was too late. They had him in a corner, too busy trying to parry the blows to retaliate. He tried to twist away to protect his face, but anything he did proved useless, they just kept coming.

He was on the point of blacking out when it stopped. Someone dragged him to his feet and pushed him against the wall. A face came close to his, hard to see with his puffed up eyes, but he could smell stale tobacco and garlic. He peered through slits. The guy had a rough, lived-in face and spoke gruffly with a regional English accent he couldn't place.

'We don't want no fucking people like you snooping around our patch. Get the fuck out of Bordeaux tomorrow or you'll get this.' He pushed a long steel blade up against Miller's nose. With a flick of the wrist his septum would disappear, just like a coke addict. He held the knife there for a few seconds before it disappeared.

'This is to remember us by,' he said. Expecting a knee in the balls, he tensed up, but instead a head-butt crashed across the bridge of his nose. A knee in the balls rapidly followed. 'You're a fucking nosey bastard, Miller,' he heard him say despite the ding-dong bells going off in his head. 'I never want to see your fucking face around here ever again. Got it, pig shit?'

# SEVEN

It was Saturday morning and even though Henderson had been living with Rachel for a few weeks, they hadn't yet established a weekend routine. Last week, after a decent lie-in, he'd nipped out to the newsagents on St George's Road for the morning papers, which they'd read for an hour or so over breakfast and several cups of coffee. After lunch, they went into town and bought something for the house, although it seemed no matter how much they spent, there was always something else to buy.

It would be different today as he was driving to Camberley to see Dennis Fletcher. Dennis lived in a large detached house in Springfield Road with a double garage to one side. He knew Henderson was coming as The DI had called in advance, and must have heard his tyres crunching over the gravel drive because when he got out of the car and approached the front door, it opened.

'Morning Dennis,' Henderson said. 'How are you keeping?'

'Good morning Inspector, good to see you. I'm fine. Come on inside.'

They went into the living room, bright and airy, lit by two big windows at either end with light-coloured wood flooring and pale coloured seating.

'Sit yourself down. Coffee?'

'Coffee would great. White no sugar, please.'

He took a seat on the settee as his host disappeared into the kitchen.

'How long have you lived here?' Henderson said, when Dennis appeared a few minutes later with a tray of cups and a coffee pot.

'About seven years. We used to move house every five or six years, all in the Camberley area mind, so it didn't interfere with Chris's schooling. As soon as I get a house just the way I like it, I get restless, you know?'

'Yeah.'

'After my wife died from cancer, I kind of lost enthusiasm for the whole thing. It's close to the M3 and the golf course and it's got everything I need but with Chris...' he paused for a moment, 'with Chris moving away and now not coming back, it's too big. When I can summon the energy, I'll sell up. Fancy a five bedroom, well-maintained property, convenient for all amenities?'

'This house would be too big for me.'

'I don't know why I even said it. I know you're based in Lewes.'

'It's not as fanciful as you might think. The Home Secretary is keen for smaller forces like Surrey and Sussex to link up, and while only CID have done it so far, I would expect other functions to move the same way in the near future.'

Dennis poured the coffee and Henderson reached over to pick the cup up.

'I hope it's not too strong.'

'It looks fine. Thanks.'

Dennis sat back in the chair opposite. 'Is there any news?'

'As I told you on the phone, we've started an investigation but it's still early days, so don't become too despondent.'

'I suppose Chris being in the water doesn't give you many clues to start with.'

'It doesn't help, and with the incident occurring several weeks back, we're still playing catch-up. Don't worry though, if there are any developments, I'll call you.'

'Thank you.'

'Do your shops not open on Saturday?'

'Oh, they're open all right. Saturday is often our busiest day.'

'Is it?'

'Yes, but can you believe the time we usually do our biggest sales is between five o'clock and when we close at seven.'

'How come?'

'It's amazing how many people head out to a party or a dinner party without a bottle of wine or spirits to bring with them. They roll up at one of our shops and after a two-minute browse, buy anything or take whatever is recommended by one of our staff. If it's an evening with the boss or an important client, they think nothing of grabbing a couple of fifty-pound bottles.'

Henderson laughed, but he'd been there himself in what felt like a previous life. 'Aren't you needed with all the experience you must have?'

'I've trained managers to run the shops

themselves. I occasionally do a stint in the local one if they're short-handed, but nowadays I spend most of my time in the garden, or, during the winter, reading.'

'The reason I'm here, Dennis, is to find out a bit more about Chris: what kind of person he was, who he hung around with, what sort of things he got up to; that sort of thing.'

He nodded. 'I understand.' He lifted his coffee cup without drinking. 'Chris was a good boy up until the time his mother died. He did well at school, played lots of sports and helped me in the shop with deliveries and at weekends. He was a popular boy and had plenty of friends, often went around to their houses for sleepovers. Then his mother died, unexpectedly and suddenly, something you don't usually associate with cancer, but she ignored the signs and when it was diagnosed it had spread throughout her body. Before we knew it, she weighed less than six stone and had been moved to a hospice to await death.'

Dennis sipped from the coffee cup, his eyes a million miles away, deep in the dark liquid. 'When she died, Chris went to bits; we both did. I went from being an ok parent to a rubbish one who ignored his son and spent his time wallowing in his own misery. Chris went from being a kind and considerate teenager, to one who drank, took drugs and came home at all hours, often in the company of one of your colleagues from Surrey Police.'

At the start of any major investigation, Henderson always ran the name of family members, initial suspects, eye-witnesses, and even the victim through the PNC, the Police National Computer. If not, something might be missed which could cause the case to unravel. When this happened, it was often in the public eye, at press conferences or in the pages of newspapers, when a grieving family member was revealed to be an ex-con recently released from a ten-year stretch for attempted murder, or a pervert whose name appeared on the Sex Offenders Register. No flags had been raised about Chris or Dennis, suggesting the offences Dennis mentioned were minor and probably earned his son no more than a caution.

'It never did get completely out of hand, but he became a local nuisance. His grades at school suffered and even his long term ambition to be a journalist got chucked by the wayside. I could always have given him a job in one of the shops, of course. I would have liked him to take over the business eventually, but he didn't want to.'

'He didn't show any real interest in pursuing a career in the wine business at this stage?'

'No. "Why would I want to become a fucking shopkeeper," was one of his less colourful comments.'

'What changed?'

'I don't know. A girl came on the scene around his eighteenth birthday and she helped, but I think by then he'd got most of the anger out of his system and was ready to move on. He enrolled at a college and took his GCSE's, and after them, took a course in viniculture at Plumpton College in Sussex.'

'I know it.'

'He stuck the course out, and I don't know if the college encouraged it or if he just wanted to know more, but it was then he decided to go to France.'

'Up to the point he seemed to have turned his life around and went to college,' Henderson said, 'did Chris have any enemies? Was there someone he annoyed or fought with during his angry phase?'

Dennis thought for a moment. 'No, I don't think so. I can't think of any time he might have come home scared or told me he felt threatened. I think whatever happened to him, was brought on by someone or something in France.'

Henderson felt the same, but he had to explore the pre-France days in case something else was lurking there.

'What about his friends and the people he associated with?'

'His friends from school and even the neighbours' kids all disappeared during his angry phase. I think he cheesed them off once too often.'

'If he was buying alcohol while under-age and using drugs, he might have come into contact with some unsavoury characters.'

'Now you mention it, I once caught him carrying a knife. I asked him what he wanted it for, fully expecting him to say it was for something innocent, like opening beer bottles or picking dirt from his fingernails. I was gobsmacked when he said it was for personal protection.'

'Protection from whom?'

'I assume from some of the people he came into contact with when he bought drugs.'

This was another line of enquiry. He would task someone with talking to the Drugs Squad at Surrey

Police and get the low-down on dealers and users in the Camberley area. Was there a violent drugs gang or individual operating locally? Were many people killed or assaulted around the time Chris was buying drugs?

'When was this?'

'Let me think. When Chris was about sixteen or seventeen. So about ten years ago.'

'I'll look into it. Is there anything else you can tell me that you think might be useful?'

'No, I don't think so. One thing you need to remember, Inspector, Chris was a good boy. He went off the rails for a few years for sure, but underneath that angry exterior he still had a sound moral compass. He didn't steal, he didn't rob pensioners or break into houses to buy alcohol or drugs. What he did, he did to himself. If he wasn't so afraid of blood, he would have self-harmed, I'm sure.'

'I understand. Can I take a look in his room?'

Dennis rose from the chair more sprightly than when he sat down, no doubt buoyed by a feeling he was helping the investigation.

If he didn't know which one was Chris's room, he could easily tell from the football and heavy metal posters, but not from how tidy it looked. However, Chris had been away from home for several months, and whoever did the cleaning had obviously been in there a number of times. The room could now be included unaltered in an estate agent's selling particulars.

He donned plastic gloves and rummaged through drawers and sifted through clothes and boxes in the wardrobe. It was a cursory search, but if he discovered something suggesting the roots of Chris's death lay here in Camberley, he wouldn't hesitate to use a forensic team for a more detailed examination.

'Did Chris have a laptop?'

'Yes, he took it with him when he went to France.'

'Would he bring it back with him whenever he returned home for a break?'

'He used to bring back everything of value. If he didn't, he said it was sure to go missing.'

Henderson had a thought. Chris was returning to the UK because he had been sacked from his job, and therefore he would have been carrying everything he owned. This would include not only his laptop and a few personal effects, but all his clothes, books and toiletries. Now, what had happened to them?

# EIGHT

'What a difference it makes, me not having to wait for you to show up. The amount of time I used to waste, going back and forward to the window to see if your car was there.'

'Did you wear a line in the carpet?' Henderson said.

Rachel nudged him on the shoulder. 'You wish, but we should have done this sooner, plus the place we're in now makes it so much easier to get into town.'

'I can't argue with you there.'

This was their first night out since moving house, a concert at the Brighton Dome. They were walking down St James's Street towards Brighton town centre, past closed shops and bustling bars. It was a busy area day or night, with groups of lads hanging around the Co-op and passing around large bottles of cider, people heading into many of the pubs and wine bars, and later on, drunks trying to make their way up the steep hill.

'It's not so nice around here,' Rachel said as they waited at the pedestrian lights to cross the Steine.

'What, the guys hanging around outside the amusement arcade, or the three lanes of slow-moving traffic in front of us?'

'The boys back there. I hate to think what they'll be

like after they finish all their booze.'

'I suppose with you living in a posh place like Hove, you've missed out on all of this, but I would see it around my flat in Seven Dials. They might be noisy and a bit unruly, but if trouble starts, the John Street nick is just around the corner.'

'Is that supposed to make me feel better?'

They crossed the road and walked up North Street before turning into Pavilion Buildings. It wasn't the quickest way to where they were going, but Brighton was one of those places where busier streets tended to be the most interesting, with a variety of people, talented buskers and exotic smells escaping from restaurant doors and windows.

The Dome didn't have the huge capacity of the Brighton Centre, and on getting closer, there were none of the large crowds that could be seen on the promenade when a popular entertainer came to town. In any case, the band that Rachel wanted to see, The Maccabees, were more indie than mainstream with a modest but dedicated following.

They were stopped at the door by security and Rachel's bag was searched, an inconvenience Henderson didn't mind after the attack at a concert venue in Paris the previous year. He thought, but didn't say, the pleasant but unarmed security team wouldn't stand much of a chance against AK47 wielding terrorists.

The previous week he'd been present at a conference about this very subject, a top level powwow attended by the police, government officials, independent security advisors and academics. The security advisors were gung-ho about video surveillance and arming security personnel at football grounds, town centres and venues like this one, but they were put in their place by government officials, alarmed at what they saw as the ruination of the 'British Way of Life.'

They headed to the bar. It was long, with plenty of standing space, but the overhead fluorescent lights cast a cold, white glow, making it look more like the inside of a students' union than a theatre. It didn't bother his fellow drinkers, as judging by their youthful looks and scruffy taste in clothes, most of them were students anyway.

He carried a pint of ale and a glass of white wine back to the berth beside a pillar where Rachel was standing, but by the expression on her face when she took a sip, he'd got the better deal as the Harvey's Best tasted fine.

'Looking around,' she said, 'I don't think we're the oldest here. Your fears were unfounded.'

Henderson was forty-three and Rachel had recently turned thirty-eight, and while he didn't expect to be the most senior citizen in the room, this was the first concert he'd been to for ages and he wasn't sure what he'd find. A quick glance to his right revealed a smattering of people in their fifties, probably getting the chance to attend concerts and other events now the kids were off their hands.

'Did you have a good day?' Rachel asked.

'Not bad. I told you about the father whose son fell from the Newhaven-Dieppe ferry?'

'Yes, we did a short piece about him in the paper.'

'I've now seen evidence to suggest that he was murdered. Before you reach for your notebook or phone to tell your fellow journalists on the crime beat, this information is not for public consumption as yet.'

'Understood, but what a horrible way to die if he was, all cold and dark.'

'It's one of the most painless ways to go, according to some experts, although I don't know how they know.'

'Even so, I wouldn't fancy it. It wouldn't be so bad on your boat as it isn't so far to fall, but on some of those cross-Channel ferries, they're so high.'

'There's something I need to tell you.'

'What, is it connected to this?'

'Yeah.'

Henderson's phone rang.

'Henderson.'

'Good evening, sir, Lewes Control here. Sorry to disturb you.'

Oh hell, Henderson thought, the first concert in years and he was about to be called out to God knows what.

'What is it?'

'I've got a caller on the line who says he needs to speak to you. Says it's in connection with the Chris Fletcher drowning.'

'Put them through.'

'Just a moment.'

'Hello, hello?'

'Hello there. This is Detective Inspector Angus Henderson, Surrey and Sussex Police.'

'Good evening, detective, at least I assume it's

evening over there in the UK.'

'Don't worry, it is.'

'Thank you. My name is Harvey Miller.'

The voice sounded strained and tired but undoubtedly American.

'Where are you calling from?'

'A hospital in Bordeaux, France. Maybe if I explain why I'm calling it might become a bit clearer. I was lying here in the hospital doing nothing and I pick up this Brit paper. In there, I find an article which says a body washed up near Newhaven a few days back has now been identified as Chris Fletcher.'

'That's correct.'

'I'm a private investigator working for a rich individual in Philly, I mean Philadelphia in the States, and he's asked me to investigate what he believes is a major wine fraud.'

'What sort of wine fraud?'

'Passing off cheap wine as rare vintage.'

'How does the fraud work?'

'I don't know the mechanics, that's what I'm trying to find out, but I know the end result. It's a bottle of wine costing two thousand of your pounds, or maybe more, but inside there's nothing but common old Vin de Pays, as they say over here.'

'The bottles are genuine but the wine isn't?'

'Yep, you got it. How they do it, how they persuade a shrewd investor like my client to buy, I don't know; but I'm working on it.'

'What has this got to do with Chris?'

'I'm a private investigator. I've been asking around, talking to vineyard owners and trying to find out if any of their neighbours are acting out of character; buying up lots of land, building expensive facilities or driving new vehicles. They'll always tell me if they know something; it's simple human jealousy.'

'Ok.'

'I'd been hitting a brick wall for a couple of weeks when I hear about this château in Blaye, outside Bordeaux, a small producer with big, smart, buildings, fancy cars, a new warehouse; the whole kit and caboodle. I hang around for a bit, wait for some of the employees to finish work and I go talk to them. Cutting to the chase, I met a guy who works at a place called Château Osanne. I think it's the same Chris Fletcher you've got in your morgue.'

Henderson had been sipping his pint but stopped when he heard this.

'You talked to Chris?'

'Yep, a couple of times. One day he doesn't show up to an arranged meet and when I ask at the château, they say he's gone back to England. I do a bit of snooping around the place later that night and I get beaten up for my trouble.'

'The reason why you ended up in hospital?'

'Yep, and forced to read every goddamn English newspaper I can lay my hands on. All the books here are in French.'

Henderson had so many questions, but the crowd had thinned and Rachel was looking at her watch and pointing upstairs. With the phone clamped to his ear, they climbed the stairs up to the circle. They'd missed the warm-up band, but judging by the racket they could hear downstairs in the bar, they didn't miss much.

'I'll need to call this conversation to a halt soon, Mr Miller, as I'm walking into a concert hall and it's all set to get loud.'

'Lucky you. It will be a day or two before I can walk again.'

'I think it would be sensible for us to meet.'

'I was about to suggest the same thing.'

'The problem for me is I can't travel to France; budget constraints and all that.'

'Tell me about it. Everybody thinks Uncle Sam's got bottomless pockets, but with Republicans in Congress and the Senate, they spend all their time trying to slash public spending. Where are you based?'

By force of habit, Henderson said, 'Brighton, East Sussex, in the South of England.'

'I don't know where Brighton is but hey, I can read a map and it will give me something else to do. This is Monday; assuming I get out tomorrow, I'll come straight over to the UK on the high speed train. I ain't staying in this place any longer than I need to. I know when I'm not wanted.'

'Smart move if the people who beat you up are still around.'

Henderson sat down. The seats in the circle were all full and downstairs, where it was standing room only, it looked packed. Many of the young people he'd seen in the bar were down there talking to their friends, hands clamped firmly around beer glasses. He wondered where the liquid and the glasses would end up when the band started and they all began to jump around. Perhaps they would be so joyous or drunk they wouldn't notice.

'I'll book into a hotel in your town and we can arrange to meet from there. How does that sound?'

'Excellent, Mr Miller. I'll look forward to it.'

'Me too. Hey, you take care.'

'You too, bye.'

A few minutes later, the lights dimmed, a roar rose from the crowd and the Maccabees came on stage. They grabbed their instruments and with barely a 'hello' launched into the first song. They were halfway through it when Rachel leaned over and pulled his arm.

'Mr H, what was the important thing you wanted to tell me about?'

Henderson braced himself. This was perhaps the first test of how they would get on as a couple living together. Rachel worked regular hours with weekends in the summer often spent at country shows, but he had a habit of cancelling well-established plans when a major crime suddenly hit his desk.

'The trip we were planning to Scotland to see my folks and do a bit of touring?'

'Yeah?'

'I think we'll have to postpone it for a couple of weeks. That phone call sounded like progress in my floater case when I thought it was going nowhere.'

She leaned over and kissed him on the cheek. Strange, he expected a slap.

'I guessed as much,' she said smiling. 'Now give your voice a rest and listen to the band.'

# NINE

The on-coming traffic cleared and DC Sally Graham floored the accelerator of the Vauxhall Astra pool car. Nothing much happened, causing DC Deepak Sunderam in the passenger seat beside her to grip the door handle when he saw another car coming towards them.

'Not much poke in this thing, is there?' she said as she guided the car back to the safety of the inside. It didn't elicit a blast of the horn from the on-coming car, but Sunderam still didn't release his tightly gripped hand.

'Do you need to drive so fast?'

'Was I?'

'You were, it was as if we were in pursuit of another vehicle.'

She laughed. 'It would help if these pool cars weren't so knackered. My little car nips in and out of overtaking manoeuvres far better than this heap of rubbish.'

'It's a good job then we're using this and not your car.'

'Have you found a place to stay yet, or are you still commuting from Guildford?'

'I'm renting a flat in Hove at the moment, but if my move to Sussex is to be made permanent, I'd like to buy somewhere.'

'Have you seen house prices in the Brighton and Hove area? You'll need to share with someone or get help from your folks. It's hard to afford anything more than a bedsit on a DC's salary.'

'My father has offered to assist me.'

'That's good. What does he do?'

'He's a heart surgeon at St Bart's Hospital in London.'

'Ah, that's why you're so skinny. You should run classes for some of those fatsos in our building and over at John Street; some of them are walking cardiac cases.'

They reached the outskirts of Newhaven where Graham ignored signs for the town centre and headed towards the docks. She and her car companion had spent the last couple of days reading through transcripts of interviews done by two uniformed officers from Newhaven with the passengers and crew of the ferry from which Chris Fletcher fell. It must have seemed like a thankless job for the two coppers who did the interviews, as they didn't know where anyone would have been on the ship at the time and how sober or alert they were.

The interviews were all done by telephone, asking if they'd seen Chris or if they had noticed the incident from which he perished, but all professed ignorance. Crew interviews had only been conducted with the captain and a few of the senior officers, but as they were most likely to be on the bridge at the time of Chris's disappearance, the detectives today also wanted to speak to other members of the crew.

Heading towards the quay, they passed numerous storage warehouses and logistics companies, either working for many of the industrial companies close by, or transporting goods on the huge ferry that loomed in front of them. Graham followed the signs for Car and Foot Passenger Check-in and stopped outside the port offices of Cross-Channel Seaways.

They waited a few minutes for General Manager Stefan Karlsson to appear. DC Graham didn't mind the wait as a steady trickle of cars were arriving and she knew that the ship, which she could see through slightly clouded windows, wasn't going anywhere for at least another hour.

'Ah Detectives Graham and Sunderam,' a tall blond man said in a loud voice as he strode towards them. He shook their hands. He had deep blue eyes, tanned skin, and the hint of a large gold chain under his shirt. The word 'charmer' popped into Sally Graham's head and this was confirmed when he said, 'You must have some Scandinavian blood Miss Graham, it is not often I see British girls with naturally blonde hair.'

'Not as far as I know, Mr Karlsson, my mother and grandmother both come from Sussex.'

'Maybe further back, eh? Come. I will introduce you to our captain.'

With a hand on her shoulder to guide her past other passengers, he led them outside and towards the cross-Channel ferry, *Brittany*. He was a tall man with a long stride and it was difficult keeping up with him. Deepak was having trouble too, but he was probably more annoyed that Karlsson was talking to her and ignoring him.

'We have 58 sailings to France per day on the south east coast of England over three routes: Newhaven to Dieppe, Dover to Calais and Dover to Dunkirk. This is the *Brittany* and it is the largest ship we use from Newhaven. It is 142 meters long, it can carry 650 passengers...'

She tuned out. At school, maths was her weakest subject, barely scraping a 'B' in her GCSE's and her eyes would gloss over at the slightest mention of numbers or a stream of statistics. Now if he wanted to talk history, or about the great book he was reading at the moment, he would have her full attention.

'... and it has a panoramic lounge and would you believe, a ship-wide Wi-Fi system.'

'Very impressive,' Graham said, grateful her inattention hadn't come to his notice.

They climbed a narrow staircase and after pushing open a door marked, 'No Admittance – Crew Only,' they walked into a room with masses of screens and dials, arranged under a panoramic window with views overlooking the bow.

'This is the nerve centre for the whole ship. It is steered from here, the engines are monitored from here, and feeds from CCTV cameras tell the crew what is going on in the passenger areas and down in the car deck. I will now leave you in the company of Captain Michael Swanley. It was nice meeting you, detectives.'

'Thank you, Mr Karlsson,' she said.

They shook hands with Captain Swanley and sat down. She was expecting to meet an old sea dog with a weather-beaten face, wild white hair and wearing a white and grey spotted polo neck, but this guy was young, no older than mid-thirties. He wore a crisp, white shirt, worn open-necked, and his close-cropped beard and styled black hair made him look more like a marketing executive than the ship's captain.

'You are investigating our man overboard, three weeks ago, I understand.'

'Yes, we are. What can you tell me about him?'

'Very little I'm afraid. We didn't find out he'd gone missing until we'd docked at Newhaven.'

'How did you find out? I don't imagine you check the names of every passenger as they come on and off.'

'No, you're right, we don't. It was another passenger who informed us. He said he knew him from previous crossings and they'd agreed to meet in the bar for a drink. When he didn't show up, he searched all round the ship and when he couldn't find him, he feared the worst and alerted one of the stewards who told me. I had a member of the crew stand with him as the foot passengers got off at Newhaven but he wasn't there. We then conducted a search of the empty ship.'

'Can you give me the name of this passenger?'

He reached behind him and handed her a piece of paper. It included the man's name, Darren Land, and a mobile phone number.

'Thank you.'

'How did this friend know he wasn't travelling in a car?' Sunderam asked.

'The victim told him he was on foot.'

'Is it easy to fall overboard from a boat like this?' Graham asked.

'Come over here and I'll show you.' They walked to the side of the large room and stood looking through the tall windows. Facing straight ahead she could see all the way up to the bow and out into the Channel, and on the left, over to the ferry port and towards the town.

'As you can see from the passengers standing there,' the Captain said pointing down at the deck where several people were gathered and waving at friends on the dock, 'the rails are roughly waist height. It's enough to stop boisterous children and an accidental stumble ending in tragedy, but it's not much of a barrier if someone really wanted to jump off.'

Graham didn't believe in the suicide theory and neither did anyone else on the team, but DI Henderson had told her their supposition of murder wasn't public knowledge. She decided not to enlighten the captain.

'Are those side areas of the ship covered by CCTV?' Sunderam asked.

'I'm afraid not, the cameras tend to focus on the busy, public areas such as the bars and gangways leading to exits, and of course, the car deck.'

'Nevertheless,' Sunderam said, 'I'd like to take a look at whatever CCTV pictures you may have.'

'You'll have to speak to Mr Karlsson about it. Well, if there's nothing else, I need to get this ship ready for departure.'

'We'll leave you in peace,' Graham said. 'Is it ok if we talk to some of the crew?'

'Be my guest, but when you hear the first blast of a

loud whistle, it's time for you to go ashore, that is if you don't want to end up in Dieppe,' he said with a smile.

They stepped out of the Bridge into a fine spring morning. The air had a delightful saltiness to it, tinged with a hint of rotting seaweed, bringing back pleasant memories of holidays in Great Yarmouth. Sally Graham used to travel regularly to France, as her boyfriend at the time bought all his beer and wine there, but they always went Eurotunnel. The next time she vowed she would take a ferry. She liked the idea of breathing clean, sea air, and as a keen photographer and bird watcher, she could take pictures of seabirds and the south coast as it slowly receded from view.

'He was being helpful, right up until the point you asked him about CCTV,' Graham said.

'There I go, putting my big foot in it again.'

'No, it's not your fault, I was about to ask him the same thing.'

'It doesn't really matter, as I think he told us all he knew, which wasn't much.'

'He did give us the name of someone who knew Chris, Darren Land. I think uniform missed it as I don't recall seeing his name in any of the interview statements.'

'Me neither. So, where's the best place on this ship to shove someone over?'

Ten minutes later and with Sunderam becoming more nervous at spending the afternoon in France, they arrived at the stern. There, and a couple of sections at the side of the ship, seemed the only outside places where the public could walk. The area was dominated by a restaurant and bar which enjoyed panoramic views through large areas of glass, not an ideal place to commit a crime. The sides looked a better bet.

'I think it happened at this level,' Sunderam said.

'What about the two decks above us?'

'No way. Someone below might see the body falling.'

'True, but it was dark, remember. Let's go into the bar and see if anyone in there saw anything.'

Despite it being a morning sailing, the bar was doing a brisk trade. She hoped it wasn't a rough crossing, or the liberal downing of pints and shorts which she could tell from the number of empty glasses on some tables, would come to haunt the inebriated.

During a lull, the barman came over to see them. He had been on duty the night Chris Fletcher died and knew all about the man who had fallen overboard. He looked closely at the picture they showed him, but it was a long shot as several weeks had passed, and since then, hundreds of customers had probably been in his bar.

'Yeah, I'm sure it was him. He told me he'd spent the last year working in a vineyard and wanted a beer; anything but wine.'

The barman, John, smiled at this little joke, revealing uneven, yellowing teeth.

'It sounds like the same person,' Graham said. 'Chris Fletcher used to work in a vineyard, but why would you remember him? I would imagine this is a busy place some nights.'

'It is, but he came in when it was quiet and we got

talking.'

'How come?' Sunderam asked. 'It looks busy enough today.'

'Don't let this fool you, it's often quieter on the way back from France. There's maybe a good bargain in fags or booze in one of the hypermarkets and they spend all their money on it. If it's booze, they sit in the corner and drink one of their bottles, thinking I don't notice. As I was saying, I was quiet and we got talking. Cut a long story short, we found out we both went to the same school in Camberley.'

'Did you?'

'Yeah, different years as he was a bit older than me but we knew the same teachers and all that.'

'Did you see him leave the bar?' Sunderam said.

'Yeah, I did. He was sitting on the stool there and we were chatting, and then after a while he said he fancied some air and went outside.'

'Was he with someone, or did anyone go out with him?'

'He wasn't travelling with anyone. Now you mention it, I noticed two geezers get up soon afterwards and follow him out. I said to René, one of the other barmen I work with, they both must have been feeling a bit Pat and Mick as they left half-finished drinks and other stuff on the table.'

'How soon afterwards? Was it within a minute, or longer?'

'Let me think.' He paused looking into the distance. 'I would definitely say it was within a couple of minutes. I didn't really think anything of it at the time, but you know, you look at things more closely when it's quiet. It gives me something to do.'

'Did you notice anything else?'

'No, I didn't because soon after, a couple of guys with money to burn as they'd been working on a building site in France, came up here and gave me a big order. Tied me up good style for the next ten minutes.'

# TEN

DI Henderson strolled through the entrance of the Queens Hotel on Brighton seafront with the confidence of a resident, and took the stairs to the third floor two-at-a-time. Halfway along the corridor he knocked on a door. There was a delay of about a minute before a tall man with untidy white hair and glasses opened it.

'Detective Inspector Henderson? Good to meet you. Harvey Miller.'

They shook hands.

'Sorry it took me so long to answer, I still can't walk as well as I used to.'

'It's ok.'

'Come in. You want a coffee?'

'Sure.'

Expecting him to call down to room service, Miller surprised him by filling a water receptacle from the bathroom and starting up a Nespresso machine, a slightly smaller version than the one Henderson had at home.

The room, which he assumed was a suite, faced the front of the building, and through long, double-glazed windows which were spotted with salt residue, he could see the Palace Pier, Esplanade and the pebble beach. It was a delightful view on a warm and sunny spring morning, but he could imagine it would be a grim outlook during January and February when winter gales came calling, some so strong they could lift tons of pebbles from the beach and dump them on the Esplanade.

'It's a nice room you have here,' Henderson said. 'You have a great view.'

'I know we Americans always bitch about the small rooms in Europe, but I kinda like them. It suits me, especially as I'm often travelling alone.'

Henderson took a seat near the window where a two-seat settee and chair with matching coffee table were placed. Looking closely at Miller now he could see bruises on his face, the stiff way he moved his arm, and the limp in his leg when he walked over and handed him a mug of coffee.

'How are the injuries, Harvey? Are you expected to make a full recovery?'

He put his own mug on the table and slumped into the chair opposite. 'I've been better, for sure, but I've had worse. Philly can be a rough place too.'

'Tell me what happened in France.'

Miller relayed the story of his talks with Chris Fletcher, losing contact, meeting Pierre, his evening of watching vans at Château Osanne and being beaten up as he walked back to his hotel in Bordeaux.

'You're sure the guys who attacked you were from the vineyard?'

'I didn't get a good look at them as it was dark and they caught me by surprise, but it was what they said. A small stocky guy stuck a knife in my face and said "We don't want your sort snooping around here," or something. The only place I'd been snooping around was at the vineyard.'

Henderson laughed. 'You do a good English accent.'

'Years of watching British TV shows.'

'How did you become involved in this?'

'This story goes back a long way. Over the years, there have been regular reports in the US papers about wine fraud, tucked away in the depths of a newspaper, but it never really broke the surface. Then Robert Wilson approached me. He's a well known party giver and fund raiser in Philly, and knows all the influential people in the town. He's proud of the wine he serves when he hosts a reception or party.'

'What sort of wine does he buy?'

'Top-end stuff from France, Italy, the US. He goes to a couple of auctions a month and spends tens of thousands of dollars each visit. Here's something you maybe didn't realise, rich folks who buy a two thousand dollar bottle of wine most times don't have any intention of drinking it.'

'You're right, I didn't.'

'It's true. They don't usually buy one bottle, but six or twelve in an old wooden case, and keep it in air-conditioned wine cellars. When friends come round to a dinner party, they show them what smart wine connoisseurs they are. Some people do it simply for investment, as at times wine has been a better long-term bet than classic cars or stamps, but you can be sure they still show it off to their friends.'

'So they buy a case of wine, don't open any of the bottles, keep it for a few years and then what, sell it to someone else?'

'The cases are worth more if they're intact; same for classic cars. A special case of really old wine might change hands every five or ten years, or some collector could lock it away for decades.'

'Ah, I get it,' Henderson said. 'If the owner never opens a bottle and tastes what's inside, he'll never know if it's the genuine article or not.'

'Precisely. This is what the fraudsters are basing their business model on.'

'Until you and Robert Wilson came along.'

'You've got to understand a little about Robert. He was a corporate raider, crash and burn, anything to shift stock prices. He's retired now and according to the man himself, he's slowed down, but the attitudes that served him well for years in business still glow bright. He buys wine to drink and keep, not sell. He's so rich he doesn't need the money.'

'I guess he found this out when he opened one of his expensive bottles?'

'He's done it a number of times. He first noticed a problem when he opened a bottle of Château Latour 1935, the year his mother was born. This from a case that had set him back nearly twenty-thousand bucks. He says, particularly with really old bottles, the wine inside could be corked or oxidised...you following me?'

'I think so.'

'A case of wine may have changed hands a few times and there's no way of knowing if any of the previous owners really looked after it.'

'I suppose it's the same with a classic car. You

assume the previous owners had the thing serviced and kept it out of the rain, but you don't really know for sure.'

'Exactly. With this 1935 bottle, it didn't taste off but it didn't taste anything special either. The wine inside looked fine, it smelled ok but it tasted like something out of a ten-buck bottle.'

'Did he try any others?'

'Sure. The same wine was in each of the bottles in the case but it wasn't Château Latour.'

Henderson did the maths. If the faking gang had been operating for a few years and selling regularly, with a profit of five hundred or a thousand pounds on each bottle, they must be making millions.

'What's the mechanics of the trade? I presume if it was easy, more people would be involved.'

'Robert buys most of his wine from auction so I assume it's coming through there.'

'Is it easy to sell wine at auction?'

'To sell anything, including wine, requires a thing that auction people call provenance. They need to know where your Picasso painting or Greek urn has come from, who used to own it, why you're selling it, the full nine yards. They don't go as far as asking you to produce a birth certificate, as people do find things in attics and flea markets, but as long as it comes from a reputable dealer or a known collection, it will be auctioned and buyers will bid.'

'I've heard of fake art being passed off at auctions but never wine. Have you tracked any of it down? Do you know, for example, the auction house they use or the name of the dealer representing them?'

'Nope, nothing yet. I was nurturing Chris as a new contact when he disappeared. What did you find out from your end?'

'Chris was first reported as a drowning, a man who had fallen from a cross-Channel ferry. When his father came to see me, he talked about his suspicions and we took a closer look at the post-mortem; an autopsy to you. I believed then, and I haven't heard anything today to contradict it, there are enough questions over his death to conduct an investigation.'

'I see.'

'Chris left his lodgings in Blaye on Saturday morning and took the train to Dieppe where he boarded the evening ferry to Newhaven. He didn't arrive in England, and the first time anyone realised he was missing was when a man travelling on the ferry who knew Chris, alerted the captain.'

'Didn't they look for him on-board?'

'They did, they searched the ship.'

'Did they conduct a sea search?'

Henderson shook his head. 'The captain, rightly or wrongly, took the view that the person who reported Chris missing was a bit drunk and might have been mistaken. According to our witness, the ship docked approximately an hour or so after the time he thought Chris fell in; no one could survive in the water around there for more than fifteen to twenty minutes.'

'It's that cold?'

'Very cold, especially in spring. His body was washed ashore on Thursday and after being identified, Chris's father, Dennis, came to see me and told me he believed his son had been murdered. So far, we've talked to the ship's crew, the guy Chris knew on board, Chris's father, local police and we're trying to make contact with the vineyard where Chris worked.'

'Good luck dealing with them. Do you think he was murdered?'

'Chris's father thinks so. I think we've seen enough evidence to suggest his death looks suspicious.'

'I'm with Chris's father, I think he was murdered too. I believe it happened because he was about the disclose what was going on at the château.'

'I wouldn't put it so bluntly, Harvey. You were beaten up for snooping around the château, and one of their former workers is dead, all that is clear, but what else do we have? Do you know something you're not telling me?'

'You didn't see the château. It's big, way bigger than you would expect for a small-time producer like them. Plus the warehouse, the grounds, the buildings all looked well-maintained. The place reeks of money.'

'I know what you mean.'

'What I did before I met Chris was talk to other producers in the area and ask them if any of the competition were doing well, you know, batting above the area's average. Loads of them talked about Château Osanne and how the owners had rebuilt the château and built a new warehouse and fences, and yet they believed the château's wines were no better than their own. They're all as jealous as hell.'

'Maybe they export to Japan and the US. From what I know from the odd visit to France, many small producers can't be bothered with export and supermarkets, and only sell through a local distributor.'

'The other vineyard owners said the same.'

'But you don't believe it?'

'The smart buildings, late night activities and the death of Chris; there's too many coincidences for my liking.'

'I'm beginning to agree with you. What do you know about the château?'

'It was started by a former British Army captain in 1885. His name was George Wolf, hence the wolf on the wine bottle label. The name of the château comes from Osanne Fevrier, the love of the captain's life. The vineyard stayed in the family until the end of the Second World War when it fell into disrepair. It was revived in the nineteen seventies by a group of entrepreneurs who revived it and then sold it, and it's been bought and sold every twenty years or so since. The current owners bought it six years ago.'

'Do you know who they are?'

'Nope.'

'It's owned by Château Osanne Ltd, a British registered company.' He looked down at his notebook. 'The company has three directors: Daniel Perry, James Bennett and David Frankland. I've never heard of the last two, but Daniel Perry's a well known villain in these parts.'

'That's interesting.'

'Anything else?'

Miller shook his head 'That's it, Inspector; it's all I've got. What about you? Where are you heading with the police investigation?'

Henderson gave him a flavour of the interviews

done, the research on the château and its owners, and his discussions with Chris Fletcher's father. A combination of Chris's post-mortem, Sally Graham and Deepak Sunderam's interview with the barman aboard the *Brittany* ferry, and CCTV pictures from the ship, convinced him, as well as CI Edwards, that Chris had not intended to kill himself, or had died in a tragic accident. Chris left the bar at the rear of the ferry to take some air and wasn't seen again. The bit missing was why, but Harvey's theory of a potentially multi-million pound fraud was the best he'd heard yet.

They still hadn't found his belongings, and the crew didn't find an unaccompanied bag when they searched the ship. He could only assume it had been stolen or thrown overboard. This still left the issue of the two men seen walking out on deck immediately after Chris. The team were searching through CCTV pictures to try and identify them, but unfortunately a camera was not positioned directly outside the bar.

'What about you, Harvey? What are you going to do now? Return to the States and make your report to Robert Wilson?'

'What, to lick my wounds and convalesce? No way; it's not my style. The night I was beaten up, I took down the licence plates of the two British trucks I saw. A cop I know in the Metropolitan Police checked them out.'

'Ok.'

'He tracked them down to a warehouse in Uckfield. I'll mosey on down there in a day or so and see what I can find. Man, if I can put a log in their spokes, I'll do it. Sweet payback, I call it.'

# ELEVEN

Henderson was driving through rain soaked streets when the sat-nav piped up, 'You have reached your destination'. He glanced at the electronic box and gave it a quizzical look.

'Don't you know, you stupid machine, that Barking Road is a couple of miles long? I don't know if I'm at the beginning or the end.'

DS Walters beside him didn't look up. She had been quiet for most of the journey up to East London as mornings didn't rock her boat, but now that she'd got her teeth into the file in her hand about Daniel Perry, she became animated.

'I've just been looking at his trial for the murder of Don McCardle and it reads like a 1930's detective novel. Even his wife is a platinum blonde.'

'Ex-wife. He got shot of her after his lawyer got him off and he walked out of jail. He said she didn't support him enough.'

'Strange, as she gave him his alibi. She told the court he was home all evening with her, the night McCardle was killed.'

'She would say that, wouldn't she?'

'You never really find out the real reasons why people divorce. They say one thing and if you know them well enough, it's often about something else.'

Henderson was well qualified to air his views on the subject as he was divorced from his first wife Laura, now living with her new husband in Glasgow. However, moving in with Rachel felt like a new start and it was time to put all that old baggage behind him, so he decided to keep quiet.

'Take a look at what McCardle's family said about the trial,' he said. 'You should find it interesting.'

Daniel Perry was a new breed of criminal: smart, well dressed, well connected and, to the outside world at large, running a number of legitimate businesses. In Perry's case, a successful building supplies outfit with branches all over London, a boat-customising company in Portsmouth, a parcel business in Uckfield, and he owned several properties and land around the East Ham area of London.

A call to a contact in the Met Police confirmed what the papers in Walters's hand only hinted at. Perry, with his flash suits and stylish cars, was as dirty as any street punk. The Met had been investigating him for years, hampered by witnesses who would never testify and a suspicion that someone on the inside of the Met was looking out for him.

Perry could have chosen to meet them at his offices in Barking or the gated property where he lived in the town, but he chose the place Henderson was driving into now, DP Building Supplies. He parked the car between two small dirty vans and got out. The main products of the business faced him, a succession of large pens filled with sand, pebbles, bricks, and aggregates.

'It's not a very exciting business, is it?' Walters

said, walking towards him.

'I must admit, unless I was doing a house up, I would have to agree with you, but maybe because it's so low-key and boring, I doubt many people look at it too closely. Let's go in and meet him.'

The rain made everything look grey and drab but inside the shop it was warm, pop music was playing in the background, jolly signage hung from the ceiling and the staff were having a laugh with a customer. Maybe they were laughing to keep him happy, as he was a huge brute of a man with a craggy face and a large spider tattoo around his neck, and looked as though he could easily pick up both assistants with one hand.

Henderson spotted Daniel Perry, talking to someone. The owner of DP Building Supplies caught the DI's eye and nodded.

'This looks an ok place to work,' Walters said, 'taking orders from customers and letting other people do the grunt work and heavy lifting, but I don't have a clue what most of this stuff does.'

'Me neither. I lived in a new-build in Scotland so I didn't have much to do in the way of repairs, and when I came here to Sussex I bought a flat that didn't need much doing to it. If I've ever been in a place like this before, I don't remember.'

'Maybe that'll change now you're living in an old house. Mind out, Perry's coming over.'

'Good morning, detectives,' Daniel Perry said.

'Good morning, Mr Perry,' Henderson said, shaking the outstretched hand

'I hope you found us ok.'

'No problem.'

'And you must be DS Walters,' he said, turning to face her, switching on a real smile and not the faux greeting Henderson received. 'So pleased to meet you.' He shook her hand and placed his other hand on top of hers. 'They didn't tell me coppers from Sussex were so pretty. You must come again.'

Walters didn't snatch her hand away as she normally did when someone made a play for her; interesting. Perry had a reputation as a lady-killer, perhaps it was true.

'Come into my office, we can talk there,' Perry said before turning and striding off. The officers followed.

Henderson looked over at Walters, trying to gauge her reaction at being man-handled by a rattlesnake. She simply shrugged her shoulders as if to say, 'so what?'

The office looked small and wasn't, he suspected, the main one for this business due to the absence of invoices requiring authorisation, purchase orders to action or a staff rota, covered in amendments and dabs of highlighter hanging on the wall. This was a place to prevent nosey coppers finding out something they shouldn't.

Perry took a seat behind the desk and they sat in two plastic visitors' seats.

'Thank you for seeing us, Mr Perry. I expect you're busy, we won't keep you long.'

'Before we begin, can I get you folks something to drink?'

'Not for me,' Henderson said, although he would welcome a coffee, as it had been an early start, but he didn't want anything from this guy.

'Same,' Walters said.

'It's a pity, the coffee's good around here. I insist on it as I can't do with all that vending machine crap.'

'The reason we're here,' Henderson said, 'is we're investigating the death of a man by the name of Chris Fletcher. His body washed up on the shore near Newhaven in Sussex, about three weeks back after falling from a cross-Channel ferry.'

'Shit happens,' Perry said in a cold voice.

'You own a vineyard in France called Château Osanne?'

He nodded.

'The victim, Chris Fletcher used to work there.'

'There are over two hundred and fifty people in my organisation. You don't expect me to know every one, do you?'

'Come, come Mr Perry. It's not every day one of your employees is killed, is it?'

Perry crossed his arms and said nothing.

'Is this the only vineyard you own?'

'I have another in Tuscany.'

'Is this a business venture or a hobby?'

He smiled and leaned forward. 'You don't know me, detective but if you did, you'd know I only do something if it can turn a profit.'

'Same with the vineyards?'

'Yep, same with them.'

'If we can focus on Château Osanne for a moment, as this is where Chris Fletcher worked, how long have you owned it?'

'About four years. Why are the police taking an

interest in my vineyards? Didn't you say this guy drowned when he fell from a ferry?'

'He was murdered, Mr Perry, didn't I say?'

Perry's face went ashen and his mouth dropped open, either in shock that an employee of his had come to such a shocking end, or, as Dennis Fletcher believed, annoyed that a planned accident had gone wrong.

'Are you all right Mr Perry?' he asked. 'You look pale.' It was as if he'd seen a ghost; the ghost of Chris Fletcher, maybe.

'I'm fine. I'm just shocked to hear that someone who used to work for me was bloody murdered. Chris Fletcher you say?'

'Yes.'

'I think I remember now hearing something about it.'

'At first, we thought he'd accidentally fallen overboard, or even committed suicide, but recent developments forced us to alter this view.'

'What recent developments?'

'I'm not at liberty to reveal this information at present, as you can no doubt appreciate sir, but I'm sure it will come to light once the killer or killers are apprehended.'

'Do you know who did it? Do you have any leads?'

'I can't say at the moment, but can you think of anyone who would want to kill him?'

He shrugged. 'I had trouble remembering the guy in the first place. How would I know if someone wanted to kill him?'

'Perhaps you can pursue the question yourself by

asking your vineyard manager and his staff if they know anything.'

'I spoke to the manager earlier this week,' Walters said, 'and he was less than helpful. You might have more luck.'

'He'll talk to me all right, don't you worry.'

'While you're at it, Mr Perry,' Henderson said, 'I'd like a list of all the employees working there.'

'In France? Don't make me laugh. You've got no jurisdiction there.'

'I'm aware of that, but if you don't, I could charge you with obstructing a murder investigation.'

'Maybe I'll just call my lawyer and ask his advice.'

'Be my guest, mate but you'd be wasting your money. You don't know me Mr Perry, but I don't make threats I can't keep.'

They eyeballed one another for a few seconds before Perry shrugged. 'Not worth the candle. I'll see what I can do,' he grumbled.

'Were you aware that Chris Fletcher was travelling back to England because he'd been sacked?'

'I didn't know, but you've got to understand something about wine making. It's not all about sniffing the aroma and spitting into buckets.'

'No?'

'Wine making is about farming; a lot of people forget that. The vine is a plant and needs to be pruned, sprayed, the grapes picked and all the rest, and this sort of work is seasonal. We hire people to come in and pick the grapes and then we let them go at the end of the season. People come and go at a vineyard all the time.'

'How often do you visit Château Osanne, Mr Perry?' Walters asked.

'A couple of times a year. I don't need to be there so much as it more or less runs itself.'

'Would you know if anything untoward was going on there, such as bullying or a high stakes poker school, for example?'

'David Frankland, my Operations Director, goes over there more often than I do and he'd tell me if something wasn't right.'

The name clicked with Henderson but he couldn't remember why. 'Where can we find Mr Frankland?'

Perry wrote down a number and handed a piece of paper to Henderson. 'He's not an easy man to track down as he's away a lot. Usually working for me, but sometimes on his own stuff.'

'Thank you. I don't have any more questions.' Henderson turned to Walters. 'You?'

'No, I'm done.'

They both stood and shook hands with a still-seated Daniel Perry.

'Thanks for seeing us, Mr Perry, we'll show ourselves out.'

'The pleasure's all mine,' he said but his cold, hard eyes did not reflect the sentiments of the statement.

Henderson reached for the door handle but stopped and turned. 'One more thing.'

'You people with your questions. What is it this time?'

'An investigator I know has uncovered what he believes to be a wine fraud going on in your corner of France.'

It was fleeting but Henderson saw it; a wave of alarm swept across Perry's face.

'Really? It's the first I've heard of it.'

'What, you don't know anything about wine fraud in general, or you don't know if wine fraud's been going on in your part of France?'

'Fraud goes on in every business. Wine's no different. We've had the owners wine storage facilities selling wines that didn't belong to them and Italians passing off cheap plonk as Barolo, but nothing like that is going on in my vineyards, I can assure you.'

'I thought not, but it's something we're keeping our eyes on. I just thought I should mention it. Goodbye Mr Perry.'

Liar, liar, liar. Perry was no card shark and how he succeeded in business negotiations with such an easy to read face, Henderson would never know. He had lied to them earlier and he was lying to him now.

# TWELVE

After staring at both whiteboards for half a minute, Henderson drew a line from Daniel Perry to Chris Fletcher.

'I think Perry's involved in whatever has been going on at that vineyard,' he said looking around at the faces of the murder team.

'He claims to know what goes on in his businesses,' he went on. 'This is borne out by newspaper reports that say he's a control freak and money grabber who negotiates for discounts when he's buying clothes and boasts he never pays over the odds for anything.'

'Why does he do that, sir?' DC Deepak Sunderam asked. 'He's a rich guy, owns a stream of businesses and properties and lives in a big house behind big gates with a young wife.'

'Maybe he can't get enough,' DC Sally Graham said.

'Maybe the wine-faking business is paying for the big house,' DS Walters said.

'Could be any of these things, but if Chris Fletcher's death is connected to Château Osanne and there's wine fraud going on there, Perry would know about it, and in all likelihood, he would be behind it.'

'When you mentioned wine-faking to him,' Walters said, 'he practically peed himself, or whatever the male equivalent is.'

'Sally why don't you bring us up to date with the passenger and crew interviews you did with Deepak at Newhaven.'

She blushed slightly as she began to speak. She was a confident officer in interviews and dealing with victims, but ask her to talk in public and her self-assurance went out of the window.

'We talked to the captain, but he didn't know much and seemed more interested in his forthcoming voyage than talking about one dead passenger. We found a barman who thought he'd seen Chris go out on deck. He remembered two men following him out shortly after but it could be something or nothing. He didn't notice anything out of the ordinary after that.'

'He didn't see Chris come back in?' Walters asked.

'No, he didn't, so as I guess he went overboard soon after.'

'Did he notice the time?'

'No.'

'Did you check the ship's CCTV? Do we have sight of these two men?'

'Sorry sarg. We checked but there aren't any cameras in that part of the deck.'

Graham paused, anticipating another question from Walters, but nothing came.

'Go on, Sally,' Henderson said.

'Yes sir. Where was I? Erm, the captain gave us the name of a guy who had been drinking with Chris earlier, someone called Darren Land. He was the first person to notice Chris missing and reported it to the crew.'

'How did you get on meeting him?' Henderson

said. 'He sounds a good lead.'

'He is, sir, as he gave us some idea of Chris's state of mind.'

'Which was?' Walters asked.

'A bit melancholy and down; understandable as he'd just been sacked from his dream job but not depressive, such that he would want to kill himself.'

'Perry became evasive on the same point,' Henderson said, 'and gave us some spiel about the seasons and letting casual labour go.'

'It was his way of avoiding getting into the reasons why they fired him,' Walters said, 'or as the busy chief executive of various businesses, he didn't bloody well know.'

'I think the former,' Henderson said. 'What else did Darren Land tell you?'

'He talked a lot about the search of the ship which was irrelevant as we know they didn't find Chris. I reckon he'd been drinking for most of the crossing as his memories were a bit patchy.'

'I got the same impression, sir,' Sunderam said.

'Do we know if Land's one of the men who followed Chris outside; perhaps the result of an argument earlier?'

'No, he wasn't one of the men. The description the barman gave of one well-built bloke and his tall, skinny companion doesn't work with Mr Land, who's small and fat. He told us he spent the entire voyage in the bar and only moved away to have something to eat or go to the toilet.'

Henderson sighed. 'He looks like a dead end. Anything else?'

'We haven't tracked down Chris's suitcase, but we recovered his backpack,' Phil Bentley said.

'Excellent. What have you done with it?'

'We went through the contents, logged them and sent his laptop up to HTCU.'

'You found his laptop? Good. Give HTCU a couple of days and if you don't get it back by then, head up to Haywards Heath and badger them. Ok?'

'Yes sir.'

'Did the contents of the backpack include Chris's phone?'

'Nope.'

'It's likely he took it with him when he went out on deck, mind you, a phone wasn't included in the items we got back from the mortuary. Sally, could you check with the mortuary again? It's unlike them to miss it, but they may have forgotten to give it to us.'

'Yes sir.'

'Phil, what sort of laptop did Chris have?'

'An Apple. Mac Air, I think.'

'Ah that's good as they keep records of phone messages. I'm interested in them and emails, social media and the websites he's visited; anything that might give us a clue what he was involved in and why he died.'

DC Bentley nodded.

'Have we covered everything?' Henderson said, looked around at the faces but no one was offering anything new. He turned to Carol Walters.

'DS Walters, enlighten us about how you got on with your calls to France.'

'The Bordeaux Police were helpful but useless.

They aren't interested in Chris Fletcher's death as they believe, not unreasonably, that it's a UK issue. When I mentioned Château Osanne and asked if anything strange had been reported there, they stonewalled me. How can you sully the good name of a fine French wine producer without evidence blah, blah, blah?'

'What about your calls to the vineyard?'

'The manager of Château Osanne, when I finally got through to him, is a charming bloke called Rene Fournier, but he said more or less the same thing. Chris died on a cross-Channel ferry when it was close to England, and as Chris no longer worked at his vineyard, it wasn't his responsibility.'

'No sympathy for the dead?' Phil Bentley asked.

'Nope. He's wiped his hands of him.'

'This just leaves us one more item to consider: the victim,' Henderson said. 'You've all seen the profile I wrote after talking to Chris Fletcher's father. Chris had troubled teenage years after his mother died and it led him into drink and drugs. I put a call into our colleagues at Guildford to find out if there was a history of violence among drug dealers and users in the Camberley area around that time.'

'I'll follow that up for you sir, if you like,' Sunderam offered. 'I know quite a few officers in the drugs squad.'

'I was just about to ask. You do that. The guy I spoke to was DS Ken Haines.'

Sunderam nodded. 'I know him.'

'Dennis Fletcher said Chris had sorted himself out and didn't detect any problems the last time his son came home on leave about three months ago.'

'It depends on how well his father knew him,' Phil Bentley said. 'We've all heard of drug addicts and dealers that parents knew nothing about.'

'I agree, and it serves to remind us to keep an open mind,' Henderson said. 'There may be wine faking going on at the château and we know Chris is dead, but we don't know yet if or how the two are related. At the moment, we've only got Dennis Fletcher and Harvey Miller's suspicions and theories to support the connection.'

**

After the team meeting, Henderson returned to his office. It was a brighter room than the old one at Sussex House, with views over nearby woods, and better quality furniture, but the more space he had, the more people were tempted to dump boxes in it.

He didn't say so at the team meeting, but they were running out of places to look for a motive that could explain Chris Fletcher's death. If the château was based in the UK, he could put them under surveillance and find out what they were doing, or obtain a warrant and raid the place. In France, as Daniel Perry so rightly said, he had no such jurisdiction. He'd considered keeping a watch on the Uckfield warehouse that Harvey Miller mentioned, but the DI could see nothing there but a dead-end, and if Miller wanted to stake it out for a few fruitless days, he was welcome to it.

If he believed Dennis Fletcher, and he had no reason to doubt him, Chris didn't die as a result of some criminal activity on his part. It was caused either by an accident aboard the ship, not likely based on what he'd heard so far, or he was killed by someone on-board. Perhaps by the two men seen heading out on deck shortly after Chris, or other persons not identified yet. The only lead they had left was Daniel Perry's head of operations, David Frankland. Henderson could try and put more pressure on Daniel Perry, as the owner of the vineyard he had to know what was going on; but with what evidence?

He picked up his jacket and headed downstairs. He went outside and made his way across the courtyard to the staff restaurant. They didn't have this level of eating luxury at Sussex House, but because so many admin and operating services were based in Lewes, the likes of 999 and 101 services, finance, HR, website specialists and all the usual functions of a large and complex business employing around five thousand people, it was a necessity.

The one disadvantage of such a place, besides adding the occasional inch or two to his girth, was that most of the top brass appeared there at some point in the day. To be fair, many of them didn't get out much on investigations and operations due to the administrative rigours of the job, and so they tried to collar people like him to try and catch up with all the news. As if reading his mind, CI Lisa Edwards spotted him and waved him over.

He put his tuna and sweetcorn baguette and coffee down on the table and took a seat opposite.

'Afternoon, ma'am. I didn't expect to find you in here at this late hour of the afternoon.'

'The ACC decided to hold one of his regular working lunches in here,' she said as she sipped a cup of coffee. 'I prefer to do it within the confines of his office with food brought in, as there are too many distractions in a place like this. Plus it's hard to talk confidential stuff with all the professional ear-wiggers about.'

'First whiff of a decent story and it's all over the Airwave sets.'

'It's the internet I worry about,' she said. 'I don't know if you're aware Angus, but many officers and detectives are secret bloggers.'

'I knew a few were doing it.'

'There's loads doing it now. You've got 'My Life as a Bobby,' 'The Bored CID Detective,' 'Death from Forensics'; there's no secrets, even here. That's enough tub-thumping from me, how are you getting on with the Chris Fletcher case?'

He gave her a synopsis of the work completed and what they had discussed at the last murder team meeting. She nodded, no doubt mentally ticking off all the things that she would do if it was her case.

'Where did you leave it with the private investigator, Miller?'

'He says he knows where the vans from the château go; the ones he saw the night he was beaten up. Somewhere in Uckfield apparently, and he's going over there to take a look. At first, I thought it was a job for us, but after some thought, I decided no, it's probably a wine delivery depot. '

'Hmm,' she said, thinking. 'You could be right. Let Miller go there and stake out the warehouse, we don't have the manpower to do such things on the basis of a hunch. I'm assuming it wouldn't be putting him in any danger?'

'He's an experienced investigator and a former crime journalist and should know what to do if things start to turn sour.'

'What about this name Perry gave you, David Frankland? Have you talked to him?'

'No, not yet.'

'Do it soon,' she said. 'I don't want this case grinding to a halt and the ACC saying he warned me it was all a waste of money.'

'I get the impression that Frankland is Perry's go-to guy for problems solving. He might be called the operations head or whatever, but if he's required to do something dirty, he'll do it.'

'He sounds like a nice bloke, but don't underestimate Perry, Angus. He's a violent streetwise geezer who might wear flashy suits and drive smart cars, but underneath, he's evil. The Met have been trying to put him away for years but something always gets in the way and they're forced to back off.'

'So I heard.'

'I assume you're liaising with them. I don't want a call from that tosser Commander Tom Waite, chewing my ear off because one of my officers dared step on to his patch.'

'I've talked to them. The message I'm getting is I can do what I want, as they've got nothing on him, but they want a piece of the action if I do.'

'They backed away from Perry after the McCardle trial collapsed. Too bloody embarrassed if you ask me.'

'This was the land deal that went wrong?'

'It went right for Perry. McCardle was a property developer who got into debt. His mistake was not financing his shortfall from banks as a normal businessman would do, but from 'friends' in East London finance companies. When he couldn't pay the interest, they threatened to break his legs. He turned to Perry. He sorted everything out and in return, acquired a strip of land containing nothing but half a dozen derelict warehouses with fine views over a stretch of the River Thames.'

'The land turned out to be worth something, I thought.'

'It did. An American bank decided they wanted to build their European HQ there and paid Perry millions for the land. McCardle, realising he'd passed up the chance to become rich, threatened to sue Perry claiming he'd been duped into selling the land. The rest, as they say, is history.'

'Especially for McCardle.'

'Yes, especially for him. Have you seen pictures of Perry's new wife?'

'No.'

'Check her out on the web if you want a treat. She's a twenty-nine-year-old ex-model, only ex because her hubby's so rich she doesn't have to work. Hits the gym at five every morning and does a couple of hours every day.'

'She deserves a slim figure if she can hit a gym at five in the morning. I know I couldn't.'

Edwards stood. 'I need to go. Remember what I

said, Angus, watch yourself with Daniel Perry. He's dirty and devious and he's got a lot of low-life friends. Make sure you build a strong case against him if you're convinced he's behind this. Plenty have tried and failed and I don't want you to be one of them.'

# THIRTEEN

It was three o'clock in the morning and private investigator Harvey Miller was in the company of Billy Rush, a career burglar he'd sought out in a seedy bar near Uckfield Station. In the US, the hungry look often gave people like Billy away, but here in the UK, it was the ferret-like way they scanned a room looking for phones, abandoned handbags and undercover cops.

They met in a car park and the back of a recently constructed housing development and walked across scrubland before dipping into a thin line of trees bordering the Bell Lane Industrial Estate. In a hushed voice, Rush explained the routine of the mobile security guards patrolling roads nearby and the position of CCTV cameras dotted around the building they were approaching.

For a couple of days last week, Miller had staked out a warehouse at the Bell Lane Industrial Estate in Uckfield. This was the place where his contact in the Met said the vans seen at Château Osanne in France ended up, and true to his contact's word, he spotted them. Problem was, close up they were run-of-the-mill delivery vans. To compound their ordinariness, the boxes he could see inside the warehouse of PFB Parcels, where the vans were parked, were boxes of wine from Château Osanne, bearing the logo of the Café de Paris, a UK restaurant chain.

This would have been enough to send a rookie investigator scuttling back to Brighton to pack his bags and hop on the next plane back to the States. Then, when he'd summoned up enough courage, he'd report back to Robert Wilson and tell him that his investigation had reached a big fat dead-end; but no. Harvey Miller always had bags of patience, persistence and sheer bloody mindedness and they received their reward when he got out of the car and went out for a stroll.

It was then he noticed that the parcel business didn't occupy the full length of the warehouse. One end of the building appeared to be sectioned off, the windows blacked out with no visible markings. He initially believed it was empty, surplus space that the PFB Parcel business didn't need, but this all changed when a van pulled up outside and someone disappeared inside the 'secret' part of the warehouse. The van belonged to Fraser Brook's Fine Wines, and half an hour later, he spotted two men loading a number of heavy boxes into the back of the van.

Billy Rush was young, late twenties, but prison had added lines to his drawn face. Like a soldier, he kept himself fit to outrun pursuers, and wore his hair short and his clothes tight to give security men and the police nothing to grip if they tried to make a grab for him.

Two nights previously, Rush had come down here and triggered the alarm system by levering open one of the back windows. He did the same last night and again tonight and it was his expectation that the harassed key holder would cease setting the alarm until an engineer arrived and repaired the fault. Never fails, he told Miller.

It was a dark, cool night with barely a sound, and as a man from a bustling and noisy city, Miller felt unnerved. No one but the odd owl took notice as the two men headed down a small slipway at the back of a large warehouse, carefully avoiding rattling four wheelie bins and ducking into the recess beside the fire door.

Rush didn't carry a tool bag, for obvious reasons, and kept everything in multiple pockets of his clothing. From his jacket he withdrew a long, thin piece of metal. He leaned over and whispered, 'Soon as I lift the bar, I'll give the door a shove. If the alarm's on it'll sound. Yeah?'

'What do we do then?'

'Run like hell back to the woods.'

'That's it? Game over?'

'Nah. We'll give it an hour or so and the key holder'll turn up. Wait'll you see his face, it'll be worth hanging around for.'

Rush delicately slipped the thin metal between door and door jamb and began moving it slowly up and down, while Miller held his breath.

'Got it,' he hissed. 'This might be a bit noisy so I'll wait for a little background noise.'

They waited for what seemed like an age until the sound of a motorbike in a nearby housing estate echoed in the cool, still air. Miller was so intent on watching and listening for any response to the clatter of the door lever, which seemed really loud, that he didn't realise Rush had opened the door and disappeared inside. Miller took one final look around and followed.

'It just seems noisy,' Rush whispered, 'because there's no one about, but if anybody heard, they would just think somebody dropped something; maybe a jemmy or something,' he said, laughing.

Miller tried to smile but he was too nervous, and it felt like a sickly grin. Not that Rush could see as the windows were blacked out, leaving the inside of the 'secret' part of the PFB Parcel warehouse inky dark. When his eyes became more accustomed he could see weak light filtering in from an open door leading out into a small corridor, an omission no doubt made by the aggravated key holder as they rushed back home to a warm bed.

Despite the darkness, he knew he was in a large, airy room and walked slowly towards the middle, trying to avoid bumping into anything or kicking a hidden object. He bumped into Rush. 'There's fuck-all in here mate, except that big work bench and some offices out through that open door. You take a look around here and I'll poke me head around the offices.'

He started to move but Miller caught his arm. 'Remember what I said earlier, Billy. Don't touch anything, they mustn't know we've been here.'

'Right on skipper,' he said before he slipped away and was swallowed up by the darkness.

Miller moved towards the work bench and laboriously counted five high stools. He sat down on one and ran his hand over the surface of the bench, which he could feel was flat and blemish-free, like melamine or porcelain and clean, clinically clean, his opinion amplified by the distinct smell of disinfectant. The five positions were lit by individual overhead lamps and each position had a mobile magnifying glass, indicating the technicians working here were undertaking intricate work.

On the shelf above the bench he felt the shape of big bottles or flasks. He had brought a little torch and decided to switch it on as the batteries were weak and he was sure not much light would escape outside. He aimed it at the bottles but it didn't do any good as the labels were all written in Chinese.

He moved the torch around him, careful to keep it low and not to let the light glint though a gap in the window paint. He could see the outline of a filing cabinet across the room from the bench. It was a document cabinet with an up-and-over roller door, closed only to the halfway point where a large folder blocked its path.

He eased the door up and pointed the torch at dark shelves. A thick, well-thumbed loose-leaf book caught his attention. He pulled the book out and placed it on the floor. If he didn't suspect this was a place used by wine fakers, he would believe this was an avid wine collector's life work. Encased within plastic sheet after plastic sheet were labels from the most famous wine houses in the world: Batailley, Beychevelle, Château Du Tetre.

A hand on his shoulder made him jump.

It was Rush. 'It sounds like from all your huffing and puffing you've found something.'

'Christ you gave me a fright,' he whispered. 'Did you see anything in the offices?'

'Not a dickey; just stationery and stuff. I'll take a gander around here, looks more interesting. What's that?'

'A book of wine labels.'

'Ah great. Prefer the real thing myself.'

Miller returned to the folder of labels. Between plastic sheets were the originals, some old and stained, others faded and scratched. Reading the notes inside, he realised it was a template for faking wine labels. The job of the technicians sitting at the high stools, was to copy the details and add ageing marks and stains, which were all described in the book, befitting the condition and age of an old wine bottle. Ingenious!

He was about to remove one of the labels and examine it in more detail when a loud rattle from the front door made him freeze to the spot.

Rush moved beside him. 'It's a bloody security guard checking the doors. Did you lock the fire door?'

'What? No,' he hissed. 'Was I supposed to?'

'Bloody hell! Come on!'

They walked quickly to the fire door, making as little noise as possible. Rush gripped his arm. 'It's too late to lock it with the bar, he might hear,' he whispered.

'What do we do?'

'Push our backs against the door.'

'Will it be enough?'

'It'll have to be, or him out there will be getting a bit of this,' he said tapping his jacket pocket.

Miller didn't stop to ask what 'this' might be and instead, pressed against the door, his trainers finding a strong grip on the uncarpeted floor.

'After he does the front, he'll come down 'ere and try the fire door,' Rush said. 'It's what he does on all the warehouses.'

A minute or so later they heard the sound of boots shuffling across the concrete. Not the smart, snappy walk of a military man, but the sluggish, lazy gait of a jobsworth, forced to depart from a warm guard house to do something that he regarded as an inconvenience and not a necessity.

Miller was wound as tense as a guitar string, when suddenly the guard let out a yell, causing him to stifle a yell in response. Seconds before, Miller heard a clang and realised the security guard had struck his shin on a long piece of metal sticking out from the bottom of one of the bins, an obstacle he and Rush had been careful to avoid.

They listened as a series of curses resonated noisily in the still air, making it clear the man was in considerable pain. Rush stifled a laugh. They waited another two or three minutes, all the time maintaining pressure on the door, when the guard moved from the bins to the fire door. As he approached, a chink of light from his torch appeared at the base of the door.

His boots scraped across the concrete outside and they heard him mutter something. Without warning, he banged his hand on the door then gave it a push. To Miller's relief, it didn't move. His boots shuffled and began to move away. Miller relaxed and was about to release his hold of the door when Rush's arm came across his chest and he mouthed, 'Wait.'

Nothing happened for what seemed like five minutes, but in likelihood, was no more than fifteen seconds, then he heard the shuffle of the guard's feet; he was still outside the fire door. A voice in Miller's head screamed, 'what the hell are you doing out there! Go, will you?'

'These fuckin' bins,' the guard said to himself. 'Me sodden leg's bleedin' so it is.'

A little more shuffling and then the familiar splash and tinkle of someone pissing against a wall. Miller looked over at his companion. Rush's hand was covering his mouth, his shoulders moving up and down as he tried to stifle a laugh, forcing Miller to turn away, fearing his merriment would be infectious. At last it was finished and the guard zipped up. Seconds later he walked away, his footsteps, moving faster this time, and gradually they receded into the distance.

On Rush's signal, Miller moved away from the door and was about to walk back inside the building when he felt a blast of cold air. He turned. Rush had opened the fire door and was peering out. 'He's gone,' he said smiling.

He lifted the bar and locked it 'That'll stop him if he comes back unexpectedly, but he won't. These guys only look at each building on their patch once a night.'

Miller headed back to the book cabinet. For the next few minutes, he looked through what appeared to be the production schedule. The heading in one column, FB, had to be Fraser Brook's Fine Wines, the van he'd spotted while sitting outside last week. If his assumptions were correct, the numbers in the 'FB' column represented the number of fake bottles Fraser Brook picked up each week; sometimes thirty, other times more.

Rush appeared at his shoulder and hissed, 'Hey, come here and see this, mate.'

Miller flashed his torch in the direction of the voice only to see that the wall, which he first thought looked blank, was in fact lined with racks of wine bottles, their dark shapes glinting in the faint light of the small torch. As he moved towards Rush, he could see he held a bottle in his hand. It was empty. 'They don't make bottles like this nowadays,' he said. 'Feel 'ow heavy it is,' he suggested, handing it to him. Miller was surprised to find how solid it felt, more like a cudgel than a bottle.

'If that don't sail your boat, cop this,' Rush said. He followed the voice and Rush handed him a piece of paper. He lifted the torch. It was a Château Margaux label printed in an old typeface and dated 1945. He wasn't an expert, but it didn't look like a recently made label trying to look old, it felt and looked like the real McCoy; stained, frayed and a little bit fragile.

In a wall display of small plastic bins three across and ten down, each bin contained dozens of labels of Lafite, Lafleur, Lafon and further over, Palmer, Pavie, Petrus. He shone the torch past the labels, to a smaller set of red bins with aged corks, and white bins full of faded and cracked neck capsules.

Emboldened now, he used the torch to walk around the room, and on the wall opposite he spotted four wooden wine barrels, resting on sturdy plinths. He tapped each in turn with the back of the torch, and the dull sound that returned suggested all were full of wine. A handwritten label stuck to the side indicated three were 'Claret' and the fourth, 'Burgundy.'

He was about to walk back to where Rush stood when he spotted some stencilled writing on the side of the first barrel. He almost cried out in triumph when he saw the line drawing of a leaping grey wolf with the words, 'Château Osanne' underneath. It was the link he had been searching for.

He walked back to Rush, his head reeling and his heart racing. 'I've seen everything I came her for. Before we go, I'd like to take some photos; the books in the cupboard and those racks of labels. I'll need to use a flash, do you think it'll be ok?'

'Sure. We should close the door to the offices and make it really pitch in here, but you'll need to shield it. I saw some technician's overalls on the pegs over there. Get everything under the overall and take the picture, but you'll need to shut your eyes when the flash goes off or you'll be blinded.'

Ten minutes later, they headed back to the fire door. Rush lifted the handle and peered into the gloom. 'The coast's clear, mate. Let's get the hell out of here.'

Outside, the cold air hit Miller's face like a wet cloth after the stuffy clamminess of the warehouse. He waited until Rush locked the door using a thin strip of wire. They then made their way past the bins, stopping at the edge of the warehouse. Miller glanced at his watch, four-thirty, but still dark. They heard nothing; no voices, no shuffling of feet, no car doors closing. With a nudge from Rush, they ran across the road and ducked into the cover of trees and bushes bordering the industrial estate.

They parted company at the car park with a firm handshake and the satisfied smile of a job well done. Miller was pleased that his beating in France had not been in vain and he was now on the trail of wine fraudsters who, based on the detail he saw in one of the books in the filing cabinet, were making millions. In all likelihood, the fear of Chris Fletcher blowing their lucrative secret was what got the poor fellow killed.

Billy Rush returned to his car, a nondescript Ford Focus that didn't attract attention, unlike his weekend transport, a yellow Yamaha trail bike. It had been a good night's work for him too. Not only had he pocketed three hundred notes from the American, he had also trousered another five hundred, found in a drawer in the office of a Mr Jim Bennett.

# FOURTEEN

'Ah, this takes me back,' DS Carol Walters said from the passenger seat.

'What?' Henderson asked, 'me driving and you taking charge of the radio, or the sight of grimy ships and docks?'

'Grimy? How can you call Portsmouth grimy? Millions have been spent on redevelopment and regeneration. It's a tourist haven for all who come to see the Mary Rose, have a tour of the harbour and see what naval ships are in dock.'

'I did that harbour trip myself a few years back, but it was a blustery day and I was glad to get back indoors I can tell you.'

'What, and you a seasoned mariner?'

'It was my own fault, it was summer and I was just dressed in t-shirt and shorts. I didn't expect it to be so cold, nor for the weather to change so quickly. How come you're being so supportive of the place, I thought Portsmouth held bad memories for you?'

'It does. I mean, I loved the place when me and him first moved here, first house together and all that jazz, but you're right, it all went downhill for me soon after. You come off here at the junction for the A27.'

Henderson did as he was told, Walters refusing to program the sat-nav, trusting her local knowledge of the place she once called home.

'The roundabout after this, take a left and then you're on the Gosport Road. Even you should be able to find Gosport now.'

'I'll have you know I'm good at this, finding places on a boat is ten times harder. On a road you've got all the signs and landmarks you need, but out there on the open sea you've got nothing, and often you can't see the land for fog or because you're out too far.'

'Just because we're going to see a boat builder doesn't mean you can sneak in another seafaring story.'

Daniel Perry's yacht customisation business, Ocean Cruising, was on Harbour Road, a better address for a company of this nature he couldn't think of. According to their website, all a customer needed to do was give them the yacht of their choice, be it a Sunseeker, Princess or Moody, and they would customise the vessel to exacting specifications. This could include luxuries such as gold taps, flat screen televisions and luxurious beds, or technical advances like a more powerful engine or larger sails.

While waiting in reception, Walters flicked through a magazine lying on the table, while he examined the photographs on the wall. They were pictures of yacht owners, many instantly recognisable as stars of television, film and the music business, picking up their modified plaything. Standing beside, smiling or shaking their hand, was a representative from Ocean Cruising, invariably Daniel Perry. Snappy dresser that he was renowned to be, he didn't resort to the traditional uniform worn by yacht club dignitaries: a dark-blue blazer, open-neck shirt and fawn coloured slacks. He wore a sharp suit, hair styled and skin tanned, with an expensive gold watch and diamond ring; but no amount of dressing up could hide the darkness behind his eyes and the malice etched on his face.

The receptionist was on a call, clearly with a new lover as she giggled and whimpered like a schoolgirl. She glanced at them and whispered to the caller, 'can't talk now, I'll talk to you later,' and put the phone down, blushing. It rang seconds later and this time she said to them, 'Mr Frankland will see you now.'

They followed her directions out into a vast hall where three large yachts were suspended under an elaborate cradling system. On each, a number of blue-coated technicians were busily working. Even though the business focussed on customising, it emitted the traditional smells of a boat builder, with that unique aroma of sawn wood, varnish and glue.

They walked into a small cluttered office. The desk faced the glass panelling behind them, looking out to the workers on the yachts, while the two visitors' chairs were directed at a wall, blank, with the exception of the obligatory yacht calendar given to them by a grateful supplier. Just as well for Henderson, as the sight of all those boats would surely distract him.

'Good morning, Mr Frankland. I'm Detective Inspector Henderson, Surrey and Sussex Police, and this is Sergeant Walters.'

Frankland rose and, it seemed with some reluctance, shook their hands.

'Excuse the bloody mess in here,' Frankland said as he sat down, 'this isn't my office.'

'Do you have an office you can call your own?' Henderson asked 'Or do you hot-desk it around the various businesses?'

'Yeah, I suppose I don't have a place I can call mine, but hell, I don't mind. When home's 10,000 miles away you learn to manage with whatever the hell you've given.'

He was similar in age to Henderson, with fair hair and chiselled, hard features. He looked strong and muscular, as if he did a physically demanding job. He was Australian, but not with a rough, country accent, something more refined, perhaps toned down for the English ear.

'So what goes on here, Mr Frankland?'

Henderson knew enough about their business not to listen too attentively, but he wanted to hear him speak. He detected a hard edge to his voice, as if maybe he had mighty problems to deal with here or didn't like talking to the police.

'What's your role?' Henderson asked when he'd finished.

'They call me Operations Director but I'm really a trouble-shooter. In this place, some of our customers are big knobs on TV or in the pop business and they want everything yesterday. Daniel's job is to schmooze the customer and keep them sweet, and mine is to make sure the buggers out there are working flat-out to meet their order.'

'Do you have the authority to change things?'

'I can sack the whole damn lot of them if I want to,

but it doesn't work like that. If the guy who runs this place or any other business in the group is a good bloke, I'll find out what he needs and get it for him. If he's a bit of a slacker, I'll give him a boot up the arse first and then ask him what he needs.'

'Maybe a softer seat,' Walters said.

Frankland smiled but not warmly.

'Do you visit Château Osanne, Mr Perry's vineyard in France?'

'If it's one of Daniel's companies, I've been there.'

'How often do you go?'

'Without consulting my diary? About five or six times a year.'

'Were you there on Friday 6th May this year, the day Chris Fletcher was sacked?'

He picked up the desk diary and flicked through it. 'Yep, I was in France 4th, 5th and 6th May.'

'Why were you there? Did they have a problem?'

'The château has a big contract with the Café de Paris. I went there to make sure the next delivery was coming out soon, as Daniel was starting to feel nervous. When Daniel feels nervous, we all have to do something, let me tell you.'

'Were you involved in the sacking of Chris Fletcher?'

'Nope. I leave all that to the vineyard manager, Rene Fournier. He's got to work with the people when I go home.'

'How do you travel to and from France?'

'I usually drive as I'm always carrying loads of things back and forwards.'

'Where do you drive to; Dieppe or Calais.'

'Dieppe, as it's closer to my house in Sussex. Plus it's a longer sea trip than Dover and I use the time to grab a meal and relax, away from bloody phones and emails.'

'Did you return to the UK on Friday 6th or the day after?'

He could lie about this if he wanted, Henderson knew, but now that he'd admitted he was in France around the same time as Chris was leaving the vineyard, they could probably pick up his name from ferry passenger records, providing he'd used his real name when booking the ticket.

'Why are you asking me this? Is there any point to it?'

'Chris Fletcher, one of Château Osanne's ex-employees, disappeared from the 6 pm Dieppe to Newhaven ferry on Friday 6th May. I'm trying to establish if you were on that ferry.'

'If I was, it would be me and about four hundred other bloody passengers,' he said.

'There is no need to raise your voice, Mr Frankland.'

'I'm not fucking thrilled to be doing this.'

'It's either we talk here or over at the police station in Lewes, your choice.'

'I hear you, mate.'

'Were you on that ferry?'

'Maybe I was, maybe I wasn't. I can't remember.'

'Did you see Chris?'

'Wouldn't know him if I did. I don't think I've ever met him before.'

'Why don't I believe you? Number one, it's your job

to know the people in this organisation based on what you've told me about what you do. And two, I don't imagine a small vineyard employs more than thirty people. How come you don't know him?'

'I don't like your tone, mister.'

'I'm merely trying to establish if you were on the ferry at the same time as Chris Fletcher. How difficult is that?'

'What then? You'll accuse me of chucking him overboard or something? Because if you are, copper or no copper, I might just lose my temper and land you one.'

'This is the UK, Mr Frankland. I don't know if it's the same where you come from, but over here even threatening a policeman is an offence.'

'Well fucking arrest me if it offends you so much, mate. As far as I'm concerned this interview's over. Now get the fuck out.'

Henderson realised they would get no more out of him today, there was little point in arguing.

'I may have to speak to you again, Mr Frankland.'

'If this is your way of saying stay in one place and don't leave the country without telling you lot first, you've no bloody chance.'

They walked out, back into the large and airy work area, the workers still beavering away, seemingly oblivious to all the raised voices of the last few minutes.

'You head out to the car, Carol, I want to take a moment and look at some of the yachts.'

'Don't be all day, sir.'

Henderson walked between two yachts and began

talking to one of the technicians. He told the DI the yacht was for a Saudi prince, and the gold taps and a huge gold mirror in the stateroom were only a couple of a thousand luxury items they were adding. He also said they were now in discussions with the prince's representatives and the boat builder, as they believed the engine originally installed wasn't man-enough to handle the extra weight.

Henderson thanked him and ducked under the bow and headed towards the entrance. Framed in the entrance, a man came striding towards him carrying a long pole which looked like a boat hook. He was a big guy, easily six foot six and built like a heavyweight boxer.

Henderson wouldn't put it past David Frankland to have put a call through to his pet Rottweiler and ask him to beat up the nosey copper for asking too many awkward questions. When the man got closer, Henderson tensed and bunched his fists.

The man stopped and roughly shoved Henderson against a wall.

'You the cop?' he said in a thick Russian accent.

'Who wants to know?'

He lifted the boat hook and pushed it close to Henderson's face. His hair was short, his face chiselled and he had one ear in the shape of a cauliflower; but there was no mistaking his expression.

'If you come back 'ere, you get this.' He pressed the cold metal against his cheek. 'Now get ze hell out.'

'What was all that about?' Walters asked when he climbed into the car.

'I don't know. Just David Frankland's way of saying goodbye.'

# FIFTEEN

Henderson made a cup of coffee and carried it out to the table in the back garden, spreading the previous day's *Argus* out before him. If he was hungry for information about the Albion, he would turn immediately to the back pages, but instead, because he hadn't read any local news for a while, he started at the front.

It was late May and the sun shone in an azure blue sky. He was determined to make the most it as June, in his experience, could be a changeable month with squally showers and cold snaps. He'd done some digging around the borders last week and while he hadn't planted anything yet, he was annoyed to see some weeds were starting to appear.

He only made it as far as page four in the newspaper before Rachel came out to join him, coffee cup in hand and looking a lot worse than he felt. When he returned home after his trip to Portsmouth, he wanted nothing more than a quiet night in, a chance to put his feet up. Their neighbours had other plans.

'Why didn't you stop me drinking last night?' she said as she slumped into a seat opposite him.

'This is often a dangerous thing to do, and in any case, why do women always try to blame their failings on their partners?'

'Conditioning; copying their mothers, I guess.'

'It was a good night, though. I didn't realise school teachers could be so much fun. They weren't like that in my day.'

'Me neither. I think the world's gone casual, away from the strictures set down in the fifties and sixties. It's like business. Ten years ago, when you interviewed a businessman they would be dressed in a nice suit, shirt and tie. Now, you're lucky if they wear a suit and you rarely see a tie.'

'Does it improve school standards, though? Is it better to have a strict teacher who makes you learn your times-tables and your French vocab, or one who treats you like a friend and never gets annoyed?'

She got up from her seat, draped her arms around his neck and flopped rather than sat on his knee. 'You're interested in schools now, Mr H? Is there something you should be telling me?'

'Not guilty m'lud. I spent the evening at a neighbour's house where my girlfriend got rat-arsed while I was being button-holed by two teachers who talked non-stop about all that was wrong with British education today.'

'Slick extraction, Henderson.'

She gave him a kiss and got up and returned to her seat. 'So, what have you got on today?'

**

Henderson walked through the reception area at Malling House in Lewes, and after calling a hearty

'Good Morning,' to Sergeant Steve Travis on the desk, stopped in his tracks when he spotted Harvey Miller sitting there.

'Hello, Harvey. How are you? Have the bruises healed?'

'Hi, Detective Henderson,' he said rising. 'It's good to see you. I'm feeling a lot better, thanks for asking. I can move much easier now.'

'That's good to hear. Is it me you've come to see or someone else?'

'You. I've got something to show you; something I guarantee you'll find very interesting.'

Henderson turned to the sergeant on the desk. 'Steve, are any of the interview rooms free?'

He looked down at his list. 'You can use Number One.'

A few minutes later, Henderson was seated opposite Harvey Miller, a grey, institutional desk and three coffee cups between them, DC Deepak Sunderam at the DI's side. He wanted Deepak there to increase the lad's experience and also to corroborate whatever Miller wanted to tell him.

'If you remember, detective,' Miller said, 'when we met at the Queens Hotel, I said I had a fix on where the vans from Château Osanne were heading.'

'Yes, I do.'

'I went over to Uckfield and sat watching a warehouse on a big industrial estate for a couple of days. It wasn't the most riveting way to spend time I can tell you, with an endless line of big trucks coming in and out all day. I was on the point of giving up when a small van drew up at the far side of the warehouse and the driver went into the secret part.'

'What secret part?'

'Let me spin back a little. I was sitting outside a company called PFB Parcels. This is where the trucks I saw at Château Osanne bring boxes of wine destined for the Café de Paris. For the first day at least, I assumed the parcel company used the whole building. When I got out the car and walked around I realised they only use three-quarters of the building; the rest of it is sectioned off, with its own entrance, but no logo and the windows all blacked out.'

'Maybe the warehouse is too big for the parcel company,' Sunderam said, 'and they sub-let it.'

'That's what I thought until I saw a van pull up and the driver go inside. The van belongs to Fraser Brook's Fine Wines and to cut a long story short, they are a wine retailer heavily involved in selling expensive wines through auction.'

'Are they indeed?' Henderson said, his interest heightened.

'Now, as you can appreciate, I had to get in there–'

'The section with the blacked out windows?'

'Yep.'

'I assume they didn't send you an invite.'

Miller nodded. 'No they did not.'

'Harvey,' Henderson said, 'I don't need to remind you, American citizen or not, that what you have done is illegal, and in any case, evidence gained by criminal means is not admissible in court.'

'It wasn't me, it was a friend; isn't that what the cons say? C'mon, I know the stuff I've got was obtained illegally but it's not as if my burglar buddy broke into a convent and stole the Mother Superior's savings. These people are nasty criminals, not just pouring crap into wine bottles and selling it for thousands, but killing anyone who tries to blow the whistle.'

'I don't think we have enough evidence to say that yet.'

'I think we do now. Won't you just take a look?'

Henderson thought for a moment. Information was the one component that this case badly lacked. They had plenty of theories but no evidence to make one of them stick, and in any case, what was the difference between listening to Harvey and one of Henderson's own narks?

'Ok, let's hear it.'

'Great, thank you. As I was saying, when I get into this building I find it's a fully functioning wine-faking laboratory.'

'How could you tell?' asked Sunderam. 'What does one look like?'

'Take a look at these.'

Miller placed a series of photographs in front of Henderson and the young DC. They weren't bad quality, as he could make out workbenches, bottles of chemicals, racks of labels and barrels of wine.

Deepak was holding the last photograph and when he looked closer, he said, 'Bloody hell sir, these barrels come from Château Osanne.'

'Yep,' Harvey said, 'they're filling old bottles with wine produced at Château Osanne. Can I tell you how I think this thing works?'

Henderson was intrigued. He had no concept in his

mind about how a wine-faking laboratory would operate, but if forced, he imagined a cold cellar full of vats, bottles and pipes. This, on the other hand, looked clean and clinical and seemed capable of undertaking optical or dental work. 'Carry on,' he said. 'I'd be interested to hear.'

Miller's enthusiasm was infectious, but seeing the name of the château on the wine barrel brought the story all the way back to Chris Fletcher. Was this the connection he was looking for between Château Osanne and Chris's death?

'Before you do Harvey, have you considered anything else? Could there be a legitimate use for any of this equipment?'

'I'm no wine expert but I've researched the web and talked to a few wine merchants in town. Now and again they're involved in rebottling an old bottle of wine for an owner because the cap's cracked or the cork leaks, but this is once in a blue moon stuff, small scale. Not a warehouse stuffed full of this sort of gear.'

'What if,' Sunderam said, 'Château Osanne is only the supplier of wine, unwittingly selling it to a gang of criminals?'

'I'd thought of that one too, but the guy who beat me up in France came from the vineyard, and I saw him come out of the warehouse and talk to Fraser Brook, the owner of Fraser Brook's Fine wines.'

'How can you be sure; how close did you get?'

'I was maybe a hundred yards away but using binoculars. Plus, when I saw the van, I looked up Brook's website and I had a picture of Brook in front of me as I was watching him.'

'Fair enough but what about the guy who beat you up in France? You said when we met, you didn't get a good look at him.'

'You're right, I didn't, but the build, size, and the close cropped grey hair of this guy were so reminiscent of the guy from Bordeaux.'

'Deepak could still be right,' Henderson said. 'The guy you saw, and let's assume you did recognise him, may well be one of the criminals but what if he was only at Château Osanne to check on a delivery?'

'I suppose he could have been.'

'It's a good point. We'll leave it open for the moment. Carry on.'

'I must admit,' Miller said, 'the pictures tell us a lot but there are still some gaps. I'll tell you what I do know. The first stage for the fakers is to obtain old bottles, as many of them are unique. I assume they must know people working in smart restaurants and clubs who save the bottles after up-market parties and meals, and they have people who do the same in other places where fine wines are bought, the likes of Tokyo, Paris and so on.'

'They don't try and replicate the bottles?' Sunderam asked.

'I don't think so, as that would take them into manufacturing. Assuming they don't, once they've got the bottle it may or may not have a label. If not, they make a label like this,' he said pointing at a photograph. 'They then fill the bottle with either claret or burgundy from the barrels, which you can see in this picture.'

'Makes sense so far,' Henderson said.

'They cork and seal the bottle using methods appropriate for the time the original wine was made, which you can see here.'

'How do they make them look old?' Sunderam asked.

'I think the technicians at the big desk you can see here, do this. It's not easy to see in the photographs but they've got boxes of labels with various degrees of staining and marking. You can make paper look old by soaking it in tea or chocolate powder or sticking it under a strong light source for a while; numerous things.'

'Right, we've got ourselves an old bottle of wine.'

'We've got ourselves an old, authentic bottle of wine.'

'How do they sell it?'

'I've checked out Fraser Brook's Fine Wines and they're involved in selling the wine collections of the rich and famous at wine auctions all around the world. We're talking about the likes of Sir John Crowley, the former First Sea Lord, and Alan James, the Shakespearean actor. I wouldn't know these folks from Abe Lincoln's grandmother but that's what's on their website.'

'I get it,' Henderson said. 'When Brook is instructed to sell a collection on behalf of say, a famous politician, he slips in a few fake bottles and everyone thinks they all came from the same collection?'

'Got it in one. Y'see, this immediately gives the fake wine provenance.'

'Which is what?' Sunderam asked.

'In the auction business the one guarantee you have that a painting, sculpture or wine bottle is not fake, is if you can verify the place where it came from. If Brook is selling fakes as part of a bigger wine collection, it automatically gives the fakes provenance.'

'Ingenious,' Henderson said.

'How does Brook ensure,' Sunderam asked, 'his company gets a big slice of the collections market? I assume to make this scam work he would have to be involved in a number of sales each year, but there must be other wine merchants trying to buy these collections too.'

'It's a good question, and one I can't answer. Maybe he has spotters all over the country working for him.'

'Or maybe,' Henderson said, 'he knows someone who has connections with the owners of big houses, like a writer at an up-market society magazine or an estate agent. The agents would know if a property has a large wine collection, and if they do, they could recommend Brook's firm.'

'I hadn't thought of that, but now I've got the faking process more or less clear in my mind, I need to take a closer look at Brook.'

'Go ahead, I can't stop you but I'll be putting Brook on my radar too, although at this stage, only as a person of interest.'

'Don't you think there's enough here to put him out of business? If you close him down, it will be like cutting off the head of a snake; they'll never be able to replicate Brook's operation in a hurry.'

Henderson shook his head. 'No, we don't have enough. We don't have any evidence that Brook is involved in the selling side. All you've seen is his van outside the warehouse. You don't know, maybe he was there about something else but I do recognise it's a heck of a coincidence.'

'Mind you, after I saw Brook and the other guy loading boxes into his van, I saw a little transaction take place that to me, could only be drugs.'

'Brook was buying or selling?'

'Buying.'

'Interesting.'

'What about this laboratory, then,' Miller said tapping the photographs. 'There's enough here to mount a raid on the warehouse, surely?'

'What's your take, Detective Sunderam?'

'I can't think of any legitimate reason for operating a place like this. We could get a warrant under suspicion of criminal activity.'

'We could, but we'll leave the connection with Brook and the auctions to one side for the moment. We'll take a decision on him after we've raided the warehouse and questioned the occupants. You never know, we might find something to implicate him as well.'

'This is great news, Inspector. Progress at long last.'

'I agree and it's thanks to some excellent work you've done here,' Henderson said, 'even if I can't condone your methods.' He pointed at the photographs. 'Can I keep these?'

# SIXTEEN

On Monday morning at six-thirty, a small raiding party assembled at a car park, close to the warehouse belonging to PFB Parcels. It didn't feel a particularly cold morning but DI Henderson heard plenty of foot stamping to get the circulation flowing, and several officers had cups of tea and coffee clasped in both hands.

The fields all around looked like photographs from Easter cards, with a light mist hugging the ground and trees glistening with morning dew. The industrial estates in this part of south-east England were located within easy driving distance of the Channel Tunnel, and if not for Council Noise Abatement Orders and vehicle movement restrictions, they would operate 24/7. Even at this hour of the morning, large articulated lorries from the Czech Republic, Poland and Germany were rumbling past, forcing those unfortunates who lived nearby to wake up early.

'Everybody listen up,' Henderson said, standing beside a throng of heavily clad officers and numerous police vehicles. 'The target is the building over there,' he said pointing to a long warehouse across the road. 'Not the first part which belongs to PFB Parcels, but the back section where there is a separate entrance. As I said at the briefing, I expect to find a wine-faking laboratory inside full of bottles, chemicals, and barrels, so be careful how you go. These wine barrels are heavy and I wouldn't want one to fall on any of you, but hell, it wouldn't half make the eulogy at your funeral a whole lot more interesting.'

They laughed. The mood of the group sounded apprehensive, not nervous or anxious, as no one had mentioned knives, guns or large dogs. They expected to enter a clean, open room lined with equipment used by technicians and calligraphers, not boxes of drugs, guarded by gun-toting hard-cases.

'Are there any questions?' Henderson asked, looking around at the helmet-clad faces. 'No? Let's go and close this place down.'

He jogged over the road behind the running black figures of his raiding team, Harvey Miller and DS Walters beside him.

'We'll let these guys move inside first and neutralise any resistance before we go in. It wouldn't do for you, Harvey, to get injured by a punch or hit over the head with a bottle, otherwise it might cause an international incident.'

'There are plenty of folks in the States who couldn't find the UK on a map, never mind concerning themselves about a wounded American citizen; I think you're quite safe.'

They arrived at the door.

'I didn't see anyone go in or out of the building, did you, DS Walters?'

'No sir, and there are no cars outside or signs of activity inside.'

'Good, there's no need to knock.'

The officer with the scratched door banger moved into position, and four whacks later, when most doors would open with two, it swung ajar.

They all piled into the warehouse. 'I'm surprised the alarm didn't go off,' Henderson said as they walked into a dim corridor.

'I think there's been a problem with the alarm,' Miller said.

Henderson turned to look at Miller's face but it was impassive. Despite his height, the DI couldn't see inside the main part of the building for all the bodies in front of him, but when he did, his mouth opened in surprise.

'Goddamn, the place is empty!' Miller said, echoing Henderson's thoughts. 'It was here a few days back, I swear to God, all the kit was here!'

Henderson walked into the bare room in a daze. 'Where is it? Where the hell is it?' he shouted to the naked walls.

The place was devoid of everything; no wine barrels, no clinical work bench and no rack full of wine labels. He'd been sold a pup by the Yank and would never be able to hold his head up in the staff restaurant without some wag calling out 'glass of wine, sir?'

Miller came rushing towards him, trying to extract something from the folder he held in his arms. 'Look here, Inspector, this is where the barrels stood, and here, this is where...'

Henderson heard but he wasn't listening. He walked away before he said something the private investigator didn't want to hear, but Miller followed him, still searching through the folder for something.

'It's here somewhere... ah here it is.'

As he pulled the picture out, the folder slipped from his hand and all the pictures fluttered to the ground in an untidy spread.

'Goddarnit!' Miller said. He dropped to his knees and started to pick them up one by one.

Henderson hardly noticed as he was too busy pondering how he was going to break this to Chief Inspector Edwards, after assuring her that the raid was a sure thing which would put the investigation into Chris Fletcher's murder on the front foot.

He walked towards a window where he could see out into the parking area. Officers were gathered in a group and enjoying a fag and a laugh; all dressed up with nowhere to go. A photograph was trapped under his shoe and he bent down to pick it up. It was of the four barrels of Château Osanne wine. The setting looked to be in the same corner as he was standing, the window to his left. He suddenly had a thought. Four barrels of wine were heavy and would drip.

Using the photograph as a guide, he knelt down and searched the floor for marks, the places where the barrels would have stood. Clear as day, he found eight parallel lines and little splashes of dark red stains that might have been blood, but he was certain they were wine. The position of the parallel lines corresponded exactly to where the legs of the trestles had been.

Henderson strode over to Miller. 'Let me have the photograph of the work bench.'

Miller pulled it out of his folder, now being held in a tight grip, and handed it to him.

Henderson turned to face the wall, the one where the work bench had once stood, now bereft of anything but odd marks on the wall, and numerous drill and screw holes, reminding him of a woodworm infection. Holding the picture up, he examined the wall.

'What are you doing, sir?' Walters said, moving beside him. 'All I see is a big empty space. I'm beginning to wonder if this is even the right industrial estate.'

'We're in the right place all right, don't you worry. Look here,' he said pointing at the wall and holding up the photograph. 'This is where the bench in this picture used to be. These holes are where the bench was attached to the wall, and if so,' he said moving to the left, 'we should find a few more about here...'

'Yep, I see them,' Walters said.

He moved further to the left, 'and here.'

'It only proves there was once a bench here, a common enough feature in any warehouse, I should imagine.'

'Yes, but not *this* bench. Look at the picture, the bench has legs, so about here we should see marks in the floor.' They bent down and there he found a small circle with three screw holes.

She grabbed the picture and located where the next leg would have been and seconds later, the third. 'Yep, they're all there. I'm convinced.'

'I think we—'

'Sir!' a voice at the door shouted.

Henderson looked over to where PC Phillips stood, helmet off and shirt partly unbuttoned. 'The workers from the warehouse next door have just turned up.'

He nodded his thanks and turned back to face Walters and called over Miller. 'I've seen enough here to convince me all this equipment was here when you saw it, Harvey. Sometime over the weekend, they must have discovered evidence of your intrusion and moved out.'

'Praise the Lord,' Miller said. 'I didn't dream it.'

**

Henderson and Walters introduced themselves to the warehouse manager, Jim Bennett, and were led into a office at the front of the building. With glass on three sides, it gave the boss a good view of trucks moving in and out of the building, and any slackers taking too long over a fag break.

'Thank you for meeting with us, Mr Bennett.'

'No problem, but it's a good job you caught me early, as this place can be like an asylum later on.'

Bennett spoke with a strong London accent, somewhere out east, and had the look of an ex-squaddie or trader on a market stall. He was of average height, thick set, with a weather-beaten, scarred face and beady eyes. His hair was grey and close cropped, a crew-cut in old parlance, and Henderson wouldn't be surprised to find out he owned a couple of leather jackets and rode a motorbike.

It took him seconds to realise this man fitted the description Harvey Miller gave him of the guy he saw a few days ago, talking to Fraser Brook. Miller was also convinced it was the guy who beat him up at Château Osanne. This could prove an intriguing discussion.

'I'd like to know more about the place next door,' Henderson said. 'Does PFB Parcels own it?'

'We lease the whole building if that's what you mean. We use this part for the parcel business, as you can see out there, and sub-contract the space next door.'

Henderson was glad he'd come clean in admitting the entire building was leased by them, as he could have stonewalled and told them he knew nothing about it. A call to the landlord would soon have exposed his bluff, forcing them to bring him in for another bout of more awkward questioning.

'How long have you been here?'

'About five years.'

'Did you sub-divide the unit, or was it like this when you moved in?'

'We did it. The warehouse was too big for what we needed at the time, so we sub-divided it and let it out to other tenants. We could do with the space now as it's bloody chockers in there most of the time, especially when we get a big delivery.'

'What sort of businesses lease it? Do you have a preference for who you want beside you?'

'Nah, as long as they pay the rent on time and they're not noisy or smelly. Short-term lets mainly. I never wanted to sign it away on a long-term deal in case I need the space for us, like now. So I won't re-let it now that lot in there have gone.'

'How do you find the tenants?' Walters asked, 'Do

you use an agency?'

'Nah, never. I've got contacts.'

'Who are, or were, the current tenants?'

'A couple of young guys working on a contract for a financial services company. They sent out mail shots, stuffed envelopes, that sort of thing. Always paid their rent on time, they never bothered us and we never heard a dickey-bird from them.'

'Their names?'

'Let me think.' He turned to look at the girly calendar on the wall with the name of an engineering business in Ashford underneath. 'Laurie Scott and Phil Taylor.'

Henderson didn't know much about many sports, but in pub quizzes he usually got the football questions right. If he wasn't mistaken, Laurie Scott and Phil Taylor played in the same England team as Sir Stanley Mathews.

'Have you got their details? How can they be contacted?'

'I've got their number in the office somewhere.' Henderson looked at the morass of paper on Bennett's desk. Even if he really wanted to search for their details, which he doubted, he would have no chance in such a messy heap. 'It's here somewhere,' Bennett said. 'Ach, I'll look for it later.'

'How long have they been renting?'

'About four months.'

'Can I have a copy of the tenancy agreement?'

'We don't bother with those, too expensive. Cash only, short-term lets, right?'

Henderson sighed at the man's barefaced cheek. It

was obviously a lie and they both knew it.

'I see you're involved in the transport of wine,' Walters said. 'Is it a big part of your business?'

'All these cases with the pink writing are bound for the Café de Paris. Me and a couple of associates own a vineyard in France and we've a big order to supply them with our wine; it's their house red,' he said with obvious pride.

Henderson had eaten there, a good lunchtime venue for a tasty baguette or a salad, but he had never tried the house wine, preferring French beer or a glass of Côtes du Rhône.

'Over the last year, they've become one of our biggest customers.'

'What's the name of the vineyard?' Walters asked.

'It's no secret, it's on the bloody label. Château Osanne.'

# SEVENTEEN

It had been a warm day and was developing into a lovely evening, the slowly descending sun glistening over the sea right outside his window. Harvey Miller had just finished his afternoon nap and no, it wasn't a dream. He had accompanied Sussex Police to the Bell Lane Industrial Estate and the warehouse that had been filled with wine barrels, books and equipment only a couple of days ago, was now empty.

Once DI Henderson had got over his understandable strop and started to think straight, he spotted the marks on the floor and the wall where the equipment had been, which proved Miller hadn't made the story up. Miller realised it would be a hard sell to Henderson's bosses as no one had a clue where the wine fakers had gone and the police had nothing to show for all their effort. There was nothing else for it but to soldier on.

This evening though, Miller decided to take a break; no more researching on the web or sitting in a car for hours. He took a shower and dressed in clean clothes that had been washed and ironed by the hotel's laundry. The plan was to have something to eat in any restaurant which took his fancy, enjoy a stroll and perhaps sit in a café or a bar with a drink and watch the world go by, anything to take his mind off today's events. Then, with a clearer head, he would decide what to do next.

He was way-laid, fifteen minutes into his walk, when he spotted the Café de Paris in the middle of a row of restaurants in Jubilee Street. He had never eaten there before, and while its connection with Château Osanne and the parcel business in Uckfield was at the back of his mind, it looked a good place to eat. All thoughts of conspiracies and murders were set aside when a pretty Polish girl brought him a bottle of the house red and a plate of various breads and oils.

A large glass or two was usually his limit now, as he was trying to reduce his alcohol consumption after too many years as a well-oiled journalist, but he wanted to take a look at the bottle. On the front, the Café de Paris logo, a pen drawing of artists at their easels on the banks of the River Seine. The overall effect would give the uninitiated the impression that the Café de Paris bottled their own wine. Only by looking at a small section at the bottom of the back label did he see the inscription: 'Bottled for Café de Paris by Château Osanne.' Beside it, their logo of a leaping grey wolf.

The wine didn't taste too bad if a bit light, and lacking the depth and heaviness of more expensive Bordeaux wines, while avoiding the bubble-gum fruitiness of its neighbour, Beaujolais. In other words, a good lunchtime drink with a ham baguette or steak frites, but a little underpowered for the beef bourguignon he had ordered for his main.

He left the restaurant an hour later, pleased with his choice of a place to eat as the food was good and the Polish girl, Magdalena, a delight. It was still light outside and, feeling a little sluggish from all the food and wine, he decided to take a walk.

He took a right at the end of Jubilee Street and headed towards the Steine. Using the map in his pocket, he crossed the Steine at the lights and walked in the direction of the sea. When he reached St James's Street he took a left, as he knew if he carried on walking it would lead him into Kemptown, a place his guidebook told him was worth seeing, with its smart little houses and interesting bars and shops.

By the time he climbed to the top of the hill, he decided he'd walked enough. Unlike most of his countrymen, he liked to walk, but hadn't done so for a couple of weeks and guessed he was out of condition. He turned down Lower Rock Gardens as he could see the sea in the distance, its hazy shimmer softer in the fading light, and knew if he followed the coast towards the Palace Pier he would soon arrive back at his hotel.

It was a warm evening and several people were lounging in doorways, drinking cans of beer and smoking, but it didn't feel intimidating as it did in the Hunting Park or Strawberry Mansion districts of Philly. There, it wasn't unusual for such individuals to be armed, and rather than swigging from tins of beer they would be passing around a crack pipe. The drugs made them arrogant and unpredictable and the guns could turn the evening into a deadly shoot-out.

When he reached Marine Parade, he crossed the road and walked along the promenade but he couldn't see much in the fading light but the white glow of breakers and the silhouette of the pier. He expected at least to smell the tang of seaweed and rotting fish, but it was the aroma of sausages and hamburgers that filled the air, food he gave up years ago to ward off an early death, toasting away on homemade fires and portable barbecues.

A car drew up alongside him. The window wound down and a guy inside called to him. 'Harvey Miller?'

'Yeah.' He walked closer. The voice sounded familiar.

'Detective Inspector Henderson needs to talk to you, urgently. Jump in and we'll take you there.'

The back door opened and he walked towards it, but hesitated. 'My mother told me never to get into car with strangers.'

The guy in the back reached into his pocket for what he believed to be an id, but instead pulled out a gun and pointed it at him. 'Get in, now.'

Miller climbed in and the car took off. He turned to look at the attacker beside him, only to see the butt of gun coming towards his head.

When he woke up, he'd lost track of time and to some degree his senses, as he had no idea how long he had been out. The haze soon cleared and he realised he was lying in the back of a car, on the floor with a pair of heavy boots resting on his back. He listened for several minutes but could only discern two voices. The man in the back with the big feet sounded young, and the driver much older, with a guttural voice as if he smoked a lot, which really didn't take too much detective work on his part as the car reeked of it.

A change in engine tone suggested the car was slowing down, and the incessant banging, not a problem if sitting in a seat, but deafening so close to the road, a sign they were travelling over uneven ground. After a few minutes, the car stopped. The weight of the legs on his back eased as both men got out. Seconds later, he was pulled out by the collar, punched in the stomach and dumped on damp grass.

He tried to stand but as soon as he did, he received a punch in the gut again and immediately regretted eating all the bread earlier in the restaurant, as he could feel it rising in his throat. The young guy stood back to light a cigarette, while the older man came closer. It was hard to see his face in the dark, but he could smell his breath which was rotten and worse than a dog after it had eaten its dinner. He hauled him upright.

'Miller, you've caused me no end of grief,' he snarled. 'Now, I'm getting it in the neck from my boss, thanks to you.'

Got them! The two thugs who beat him up in Bordeaux.

'How? What did I do?'

From nowhere, the assailant's head crashed into Miller's forehead, causing him to jerk back and bang his head on the side of the car. It hurt like hell but due to the bad light, Dog-breath had missed his intended target and Miller's nose remained intact.

'I ask the fucking questions around here, sonny. When we came across you in Bordeaux I told you to get the fuck out of our hair, remember?'

'Yeah, but–'

'Yeah, but nothing, ya useless scumbag. I've had enough of you. This is where it ends.'

Miller felt he was standing in a piece of open ground like a park, as he couldn't see any street lighting or the headlights of cars, but the darkness could not disguise his assailant's next intention. A shiny metal blade glinted. The young guy behind Dog-breath stood relaxed as he smoked his cigarette, as if carving up private investigators was something they did every day.

Miller cowered back as if his legs were giving way then swung a fist as hard as he could. By the satisfying crunching noise it made, he was sure he'd hit the knife-holder's nose. He pushed him backwards into the smoker standing directly behind, and without looking to see what happened next, took off.

Away from the car and the path it was parked on, he could see in the dappled moonlight a wide expanse of grass, and not far up the slope, a dark shape: a copse. His first instinct was to hide in the trees but decided against it as he needed to put some distance between himself and the two goons; he kept going.

He had been running for no more than five minutes, aiming towards the line of trees further ahead, when his foot caught a divot and he sprawled on the wet grass. He tried to stand and run again, but the pain from his ankle screamed for him to stop. He'd been a keen long distance runner in his youth, but a dodgy ankle had cost him a place in the NCAA Championships. It was this ankle that had brought his run to an end, but if he didn't get up and carry on, it would cost him more than a lousy medal.

Lying there, only his heavy breathing interrupted his thoughts, but there was something else. He listened again. It was the sound of his two pursuers calling one another, and by the tone and volume of their voices, they had split up. Dog-breath sounded further away but the young guy didn't seem so far behind his victim.

Miller forced himself upright, his left leg shaking and the sweat soaking his forehead as if he'd been running for an hour. Taking a few steps at a time and then stopping, he hobbled up the hill into the cover of the trees. He wasn't sure if his pursuer was wearing night-vision goggles or was just bloody lucky, but only a few minutes later and accompanied by the sound of clumsy clumping and heaving wheezing, he came the same way. Miller searched around for a weapon but the only things he could find were puny branches and twigs.

Moving away from a tree that was giving him much needed support, he looked further afield and located a solid, heavy branch. Wielding it like a club, he waited. The young guy crunched over twigs and pine needles as he entered the woods, talking loudly all the time into a mobile phone, to someone he called 'Da.' Dog-breath.

If a rush of adrenaline had helped Miller to escape from the two goons and run up here, it was a rush of fear that gripped him now. He was capable of taking on the young guy with the club, providing the gun stayed in his waistband, but the restriction imposed on Miller by his injured leg prevented him facing his pursuer in open confrontation.

Several minutes passed when he didn't hear the awkward movements of his tracker, and after allowing another five, he ventured away from the cover of the woods. Keeping within the shadow of the trees, he could see the lights of a city in the distance and headed towards them using the makeshift club for support. He was getting the hang of it now and walked with a steady rhythm, the short club pressed into the upper part of the slope, easing the passage of his weak leg.

Up ahead, the ground seemed to narrow and he realised he was approaching one of the park's entrances. His spirits soared, as this meant he would be close to an access road. When he reached it he would head towards the public road and hope that some kind soul would offer him a lift or point him in the direction of a bus or train.

Hearing a sudden noise, he turned. Before he could respond, a heavy thump on the back knocked him to the ground.

Instinctively, he rolled away, but before he could get up a figure leapt at him, punching with both fists. He lifted his hands to protect himself and was surprised to see he was still holding the club. He jabbed at his attacker at the same time as Dog-breath lunged forward. With a resounding whack, Dog-breath's head made direct contact with the end of the club and his body instantly went limp.

Miller pushed the heavy lump off and stood, taking deep breaths in the cool night air, trying to calm the dizzy spin going on inside his head. Feeling better, he bent down and felt for a pulse. His attacker wasn't dead but was sure to have a thumping sore head and painful nose in the morning.

Miller stood and picked up his club. He started to walk away but turned, wielding the club in a defensive stance as he was sure he'd just heard a voice. There was no one there. He stopped to listen. He heard it again and realised it was coming from the prostrate man. Miller bent down, reached into his pocket and fished out his mobile.

'Da, can you fucking hear me? Say something for Christ's sake.'

'What?' Miller said in the deepest, most gravelly voice he could manage.

'Thank fuck for that, I thought you were lost. I'm saying, I'm heading back to the car. We'll never find the bastard now. A' right?'

'Yeah.'

'See ya in few minutes.'

Miller threw the phone on the ground and stamped on it once, twice, three times until bits of it broke off. If he faced trouble getting back to his hotel in Brighton, he sure as hell wasn't going to make it easy for this pair of goons.

# EIGHTEEN

'What a bloody debacle,' CI Edwards said, throwing a copy of *The Argus* towards him.

DI Henderson picked it up. She'd left it open at page four. The editor had the good sense not to put a photograph of an empty warehouse on the front page, but the headline above it, *Police Draw a Blank,* in bold, thick type screamed its humiliating message.

A quick glance told him it didn't just focus on police incompetence but explained why the raid was carried out, what they expected to find and what they believed had happened to the equipment. It included his own curt quote after speaking to the PFB Parcels manager, Jim Bennett, but the overall tone of the article was negative; the police late for the party, as usual.

She pushed her chair back, an exasperated expression on her face. 'I've got a bloody meeting with the ACC in half an hour to explain how we dig ourselves out of this hole. So come on Angus, how do we?'

'There's no getting away from it, Harvey Miller's pictures show a fully functioning wine-faking laboratory and it's not there now. So between the time he was inside the lab taking the pictures, Wednesday, and our raid on Monday, they've scarpered.'

'Why the hell did you leave it until Monday? Couldn't you have done it earlier, Saturday or Sunday, then we might have caught them and avoided this embarrassment? Is your head still on this case or are you too focussed on your house move and your newly found domestic bliss?'

'Of course my head is still on the case. I only found out about this on Friday, and if you remember, we had a big drugs bust in Worthing and the terrorist emergency at Gatwick, both during the weekend. We couldn't spare anybody.'

She sighed. 'You're right but I'm not sure I should remind the ACC, as the job at Gatwick was on his say-so. How did they know we were coming? Could it be one of us?'

'I don't think so. It's a small team and I know them all well, except Deepak Sunderam as he's quite new.'

'How is he getting on? He came to us with glowing credentials.'

'He's a bright lad; he should do well.'

'Good to hear. I'll mention it to the ACC as he's very supportive of integration between us and Surrey and it might take his mind off this. I hope you're right and we don't have any leaks, as it would just give the bloody press more ammunition to shoot at us.'

'If we accept it wasn't one of us, I think Harvey or his burglar must have moved or taken something.'

'It must have been something important to make them up-sticks like they did.'

'Maybe Harvey helped himself to a bottle of wine, or his accomplice nicked the tea money.'

'All the same, Angus,' she said sitting back in her

chair, 'they've put into motion a pretty slick contingency plan. It smacks of military training if you ask me.'

'Now you mention it, I'm forced to agree with you.'

'Two things,' she said, leaning forward to eyeball him. 'I know you think there is a connection between the fraudsters and Chris Fletcher's death. If there isn't, and I'm playing Devil's Advocate here, is chasing the people behind the wine-faking operation worth the candle. If so, who do you think's behind it?'

'I take it you're thinking ahead as to how we present this case to the CPS, is prosecuting them in the public interest?'

She nodded. 'They might say it's only bottles of wine. Solving this will only benefit the rich.'

'If the fraudsters were selling a couple of bottles a month I would say no, but this is a big operation. Harvey did some calculations based on the ledgers he saw inside the place and reckons they're netting between five to six million a year, and they've been at it for four, maybe five years.'

'If it's that big an operation, how come no one noticed anything until Miller came along?'

'Apparently, rich people don't always drink it.'

'What? They buy the stuff to show it off?'

He nodded.

'Oh to be so rich.'

'Finding out who's behind it is proving a more difficult question. We know the château that supplies the wine for the fakes is owned by Daniel Perry–'

'His involvement worries me, and probably explains why the operation has been so successful.

He's a dangerous guy who isn't frightened of anyone. Officers I know at the Met believe there's a lot of bodies out there that we don't know about but they won't investigate him.'

'As I said, Perry owns the vineyard, and don't forget Chris Fletcher used to work there.'

'Therefore, you think his death is connected with the fraudsters?'

'Could be. Also, Harvey Miller was attacked by a couple of guys in France and he thinks one of them was Jim Bennett–'

'The guy running the parcel business?'

'Yep, the other guy is as yet unknown. Also, the barman on the ferry said he saw two men following Chris out the bar not long before he disappeared.'

'Ok, you've given me a couple of good points I can try and mollify the ACC with. What about the technicians working on the bottles and labels? What do we know about them?'

'Nothing. It's not the sort of skill they're likely to advertise for in the Situations Vacant page in *The Argus*.'

'They might be getting them from prison, ex-cons skilled in fraud and forging.'

'I counted five stools in the photograph of the workbench inside the laboratory, and if I asked every detective in the building to name a forger, I bet they couldn't come up with more than two.'

'There's not many of them around that's for sure. In which case, they must be using people-traffickers to give them five young things and train them up.'

'Could be.'

Edwards's face lit up for the first time and she added the point to her notes. 'The ACC will buy it. He gave a speech a few weeks ago when he said people-trafficking was one of the biggest challenges facing regional police forces.' She cast her eyes over her short list. 'I need something else. How are you going to move this forward?'

'We'll dig into PFB Parcels, research Jim Bennett and talk some more to Daniel Perry.'

'Remember my previous comment about Perry.'

'I will. I'll tread softly, softly.'

'Good. Any more?'

'Harvey's given us the name of a wine dealer he believes is selling the fakes. I'm not clear on my own mind what I'll do about Fraser Brook, but it's certainly another lead.'

'It's not much but it should be enough to keep the ACC if not happy, at least off our backs. Finding an empty warehouse was intended to bring us to an abrupt halt and it has. However, I have every confidence you'll find a way to track them down.'

**

Henderson returned to his office. He would gather the team together soon to try and find a way to gee them up after the disappointment of the raid, but for the moment, he needed some time on his own and give some thought to where they were heading. He had given Edwards some action points of what he intended to do next, but he wasn't sure they would lead him to the wine fakers. He needed something else.

He picked up the phone.

'Morning Harvey, Detective Inspector Henderson.'

'Ah, good morning Inspector. How are you this fine morning?'

'I would feel a whole lot better if the men behind the wine-faking operation were behind bars.'

'Ah, it was not be. Close but no cigar, as my old editor used to say.'

'Have you given up on your investigation?'

'No. I still have a few leads I need to shake down. In fact, I'm even more determined than ever to see this through after last night.'

He went on to explain his abduction and chase across Wild Park, a 140-acre nature reserve on the outskirts of Brighton.

'Did you report it?'

'What for? I assume nobody saw me being bundled into the car and it would be my word against them. A decent lawyer could drive a truck through that sort of evidence.'

'You're sure it was Jim Bennett?'

'Yeah, and his son.'

'Nevertheless, I'll send someone over to your hotel to take a statement. At the very least, it will give me a reason to re-interview Jim Bennett and have some fun picking holes in his alibi.'

'I'd like to be there, I'd be interested to see if I made a mess of his face; I hope I did anyway.'

'I'm surprised to hear you want to continue; don't you think you've done enough?'

'We haven't caught anybody yet.'

'I'm not saying this because we drew a blank in Uckfield and I'm winding up this investigation, because I'm not, but I think it's becoming too dangerous for you. I mean, you were beaten up in Bordeaux and last night they tried to kill you. It sounds like you were lucky to escape.'

'Why have they turned violent? What do you think has changed?'

Henderson sighed. 'I believe they've realised we can now see a connection between the vineyard, the Uckfield warehouse and Chris's murder, and they'll stop at nothing to protect their interests. Last night just demonstrated they've upped the ante.'

'You could be right. Bennett didn't bring his knife out to warn me, like he did in Bordeaux. I think he was intending to kill me.'

'I also keep playing over in my mind the way they upped-sticks after they discovered something was out of place on Friday morning.'

'I told you before, I took nothing and moved nothing that I was aware of.'

'What about your burglar?'

'I didn't watch him every minute for sure, but he didn't leave there with a bottle under his arm.'

'What about something smaller, like money, drugs or guns?'

'As I say, I didn't see everything he did but I warned him not to touch anything or take anything before we set off.'

'Perhaps the temptation was too great.'

'Maybe.'

'The point I'm trying to make is this. It took a firm,

disciplined approach to realise something was missing and to clear out of Uckfield and start again somewhere else. They're making so much money I can understand why they would want to carry on, but that level of self-control suggests military training.'

'I see what you're getting at. Military to me means guns, violence, a single-minded determination to carry on.'

'Therefore, it makes it more dangerous for you to be poking your nose in their business.'

'Thanks for your concern, I mean it, but as you've said to me before, I'm a private citizen. You can't stop me.'

'You've proved yourself to be a dogged investigator and uncovered something we couldn't, but Harvey, the rules have changed. I think you could be putting your life in danger. Leave it to the police.'

He put the phone down a few minutes later and headed into the Detectives' Room, pulling the murder team together. 'Right people,' Henderson said, addressing them. He started out by explaining Harvey Miller's abduction and why the American was refusing to return home. He instructed Phil Bentley to take a statement from Miller and with the DI, they would re-interview Jim Bennett.

'The folks who weren't on the raid at Uckfield,' Henderson continued, 'will now have digested the news, but we have sufficient evidence to believe it was exactly as Harvey Miller's photographs showed. The rapid evacuation of the laboratory to a place unknown makes me think these people are more professional than we first thought. Sally, you've been researching

Jim Bennett, what did you find out?'

'He's fifty-two comes from East Ham in London and joined the Army at eighteen. He saw service in Northern Ireland and completed one tour in Iraq. Left seven years ago and now works for Daniel Perry's company, DP Enterprises.'

'What as?'

'Managing Director – Logistics. I think it means he's the boss of PFB Parcels.'

'Anything else?'

'His son Kenny,' Graham said, 'is twenty-eight and also works for the parcel company.'

'What do we know about him?'

'He has a few minors for dope possession and shop-lifting, but nothing more. He works in the warehouse.'

'Good work, Sally. According to Harvey, the two people who abducted him last night were the same two that beat him up in Bordeaux. I'm more or less convinced, it was Bennett and his son. They might also be the two men who followed Chris Fletcher out on deck and killed him, but as we all know, it's just supposition. We don't have any evidence. Not yet.'

He looked around again for Phil Bentley, not hard to spot in such a small group. 'Phil, give us the low-down on Perry.'

Bentley sat up from his slouched position. 'He's not a difficult man to research. He's been in the papers a lot over the years and he's got previous, not to mention a few three-inch thick files at the Met.'

'Skim over the newspaper stuff as I think we've all heard it.'

'He's had a few minor scuffles with the law for violence and drugs, and did time when he was eighteen for carving a bloke up, but his big day in court was for the murder of Don McCardle, for which we know he didn't stand trial. Not so much as a speeding ticket since.'

'What about the Met?'

'They've been watching him for years hoping he'll make a mistake. They suspect him of trading in drugs and guns, and beating up anyone who gets in his way.'

'Do they have an active investigation?'

'Not as far as I know,' Bentley said. 'Perry's lawyers pursued an unsuccessful harassment case against the Met after the McCardle case, and threaten to do so at the slightest provocation. I'm told they keep their distance.'

'So, people, how do we get a lead on where the wine fakers have moved to?'

'Follow the vans leaving PFB Parcels?' Bentley suggested.

'Not a good idea,' Walters said. 'They're bog-standard delivery vans travelling between the vineyard in France and the Uckfield warehouse, and from there to the restaurants of Café de Paris.'

'What about the wine dealer, Fraser Brook?' Sally Graham said. 'If he's doing what we think he's doing, adding fake bottles to valid wine collections, he must be picking the fake bottles up somehow.'

'Good point,' Walters said. 'Mind you, he could be getting a delivery from PFB Parcels or some other distribution service.'

'So, my suggestion to follow the vans isn't such a

stupid idea after all,' Bentley said.

'I didn't say it was stupid; it might turn out to be useful if we watch his shop and one of the vans turns up, but I think it would be too public for him. His staff would soon twig what's going on. In which case, my money's on him going there himself.'

'Whichever way we look at this issue, it points to Brook,' Henderson said, his initial reticence about investigating Brook gone. 'I want that man under surveillance,' he said.

'The next big sale he's doing is Barcelona in two weeks' time,' Walters said, 'but as the catalogues are published weeks ahead of time, he already knows what he's got in the auction.'

'Maybe it doesn't matter,' Henderson said. 'Harvey saw him loading bottles into the back of his van. I think he goes there when fakes are ready. If he received too many, it would mean one auction would be carrying too many fakes.'

'Phil, I want you and Sally to take on the surveillance job. Brook's shop is on the King's Road in Chelsea, so I suggest trying to get some space above one of the shops opposite. It might be a thankless task if all you see is customers going in and out, but if Harvey's right and he goes to the wine-faking laboratory every week to pick up fakes, you could strike lucky.'

# NINETEEN

Harvey Miller walked down King's Road in Chelsea feeling a touch self-conscious amongst the slim, stylish women carrying the results of their morning shopping binge. If this wasn't enough emasculation for one morning, there were guys cruising along the road in open-top sports cars that cost more than his apartment back home, looking like male models from a clothing catalogue with their designer shades, three days growth and bouffant hair cuts.

This overabundance of chic didn't make Miller want to slim down, or give him a sudden desire for a complete makeover, and in fact his dress sense hadn't changed much since his days at college. However, when he went into a coffee shop, he didn't order his usual Caffé Mocha and instead opted for an Americano.

The morning rush of yummy mummies with their loud voices and precocious kids had subsided, and he was able to take a seat beside the front window which afforded a good view of Fraser Brook's Fine Wines across the street. His plan was to stay there in Starbucks for an hour or two, sipping coffee and reading *The Times* and when he had outstayed his welcome he would move to the posh burger place next door.

Back home, he would avoid 'designer' burger places like the plague, but this one had the same view as Starbucks and he could suffer a pretentious burger for one day in his life. After lunch, he would stroll along the road looking in clothes and kitchen shops, gaping at things he didn't want to buy, before returning to Starbucks for an afternoon caffeine hit until the wine shop closed.

At least, that's what he had done for the last two days, like some lonely apartment dweller desperate to hear human voices and needing some social interaction, even if it was only with strangers. He sipped his coffee, his face blanching at the bitter taste, already missing the dollop of whipped cream that was the usual accompaniment to his cup of choice.

The last few days could turn out to be a big waste of time if Brook only dealt with the fake wine bottles outside shop hours. He owned a warehouse in Hammersmith where Miller believed he ran his web-based business and stored the valuable collections he bought from the houses of rich individuals. There was nothing to stop Brook turning up there at the dead of night with a delivery of fakes, but countering that argument, Miller had seen the wine dealer pick up bottles at the Uckfield warehouse in the early afternoon, making him think Brook wasn't all that bothered about being so secretive.

The call he received a few days back from Detective Inspector Henderson about the threat posed by Daniel Perry, and the DI's belief that the criminals had stepped up a gear, had obviously fallen on deaf ears, as he was here in Chelsea watching Fraser Brook.

However, he did give more thought to the way they had abandoned the Uckfield operation at the first sign of trouble. He hadn't reckoned on dealing with military-trained personnel before, but if this was the case, he would have to be more careful. Not only did many former soldiers know how to access weapons, they knew how to use them.

Back in the day, while still working for the *Philly Inquirer*, he'd investigated the death in training accidents of two local boys killed at Fort Hood in Texas. He was denied contact with anyone at the base and so he did his usual mooching around bars and steakhouses, looking around for a cooperative face. More than once, he was threatened with a knife and a gun. His car received a couple of bullet holes, and towards the end when he felt nearer the truth, he was kidnapped, beaten and stripped before being left ten miles out of town.

At present, his view of Fraser Brook's Fine Wines was obscured by two buses. With a rumble and shake of the glass in the big window, the buses moved away towards their destination. He glanced to the left and right of the shop at the sea of faces walking along King's Road, and there he saw the dapper figure of Fraser Brook striding purposefully away from his shop.

Miller wasn't so young he could 'spring into action,' as his younger self could do, but he left the coffee house faster than when he went in. Crossing the street and walking quickly, he soon spotted Brook, who then disappeared down a side street. Miller followed but when he turned down the same street,

Brook was nowhere to be seen.

He was perplexed. Had Brook turned the corner and started to run, knowing he might have a tail? He didn't think so as it was a long street, and even if Brook was running, he should still be able to see him. Miller carried on walking and glanced into all the shops and doorways he passed. Up ahead, a man emerged from a doorway, wiping his nose with his hand as if dealing with the aftermath of a sneeze, or having just snorted a line of coke. It was Brook.

Miller increased his pace and closed the gap between them but not so much that a suspicious Brook would spot him. He crossed into Cale Street and outside a row of garages, the wine merchant stopped, causing Miller to duck into a doorway. Rather than stand still and look conspicuous, he whipped out his mobile and leaned against a wall, pretending to answer a call.

Brook didn't look his way but began rummaging through his pockets for something. A few seconds later he found what he was searching for and with a smile of satisfaction, he unlocked one of the up-and-over doors. Miller waited a few minutes, ambling closer and closer until Brook reversed out his firm's van, the same one he saw in Uckfield.

When Brook headed back to close the garage door, Miller walked behind the van and in a practised movement, bent down to pick up a deliberately dropped coin and attached a magnetic tracker to the underside of the van. Miller had parked his hire car a few streets from here and with the tracker in place, he was confident of catching the wine dealer up.

**

DC Sally Graham spotted the chubby, middle-aged man walking behind Fraser Brook, but didn't think anything of it. When Brook's van came headed away from lock-up, she started the dirty, nondescript Ford Focus and followed.

'See, what did I tell you?' Phil Bentley said from the passenger seat. 'Watching Brook's garage was a better bet than sitting in a posh burger bar all day watching his shop.'

'How right you were, Mr Bentley. Go to the top of the class and award yourself a Jelly Baby.'

They crossed the Thames at Putney Bridge and drove though Battersea.

'Where's he going?' Bentley asked.

'If I knew the answer, Mr Bright Spark, there would be no need to follow him, would there?'

'What I mean is, heading in this general direction, where do we think he's going; you tetchy mare.'

'Take a butcher's at the map and give it your best shot.'

They drove on a section of the South Circular for a few miles before Brook took a right into Keswick Road.

'It's the A3 then,' Bentley said, a smug look on his face.

'Let's just enjoy the day out and see where he takes us, keep all the one-upmanship for the office.'

They continued along the A3 through Wimbledon. The road was fast, three lanes on one side and three on the other, but instead of bland, concrete culverts and nameless industrial estates, common to many motorways, the trees and bushes of Richmond Park were on the right, with the expanse of Wimbledon Common on the left.

Sally Graham wasn't a book-thumping liberal, going on endlessly about the destruction of natural habitats and the desecration of the Green Belt, but areas like this where the car took precedence over people, and roads like this sliced their way through such a beautiful landscape, made her sad.

'Are you going to Seb's birthday booze-up tonight?' Bentley asked.

'Are you asking me out on a date?'

His face reddened. 'No. I'm only doing, what's it called...making conversation.'

'I intend to. Depends when we finish here. Where's he having it?'

'Druid's in town.'

'I thought so but wasn't sure. I've never been there.'

'Yeah, but you're not much of a boozer, are you? Early start and out with the binoculars, more like.'

'Don't mock my hobby, it's very interesting. No, I used to go out boozing but I don't do it any more as I don't like paying money to drink some gut-rotting chemicals that make me feel like crap the following morning.'

The traffic moved fast and it was easy to follow Brook's van, clean and bright in a sea of dirty white vans and ugly lorries. A few minutes later they arrived in Guildford, a place she knew well as she often enjoyed shopping there.

'You've got to watch the one-way system around here,' Bentley said. 'Get in the wrong lane and we're stuffed.'

'I know, I've been here before. Trust me.'

'In driving, oh I do.'

'What nothing else?'

'I...I didn't mean that.'

'C'mon, what?'

She couldn't turn to look at him as they were in the middle of town with cars and buses all around, but she was sure he was blushing again.

'I better call in,' he said picking up his phone.

Brook took the left hand lane, the A281 to Horsham, and she followed four cars back. The three lane highway of the A3 was long forgotten as they bumped and twisted along roads with missing bits of tarmac and numerous pot-holes.

Bentley finished the call. 'Henderson says we're only to follow Brook to his destination and report in. On no account are we to stop and take a look in the house or pub or whatever he's heading to. He also said, if we can get a result and find where this new wine-faking lab is, you and me can award ourselves a pub lunch and charge it.'

'Great. I quite fancy a plate of scampi and chips, a change from the tuna salad I often buy from the canteen. Brook doesn't look like a criminal, more like a lawyer who reads your granny's will or gets you to sign the papers when you buy a flat.'

'It's the quiet ones you watch, although the DI says it's not Brook we need to worry about, but the company he keeps; like Daniel Perry.'

'I've heard all about him.'

'What do you think about the boss moving in with his girlfriend?' Bentley asked. 'Are you the soppy romantic type who thinks it's lovely he's found happiness after divorce, or do you wonder why it took them so long?'

'The second one, although I never thought it would happen.'

'Were you in the sweep?'

She shot him a look but he was laughing.

'Had you there, Sally. Why do you say you didn't think it would happen?'

'Some guys, when they get divorced, feel they need to move in with a woman right away as somehow they can't live on their own—'

'Like me, you mean.'

'If the cap fits, Phil. The boss is at the other end of the scale, if you ask me. He's a guy who could happily live on his own, so moving in with Rachel is his choice.'

'I think I know what you're getting at.'

'When I say he can live happily on his own, it's with the proviso there's a good canteen at work or an Asda nearby, as I believe he's not much of a cook.'

'How do you know? Been up to his flat have we? A cosy late night supper was it?'

'If I wasn't driving, I'd give you a slap, Phil Bentley. For your information, Rachel told me.'

'Careful down here,' he said, nodding at the road ahead, 'there's a couple of roundabouts to negotiate, but I'm betting he heads to Horsham.'

'Hold your peace back-seat driver. I can handle it.'

'Whoa, did you see that? He's not going to Horsham at all, he's heading to Loxwood.'

'Where's Loxwood?'

'It's a big village to the north of Horsham. You must know it. Phil Collins used to live there.'

'Who's Phil Collins?'

# TWENTY

Harvey Miller parked his car in the shelter of a tall hedge, confident it couldn't be seen from the house. He waited until it got dark, Brook's van long gone with what looked like the same sort of wine cases he'd spotted in Uckfield. He thought of calling DI Henderson, but the chances of getting them to raid this place, Forest Farm in the village of Loxwood, without any concrete evidence, were zilch. He put his phone on silent and secured it in his pocket, zipped up the light jacket and began to climb the fence.

His progress across the field was sheltered on the left side by a broken fence intertwined with a thick, thorny hedge, while on the other, facing the farmhouse, the field was open and without obstacles. The lights of the house in the distance twinkled, its outline discernible at the top of a small rise, but did little to illuminate the way ahead; in many of the windows the curtains were closed and in those that weren't, the lights were off.

The dampness of the grass caused him to slip on occasion, and once or twice his foot got caught in what he thought was a rabbit hole. This made him think whoever owned the farmhouse didn't keep animals or grow crops, but kept the field for his kids to play, or as a buffer to hide the house from nosey neighbours.

Ten minutes after starting out, he drew level with the farmhouse about fifty feet to his right. On flatter, drier and firmer ground, he stopped to catch his breath. He knew from his earlier recce there was a large stable block on the other side of the house, but he couldn't hear the sound of horses. He edged around the silhouetted house, looking and listening for a slumbering hound about to emit a loud bark, or any movement from inside the house.

Moving clear, he could now see the profile of the large barn into which Brook had disappeared earlier, and again exited carrying heavy boxes. This convinced him he had found the new site of the wine-faking lab. He stood squinting in the faint moonlight, but little penetrated the canopy of trees rising up at the back of the property on a shallow slope.

The barn itself was large and unlit, and the long shadows it cast made it look menacing. If the laboratory had been relocated here, this building looked as good a place as any to become its new home. It was isolated and no one would notice the coming and going of technicians and Brook's wine van.

He decided not to head directly towards the barn and risk standing on a child's squeaky toy or stumbling into a row of bins, and instead he made his way through an unkempt back garden to a five-bar gate separating it from the land beyond. He climbed over and to his surprise the field was filled with young spikes of corn. He felt the cobs; small and immature, but even the south of England didn't get the same amount of sunshine as the southern United States where the cobs at this time of year would be twice as big.

Using the cover of the field he approached the darkened building from the northern end. His senses were heightened at the risk he took in coming here, but he didn't get his reputation, firstly as a tenacious reporter, and latterly as a dogged investigator for nothing, and besides, he wanted payback.

He heard scratching and scrabbling, causing him to hunker down on his knees, below the height of the corn stalks. Hearing it again, he realised it was coming from the wooded area to the left, most likely a bat or owl moving through the branches, or a fox or cat digging under the leaves to find the source of some strange scent they had just detected.

He moved slowly around the back of the barn looking for a door which would allow him to utilise some of the tricks he'd picked up over the years, and from his new burglar friend, Billy Rush. A concrete path ran alongside the back of the barn making the going easy and giving him a few inches in height, although it was so dark he almost failed to notice the window. He moved back to take a closer look and could see it was blacked out, not by curtains or blinds as he couldn't see any tell-tale wrinkles or folds, but by paint. He searched around the edge of the window, looking for a chink of light, but couldn't find any.

He felt around the wooden frame until he found a small gap where the wood had expanded either due to excess moisture or a bad painting job. He removed a screwdriver from his jacket and inserted it into the gap. He eased the screwdriver blade back and forward causing the gap to widen, and slowly worked it closer to the locking arm. A minute or so later he was there. All he had to do now was give it a big thump and with a bit of luck the arm would pop up, the window would open and he would be able to see inside.

He didn't care if he made a mess of the frame and they suspected that someone had been snooping around, as it wouldn't be spotted until morning, and by then they would all be in jail. His plan was to take a quick look inside and if it was kitted out as he expected, he would high-tail it back to the car and call DI Henderson. There would be no heroics and no photographs, and no two guys kicking the crap out of him up a dark alley. If the wine-faking lab had been relocated here, it would be up to the cops to deal with it.

He took a deep breath and was about to apply the pressure when he heard a loud swish. Before he could look round, an excruciating pain shot up his right shoulder, forcing him to release his hold of the screwdriver and fall to knees in agony. A boot smashed into his midriff, then another, and another until he slumped to the ground.

**

Henderson drove around the park that gave Queen's Park its name, trying to find a parking space. He used to have the same problem when he lived in Seven Dials, but the new house in College Place had a designated parking spot. Only one, mind you, and it was often a point of negotiation, not to say contention, whether he or Rachel had the use of it.

The call from Phil Bentley to tell him that he and Sally Graham had arrived at Fraser Brook's destination, Forest Farm in Loxwood, came at four-thirty. He instructed them to withdraw, but as it was still light, he decided he wouldn't go up there until later. It was now nine o'clock with thick cloud cover, and dark, so he hoped DS Walters had finished her evening meal and was prepared for an evening stake-out.

He eventually found a space, vacated by a young guy and his girlfriend heading out for a night on the town in a boy racer Astra. As usual, Walters wasn't standing there waiting for him and rather than sit in the car like a stalker or a PI casing out the nearby apartment of a divorcee, he walked to the door and rang the bell. A few seconds later, she buzzed him up.

'You've decorated since the last time I was here,' he said, walking through the hall.

'It started after I had a leak in the kitchen. I repainted in there but it made the rest of the flat look shabby, there was no way I could leave it. I had to paint it all.'

'You've got the place looking good. Perhaps you could come down to our house sometime and give me your estimate?'

'Don't even joke. Do you have any idea how much I hate decorating?'

She pointed him in the direction of the lounge. 'Take a seat. I'll only be a few minutes. You did say we wouldn't be there all night?'

'I did. My plan is to go over there and take a look. If someone is there and it looks as if they're not moving, I'll call in the guys I've got standing-by to watch the place. If it's deserted, we'll take a look around. If we find what I think we'll find, I'll call in the SOCOs and we can go home.'

'So whatever happens, I don't need a sleeping bag, flask of coffee, a bottle to pee in; any of that stuff?'

'Nope,' he said shaking his head. 'You have the word of a compulsive liar.'

She returned a few minutes later, decked out in a fleece, gloves and woolly hat.

Henderson laughed.

'What's so funny? I don't like feeling cold.'

'When I was parking the car, a young couple were heading out into town. He was wearing a t-shirt and jeans with no jacket, and she a short skirt and not much else. You look like you're prepared for a polar voyage.'

'Yeah, but they're probably going to boogie all night in a hot club, while I'll be sitting in a cold car or walking around a dark house out in the sticks.'

He stood. 'Don't say I don't take you to all the best places.'

They walked to the car, and after a bout of to-ing and fro-ing as the car behind, which wasn't there when he arrived, had parked mightily close to his rear bumper, they set off for Loxwood.

'How do you like the new offices?' he said as Walters fiddled with the radio, trying to locate a station with music to suit her ever-changing mood. He didn't know what it might be tonight, but long experience had taught him where women were concerned, certain questions weren't worth the asking.

'It's much better than Sussex House what with all the new furniture, and bits that don't come off on your hand as they used to, and there are more interview and meeting rooms. I miss being close to town though, and having a supermarket right there on the doorstep. On balance, the advantages outweigh the disadvantages. What about you?'

'I'm with the advantages outweighing the disadvantages. Is it a generally held view? Do most of the other detectives feel the same way?'

'Yeah, I think so. You know what our people are like, if they're unhappy about something they never stop talking about it.'

'I do. What about Gerry Hobbs? For the last couple of weeks he's been walking about with a face like fizz; a half-chewed caramel as my brother would say.'

'I'd like to meet him, your brother, he sounds funny.'

'He is, or should I say, was. Ever since he became an estate agent the barrack-room humour has gone out the window. Now, it's all about house prices and letting potential.'

'Gerry's sour face has nothing to do with the new offices. His youngest just started nursery and his nutty wife thinks because Gerry laughs and jokes with one of the teachers when he drops the lad off, he must be sleeping with her.'

Henderson laughed 'Maybe he is and she found out.'

'I don't think so, he's not the type.'

'I think the one big disadvantage of the new offices

is being so close to the top brass as they can drop by any time they like and see what you're doing. When we were in Sussex House, I could lie and say I had something important to do and miss another riveting finance meeting or a seminar on how to use PCSOs more effectively, but not now.'

'Poor you.'

It didn't take long to reach Loxwood, nor to find Forest Farm as the property was situated on the outskirts of the village, the house sign clearly prominent. It was obvious the house was occupied, they could see the glint of car windows in the driveway and several rooms in the farmhouse were lit.

He drove past the front drive and parked in a lay-by. The presence of a strange car at this time of night was unlikely to raise the hackles of the local Neighbourhood Watch Nosey Parker, as Forest Farm was outside the village, there were few neighbours and the road wasn't busy. For any car that did go past, it would be hard to spot them as the drivers would be concentrating on negotiating the sharp bend, and the high hedges at the side of the road blanketed Henderson's car in shadow.

'What now?' Walters asked.

Henderson fell silent for a moment. 'We'll give it until eleven and if the farm still appears to be occupied, I'll call in the overnight team. If everybody leaves because their work for the day is finished, or they're heading out to the pub, we'll go up to the house and take a look around. When that's done, we'll go home. How does that sound?'

'Fine.'

'So, why the disappointed look? Is this little recce into the countryside messing up a big date with someone new, or are you missing your favourite programme on the box?'

'No, nothing so important. But if I'd realised we were going to be here for a while, I would have packed a flask of coffee and some biscuits.'

# TWENTY-ONE

Slowly and groggily, Harvey Miller regained consciousness. He had been so out of it, whoever slugged him could have taken him to a place miles away and he would have been none the wiser; but no, he was still there, lying on the ground outside a barn in Loxwood.

A face leaned towards him: young, scruffy and smelling of beer. 'Get up you scummy bastard.'

With great difficulty, he got to his knees. Leaning against the wall of the barn for support, he pulled himself upright. He stared malevolently at his attacker, wishing the pain would recede from his midriff sufficiently for him to raise a punch and sink it hard into his face. He was glad he did nothing, as he now saw the gun.

The man raised the weapon and poked the barrel towards him. 'This way fucker,' he said jerking his head over to the left, 'and don't try and scarper. This baby's loaded.'

Miller started to walk, and as he did so, assessed his escape options. He would bet the kid wasn't a good shot, and in the dark most people couldn't see a barn door, never mind hit one with a handgun, but where could he run to? There could be big fences all around this place, just like at Château Osanne, and he didn't rate his chances hiding out in open fields with someone chasing him who knew the lie of the land better than he did.

Away from the shelter of the barn, the contours of the house appeared before him, many lights burning behind closed curtains and blinds. Close up, it looked to be a large house, old but extended several times.

'Over there,' the kid said, indicating a door at the back.

He walked towards it, his ears picking up the sounds of other voices inside the house.

'Open the door and get in,' his antagonist said, poking him in the ribs with the weapon to remind him, as if any reminder was necessary, that he still had a gun.

He did as instructed and stepped into the kitchen. Before he had time to assess his surroundings, a foot kicked him in the back and sent him sprawling over the cold, unforgiving, quarry-tiled floor.

'Looksee here, Dave. I caught this bastard trying to break into the barn when I went out for a smoke,' Gunboy said.

Someone stood, the legs of the chair scraping noisily over the floor and walked over.

'Let's beat the fucker up and teach him....well bugger me. If it isn't our old friend, the Yankee investigator from Bordeaux, what's his name again...'

'Harvey Miller,' another voice said.

'Christ so it is!' Gunboy said. 'If I knew it was him I'd have put a bullet in his noggin.'

Miller pushed himself upright. He immediately recognised one of the guys sitting around the table as

Jim Bennett, the guy who beat him up in Bordeaux, and the kid with the gun, aged about mid-twenties and looking like a close relation, the other attacker. Hearing him speak and looking closer, he could see now it was the same father and son team who abducted him and took him to Wild Park.

The other man sitting at the table and staring at him with malevolence, the one they called Dave, was the rude Aussie who gave him the brush-off outside the gates of Château Osanne. It was all coming together, but could he get out of here to tell anyone?

Bennett rose from the chair. He was short and squat, a less imposing figure than the tall Aussie. He walked towards Miller and kicked him in the leg. 'What the fuck are you doing round here?' he said, a gun tucked into his trouser waistband like a Mafia hit man. If there was a God, the weapon would suddenly develop a malfunction and blow his bollocks off, but it didn't happen in the movies and it didn't happen here.

'I was trying to find out where you lot had moved to.'

'It didn't take you too long to find us, did it Sherlock? How the hell did you do it so quickly?' Dave said, his casual tone gone and genuine concern creeping into his voice.

He had nothing to lose by telling them. Brook was one of their own, and he didn't care if it landed him in a pig sty with his ears being fed to his porky friends. 'I followed the guy from the wine shop, Brook.'

'Brook! I might have known,' Bennett spat. 'He's about as covert as Danny La Rue at a fucking vicars convention. What a prat.'

'We need to fix this,' the Aussie said, his face stern. 'I'm not having this new operation fucked up by anybody; no way. Jim, give me your gun, I'll take him outside.'

'Hang on a sec, Dave, not yet. I'd like to shoot him myself but Perry needs to be told first. He said after last time, we had to tell him about anything affecting business.'

He nodded. 'You're right. He went ape-shit when we were forced out of Uckfield. I'll ring him now.' Dave turned and disappeared into the darkened hallway.

Bennett had a lived-in face, more suited to receiving a punch in a bar room brawl than sipping beer and coffee in this large and modern farmhouse kitchen. Dave was taller, better looking but with an air of hidden menace. With these two thugs around, Miller wondered what Gunboy did, as he was decades younger, and looked like a refugee from an American football game with his baggy, blue jeans and yellow bomber jacket. He was tall and thin with an ungainly walk, imitating the movement of LA rappers or his long bones hadn't fused properly.

A few minutes later Dave re-entered the kitchen. 'He couldn't talk; said he'll call back in five. He said to take him down to the barn and tie him up in the office. He started whispering and went all husky like a fucking spy. I'll bet he wasn't at the theatre like he said, but shagging that gorgeous wife of his.'

Bennett laughed. 'Payback for all the money he spends on gym memberships and facials, I call it.'

Bennett turned to his son. 'Kenny, take this

scumbag out to the office in the barn and tie him up, but don't shoot him unless he tries to escape; you hear me?'

'Right Da. I'm not to shoot him but if he tries to leg it, I can. In the meantime, can I break something like his arms or his yapping mouth?'

'Not yet, big man. There'll be plenty of time for that later once we decide what we're gonna do with him. Get a shift on and get this toad out of my sight.'

'Take this,' Dave said handing Kenny a rope.

The young runt prodded Miller with the gun until he got to his feet. He was led out of the kitchen and back towards the barn. The pain in his shoulder from his fall on the floor had eased, but the boy took great pleasure in kicking him several times, laughing when he was sent sprawling over the damp grass.

This situation he was in, away from the house with only Kenny Bennett for company, provided a better chance to escape than before, as it was clear the boy wasn't the brightest bulb in the light box, and he was treating this incident like a game. However, the boy held the gun in a steady grip and kept his distance from his prisoner, much like the US police manuals instructed. It was close enough for him to take a clear shot but far enough away that the prisoner couldn't turn and attack him with a boot or a fist.

When they reached the barn, Kenny unlocked the door and switched on the lights. What a revelation! Half expecting to find another empty space, Miller was amazed to see it was almost an exact replica of the operation at Uckfield, with a long technicians' workbench, barrels of wine, empty wine bottles; the whole kit and caboodle. It was the confirmation he came here to find, it was just a shame he couldn't pull out his camera and take some pictures. He was pushed towards a small office at the back and instructed to sit in the visitor's chair.

The office was much as he expected from a gang of criminals, unlikely to be sitting in there diligently filling out their sales tax records or writing up employee appraisals. It was sparsely furnished with a desk, chair, coat stand, filing cabinet and visitor's chair, no computer or photographs of the wife and kids on the desk, and most likely used by the boss to get away from the smell of chemicals and put their feet up for five minutes.

Kenny wrapped the rope around him before tying it to the chair. Risking a smack on the face Miller asked, 'Did you and your pa kill Chris Fletcher?'

'What of it?'

'Why did you kill him?'

'He was goin' to the cops, wasn't he, just like you. And d'ye know what, you're gonna end up just like him. He got eaten by the fishes, you'll get yours from the rats and foxes.'

'My, what a vivid imagination you have.'

Kenny finished tying the rope and turned the chair towards the door before standing back to admire his handiwork.

'You thought you could come here and have a snoop around, did ye?' he said. Miller's eyes were drawn to a gap in the centre of his teeth where he was missing the left incisor, and failed to see the hand sweeping up to slap him hard across the face.

'Our business is our fucking business and we don't want you or any other scum coming here to spy on us.' He slapped him again. He was obviously enjoying himself, beating up a defenceless man. If Miller's hands were free, he would show the skinny runt how hard he could punch. 'When them indoors decide your time's up, I hope I get the job of doing you in. I'll enjoy it and no mistake.' He bunched his fists and punched Miller in the stomach. He was about to thump him again when the door opened and his father walked in.

'What the fuck you up to, Kenny, you bloody clown?'

'I was just...subduing the prisoner.'

'Subduing him? You were fucking having fun that's what. Christ, no wonder Dave calls you a psychopath.'

'What's wrong wi' you? You were jolly hockey sticks but five minutes ago.'

'It's Perry; he's going ape-shit. Dave's on the phone with him right now.'

'What, about this guy?'

'Could be, I don't know. I could only hear part of it but it didn't sound good. Dave doesn't look too happy.'

Bennett looked and sounded agitated and if Miller was reading the signs, seemed to be expecting trouble. If the boys wanted to indulge themselves in a bout of argy-bargy and shoot one another, they could just go right ahead and fill their boots, but he'd rather not be tied to a chair as there would be nothing he could do to get out of the way of a stray bullet.

The kitchen door slammed and Dave came striding

into the barn. His face was stern but he didn't look as though he was about to plug Bennett or his son; shame.

'What's going on?' Bennett asked.

'You wouldn't believe what Daniel's told me.'

'What?' Bennett asked.

'Brook and Landseer have been thieving.'

'Thieving? What? From who?'

'Thieving money from us, you idiot.'

'How?'

'Listen up, mate. Landseer had a problem with his personal laptop and Daniel suggested one of his IT guys take a look at it. The guy got it working and gave it back to Daniel. Cut a long story short, Daniel found a folder with emails between Landseer and Brook talking about the bottles they were earmarking for themselves. They've been skimming off thirty to fifty grand every sale.'

'C'mon Kenny,' Bennett said to his son, 'you were good at maths at school. What's fifty grand a sale over the last four or five years?'

'About two, two and a half mill,'

'Fuck me; the cheating, lying tossers,' Bennett said. 'I might have guessed Landseer would pull something like this. I've never liked estate agents and after hearing this, I bloody hate them now.'

'The thing is,' Dave said, 'it wasn't the fake bottles they were skimming. Brook buys a collection with Daniel's money of say, five hundred bottles. We don't know if it's five hundred and twenty, or five fifty bottles, do we? We leave it to Brook. We don't care as long as he buys them, adds in the fakes and sells the lot.'

'Yeah, but we know how much he makes in a sale, don't we?'

'Sure, and we can look it up on the auctioneer's website if we want to, but this is where Brook's been crafty. He's been shifting bottles out of the collection into his own stock then adding them to the sale as if they were his own. They've probably ripped us off for more, probably about three million.'

'Fuck!' Bennett exclaimed. 'We're being turned over good-style. I might have known a sleazy coke-sniffing bastard would pull something like this.'

'How do you know Brook takes drugs?'

'I...I don't know. He must have told me.'

Dave rounded on Jim Bennett, pointing a menacing finger into his face. 'I hope you're not up to your old tricks, mate. Daniel's been clear on this point, no drugs around this business – full stop. Cops will pull out an armed response team and a fucking helicopter for a big drugs bust, but they don't give a toss about a few bottles of wine. D'ye hear me, both of you? No drugs.'

'I hear you, Dave; got it.'

'Yeah, me too,' Kenny said.

'What are we gonna do about them?' Bennett said, his voice less steady than before. 'What does Perry think?'

'He says we're to top the pair of them tonight. We don't know what sort of warning our investigator friend here gave them. Brook might not be so clever to notice someone like him following his van here, but he's smart enough to look after nicked millions.'

192

'Right! Let's go and do them,' Bennett said, his face animated. 'Let's get these bastards.'

'Action!' Kenny said.

The three men headed for the door, causing Miller's hopes to soar. Their departure would buy him time to think how he could escape.

'Hang on fellas,' Bennett said. 'What about him in there?'

'Leave him until we've sorted this thing out, he's not going anywhere,' Dave said. 'Lock the doors and kill the lights. We don't want the fucker getting too comfortable.'

'I'll do it, you two go on ahead,' Kenny said.

Kenny back came into the office and stood at the door, a cigarette dangling from his mouth. A vicious smile played across his lips as he enjoyed once again the bedraggled sight of Miller slumped forward in the wooden chair, his thick frame dwarfing the chair's beech framework.

'We won't forget about you ya sneaky bastard,' he said. 'You're gonna get this.' He made the shape of a gun with his fingers, pointed it at Miller's head and made a 'pow' sound with his lips. 'In the meantime, enjoy your stay.' He walked up to him and kicked him in the chest. The chair spun slightly before tilting backwards towards the desk and, almost in slow motion, the edge came up to meet him.

His head smacked the edge of the desk with a bang and a shower of fireworks exploded inside his head. Seconds before he hit the floor and the lights went out, he heard a loud crack.

# TWENTY-TWO

Harvey Miller woke but felt as if he was walking towards a tunnel through a thick bank of fog. The room was dark and he was lying on the floor on his side, his upper body and legs tied to a chair, and half-underneath a desk. The thump, thump in his head reminded him of his encounter with the edge of the desk sometime earlier, and with some difficulty, he spat out a clot of blood making him gag.

He remembered the kick from Kenny Bennett, the bang on the head, and the crack. The crack, where did it come from? He felt a wave of panic as he thought it might have been his leg, collar bone or God forbid, his spine. For several minutes he lay there motionless in the darkness breathing hard, trying to calm down and steady his nerves before summing up the courage to move.

He shifted position, anticipating all the time the sudden jolt from a broken bone or the gnawing throb of a damaged tendon or muscle. He felt nothing. Despite the ropes, he managed to lift his left leg a little and to his surprise, it moved without pain. Shifting his weight, he tried the other, which felt dull and lifeless where he had been lying on it, but with some relief he also found out it was not broken or damaged.

Bennett had certainly made a good job of tying him

as he couldn't move his body, but while the bindings around his right wrist were tight, there was more movement with the one on the left. He then realised what the crack he heard was all about. The back of the chair had broken, not his spine or arm. He moved his back and shoulders trying to ease them free but even though the chair felt much looser than before, part of it seemed still connected to the base. With great difficulty, he tried to look over his shoulder and see if there was anything more he could do.

It was a basic beech wood chair with a framed back, attached to the base by two wooden posts. He could just make out that the post on one side had completely snapped, leaving a jagged stump. On the other, a large crack ran diagonally across it. It looked ready to split, but despite heaving his shoulders from side to side, he couldn't break free.

It took ten minutes to manoeuvre the top of the chair under the bottom of the desk, and with fists clenched and his feet hooked under the base of a radiator, he eased his shoulders forward with as much strength as he could muster. The veins on his forehead bulged, unused stomach sinews and tendons protested and sweat dripped in little streams down his face as he pulled and strained doing the toughest exercise he'd done as an adult. It resisted and resisted until he heard it splinter and then a loud crack. He kept the pressure on, when suddenly he jerked forward as the back of the chair parted from the seat. Boy, did that feel good!

His hands weren't together but tied behind him on to the wooden posts of the chair, and by squirming and leaning hard against the desk, he began to push both through his bindings. He was almost there, an inch or two to go, but it wouldn't move any further. What he needed was something to hold the frame steady.

He scanned around in the dark, easier now that his eyes were becoming accustomed to the gloom, and with a picture in his head of the office layout before the lights went out. He spotted the ideal candidate. It was a long, metal door stop, designed to prevent the handle of the door swinging back against the glass partition. Unfortunately, it was at the other end of the room.

Hot, tired and with pain coming from so many places, all he had to do was think of the jolly trio's return and it gave him a renewed burst of energy. He squirmed along the carpet, made easier now with more freedom to bend his torso. It didn't take long and he soon hooked the chair back under the door stop and pulled. His bindings parted from the chair back at the first attempt. With only a little more wriggling, the rope fell easily from his hands. He set to work on his leg and, after a few minutes, threw the rope into the corner as if it were a poisonous snake.

Free at last, he sat in the darkness rubbing his bleeding wrists, thinking how to get out of the barn. A few minutes later, a strange new aroma assailed his nostrils, different from the wet grass smells of the country or the dull woody notes of a barn made entirely of oak. This smell was acrid and bitter; like the smoke his neighbour used to send over his garden whenever he decided to burn leaves instead of composting them.

It started like the smoke from a far-off chimney, but grew stronger in tandem with his rising anxiety. He tried to open the door between the office and the laboratory but found it locked. He moved to a window overlooking the laboratory and parted the vertical blind. He could now see the source of the smoke. In the corner of the laboratory, beside some bottles of chemicals, orange flames were licking upwards. He watched, frozen to the spot, fascinated as they grew larger, feeding on the bottles like a hungry alien. When the bottles burst in the heat, the flames moved upward, tearing ravenously at the wooden frame of the barn.

He snapped out of the spell and searched for a way out. The door between the office and the laboratory was locked, maybe not a bad thing because if he opened it, the draught would create an upsurge of oxygen and invite the fire towards him. He ran to the office window facing the front of the barn, but to his utter dismay it was double-glazed and locked; no key.

There was nothing lying around with which to break it, save for some pieces of broken chair. He tried, but they simply bounced off the toughened glass. The flames were now licking at the office door, the noise and smell of burning wood almost overpowering. The window between the office and the laboratory suddenly shattered with a deafening crash. Flames licked inside the office, the vertical blind turning to dust in seconds and smoke and flames billowing under the door before changing it into a ball of flame seconds later. The heat was intense and

Miller was sure his clothes were about to melt around his body.

The only other heavy object in the place was the main office chair, an expensive and thickly padded monster which would not look out of place in the offices of an investment bank. Summoning up his last reserves of energy, he picked the chair up and launched it at the window. The glass cracked but didn't shatter. He lifted the chair again, with difficulty this time as it felt heavier than before, and swung it towards the window. This time both panes of glass shattered. Using the wooden leg from the broken chair, he poked at the jagged peaks of glass, trying to clear a path, hard to see as smoke and sweat were clouding his vision.

The sudden intake of fresh air from the broken window gave him an instant burst of energy but increased the intensity of the fire, now roaring behind him with the aggression of an angry lion. He could smell his hair sizzling and his flesh burning as he climbed into the ragged opening. He was nearly there, the cold fragrances of the night leading him on, but when he tried to move, he couldn't. He tried and tried but couldn't progress any further. Part of his clothing was caught on a shard of glass.

**\***

DI Henderson and DS Walters watched as a Range Rover bounced down the drive, and on reaching the tarmac, shot off down the road, heading north.

'They seem to be in a bit of a hurry,' he said.

'They do, but there's still a few hours until closing time,' Walters said. 'What's the rush?'

'Not everyone thinks about life in terms of drinking time, Sergeant Walters. There may be something interesting on the box, or maybe the driver's been told to get home now as his dinner's getting cold.'

'I take it the nosey copper in you now wants to wander up to the house for a look?'

'You know me too well, Sergeant Walters. Let's go.'

They got out the car and walked along the road to the entrance of Forest Farm. They turned into the drive when Henderson stopped. 'There are still lights on in the house.'

'So I see. Which means what? Someone could still be there?'

'Could be,' he said, 'or the householder is a bit cavalier about wasting electricity.'

'Or maybe there's been a spate of burglaries in the area and the householder leaves a light on for added security, as our colleagues in uniform advise. What do you think we should do?'

Henderson's phone vibrated.

'Hang on. Hello, Rachel.'

'Angus, where are you? You said you were coming home early tonight. I'm cooking you something special.'

Henderson racked his brains. It wasn't his birthday, her birthday, Easter, Valentine's Day. Nope, he would have to come clean.

'What are we celebrating?'

'We've been living together for two weeks.'

He was tempted to say, 'I thought it was something

'important', but resisted.

He went on to explain what they were doing in Loxwood, how long he thought it might take and when he expected to be home. With a warning not to be late as her 'special' lasagne would spoil if cooked too long ringing in his ears, he ended the call.

'Are you in some sort of trouble? I told you this would happen once you two moved in together.'

'I could be if we don't get a move on. How long was I talking on the phone?'

'Five, six minutes, I don't know. Why?'

'In this time, did the lights of the house change or did you spot any movement?'

'Nope, nothing's changed, nothing at all.'

'Let's go, but at the first signs of life or a dog, we back away and return tomorrow, hopefully with a warrant.'

'Only to find that Brook was here delivering the owner's legitimate wine order.'

'No chance. Phil said wine deliveries are done in big vans from the warehouse in Hammersmith. Brook is the boss, he doesn't do deliveries. He was here about something else.'

'I was joking. I hope they don't have a dog. I hate dogs.'

'I'm not too fond of big Dobermans or Alsatians myself, but as they don't have a front gate I suspect they don't have one, or if they do, the brute is safely locked up inside.'

'This driveway's a mess, don't you think? It's full of potholes. It's a good job there hasn't been much rain lately or we'd find ourselves stepping into some deep puddles. '

'If they've been making shedloads of money by wine faking, they sure don't spend it on tarmac.'

They walked in silence for a few minutes, their progress slow as they tried to sidestep the worst pot-holes, Henderson using his trusty Maglite to provide some guidance.

'I've been looking in the windows all the time we've been walking,' Henderson said, 'but there hasn't been any movement inside and I can't see any flicker from a television.'

'Me neither. Hang on, what's that at the side of the house?'

Henderson moved to the other side of the drive to see what Walters was referring to. There was an orange radiance, unsteady at first but solid now and getting stronger.

'I thought maybe it was the light of a torch or the glow of one of those sunlamp things,' she said.

'I don't think so, it seems to be getting bigger. I think it's a fire.' A sudden glow improved visibility. 'It's a fire, the building's on fire! C'mon!'

They started running towards it and in a practiced movement, Henderson pulled out his phone and called the emergency services. The ground levelled as they came closer to the house and he realised, for the Fire Service at least, they would be too late to save the wooden barn at the side of the house as it was engulfed in flame.

They would still be required though as the fire was singeing the branches of trees nearby, the barn was only five metres from the house and he had no idea if close neighbours were on the other side of a line of conifers behind the barn now glowing an eerie shade of orange.

They were close to the fire now, the searing heat in marked contrast to the coolness of the evening, but still no one came out of the house to investigate.

'Carol,' Henderson shouted above the roar of cracking glass and timber and the occasional small explosion, 'bang on the door and see if anyone's at home. Get them out of there, fast!'

She ran towards the back door as Henderson gave the barn a wide berth and tried to see what had been going on there. He hoped no one had been trapped inside, as in the short time since they had spotted the flames it had gone from a small fire to a major blaze, flames shooting ten or fifteen metres into the air.

He then noticed the body hanging out of a window. That end of the barn hadn't become totally engulfed yet, but soon it would be. He ran towards the motionless figure. He seemed to be unconscious. It looked as though he had tried to escape through the broken window but his clothes had got caught on the frame or a piece of glass. He hauled at his shoulders and as he did so, he could now see what was impeding his escape.

Walters came running towards him. 'There's no one in the house.'

'The guy's got stuck trying to get out. Untangle his trousers and lift his leg over the glass while I pull.'

The heat was like nothing he had ever experienced before. Sweat was pouring down his face and any moment now he was sure his clothes would spontaneously combust. Everything he touched was hot enough to cook a roast: the window frame, this man's body, Henderson's head.

He was a big guy but Henderson found the strength from somewhere to pull, and with Walters lifting his leg over a shard of glass, they gradually eased him out of the window. The fire had engulfed the whole barn now, and the area from which the man had been pulled was now filled with orange, angry flames, consuming everything in their path.

Henderson took a firmer grip of the injured man's shoulders and hauled him across the grass close to a line of trees where it felt cooler. Only then did he let him go and flop down exhausted.

Walters rushed over and attended to the victim. She drew out her torch and shone it into his eyes to check for life. 'Bloody hell, sir. It was hard to tell at first with his face all smoke and dirt, but it's Harvey Miller!'

Henderson got up and staggered towards her. He looked down, wiping his eyes with the back of his hand. Even this far from the fire, the smell of smoke and the heat made his eyes water. 'You're right, so it is! What the hell is he doing here? How is he? Is he alive?'

'I'm getting no pulse.'

Henderson lifted his arm but he couldn't find a pulse either. He placed one palm over the back of his other hand, interlocked his fingers and put them on Harvey's chest. He began to pump in a series of short, fast, downward compressions.

After about thirty pushes, he stopped and bent

down to give him mouth-to-mouth resuscitation. Harvey's face was black and his lips were raw and cracked. Henderson pinched the victim's nose and blew air into his lungs and watched as his chest inflated twice, before returning to administer another series of chest compressions. He repeated this routine three or four times, before he felt a hand on his arm.

'You can stop now, sir. I think we've lost him.'

# TWENTY-THREE

A few minutes after eight forty-five in the morning, Fraser Brook set off for work. It was Friday and he felt happy. Even though he owned a business that was open seven days a week, for the last six months he only worked a five-day week. This was partly because he was making so much money now selling wine collections, but also he wanted to see more of his friends. The new hours suited him to a tee as the jaded feeling he used to get on a Monday morning, and once again on Saturday, were long gone. Every day when he went into work, except after a heavy night, he headed there in a cheerful state of mind, prepared to attack anything his business could throw at him.

Aside from dealing with the usual list of issues plaguing his daily routine, Friday in the office also meant he would help the boys set the shop up for what was often the busiest day of the week. Rather than do paperwork in his office, he worked with Sam on the shop floor trying to decide which wines to put on display and how to market special promotions.

Only last week he received a call from a négociant friend in Bordeaux who had ten cases of a cabernet-based wine from a small château in the Cotes de Castillon, an area near Bordeaux that Sam and Brook believed offered excellent value for money. They had sold the wine before and were pleased with the feedback received from customers, so he said yes, especially when he knocked two Euros off the price of a bottle. This weekend, it would be the lead promotion, allowing customers to pick up an excellent seventeen-pound bottle of wine for only nine pounds ninety-nine. Sam liked a wager and they shook hands on a twenty-pound bet. Sam was confident he could sell all the wine by five o'clock on Saturday afternoon; Brook was sure there wouldn't be a trace of it left by one.

The sky was overcast and drizzly as he emerged from Sloane Square tube station. King's Road was full of annoying umbrellas trying to gouge a piece out of his skull, and tourists wearing hideously coloured plastic macs and anoraks bought from the Disney store and Legoland. He intended to work over lunchtime, so he walked into a small supermarket to buy a newspaper and some sandwiches. He resumed his journey, taking extra care to dodge puddles and the splashes from passing taxis and buses, when his phone rang.

'Hello Sam, how are you this not so fine morning?' he said.

'Fraser,' a voice hissed, 'I'm in the loo.'

'Sam,' he said, smiling, 'if every staff member called me up every time they went to the toilet I would never get any work done.'

'No, no Fraser, listen. I'm in the loo to get away from *them*.'

'Who's 'them'? The rent's up to date and I don't owe anyone money that I know of. Stop being so Dick

Tracy.'

'Jim Bennett and his loopy son. They're waiting for you downstairs.'

'Jim and Kenny have been to the shop before, Sam. What's the difference this time?'

'You should see the look on Jim Bennett's face, it's like thunder! He's pacing up and down like a bull and muttering to himself. He's very angry and I think it's directed at you. If I didn't know any better, I would suspect you've done something horrible to him and he's here to pay you back.'

He was a sensitive lad, Sam, and alarm bells started ringing in Brook's head before he finished the sentence. What he wanted more than anything was some coke to calm his nerves, as the needle of his personal 'stressometer' was hitting the red area at the far end of the dial. His last hit was over an hour ago, but he forced himself to ignore it. He needed to focus.

He stopped walking and stood in the shelter of a shop doorway, 'Sheik Gowns at Smart Prices' the large poster declared.

'Right Sam,' he said as calmly as he could. 'Let's go back a bit. You say Jim Bennett and his son came into the shop. Are you sure it's them?'

'Yes! I'm positive. I've seen them both before. Remember the time they came into the shop with boxes of wine, and another couple of times Jim Bennett came in for a business meeting with you. A short guy with an ugly craggy face, and his son is tall with slouching shoulders and terrible taste in clothes. I *know* it's them.'

'You're right Sam, I'm sorry to doubt you. Right, so

they are downstairs in the shop and Jim Bennett looks angry.'

'Yes!'

'What did he say to you?'

'Well, the two of them sort of burst in not long after we opened and demanded to know where you were. When I told them you hadn't arrived for work yet, the older Bennett said they would wait. When I offered to call and jog you along, he near wet his pants: no calls, he didn't want you to know they were there, it was a surprise. I've been to surprise parties before but not when the host looks like he wants to cut your throat.'

'Tell me *exactly* what Bennett said to you.'

'Excuse the profanities Fraser but he said something like 'where the fuck is Brook?' When I said you weren't in, he said, 'I need to speak to him urgently. We'll wait here for the slimy bastard.' It doesn't sound much like a social call, does it?'

Brook slumped against the shop window. Bennett never called him 'Brook' or swore at him, and rarely used bad language with other people in his presence. It was always 'Fraser' or 'Mr Brook'. These people respected him. He was their wine expert, the man who brought in all the lovely money. Something clearly had gone wrong.

'Well done Sam, thank you for telling me.' He was about to add, 'you saved my life,' but decided against it as he wasn't out of the woods yet. 'I'm in the dark as much as you are, as I've no idea what this is about, but you'll understand if I don't come into the shop for the next few days. It will give them time to calm down, but don't say anything to them. If we let them stew for a while, they'll soon get fed up and get out of your hair. Does this sound like a plan?'

'Yes it does.'

'Good. If they start throwing their weight around or get aggressive with you guys or any of our customers, you go ahead and call the police or hit the panic button. Their gripe is with me, not with you or the shop. Is this clear?'

'Right, Fraser, thanks. I feel better now I've talked to you. I must get back to the shop now as I'm not sure Anders can cope for long on his own. You know how intolerant he can be. Good luck.'

Keep calm, Brook said to himself as he stared at a shop window filled with ladies dresses and shoes. He was not in panic mode yet as he still entertained the possibility of a misunderstanding. It had to be something to do with the wine-faking business. The other dealings they had together, such as the dope Bennett supplied, or the wine barrels and bottles his parcel business brought into the UK were areas that could never generate animosity between them. He needed to speak to Landseer.

Landseer's mobile rang and rang but eventually diverted to voicemail; Brook didn't leave a message. He called Landseer's home, and again there was no reply. He called his office at Landseer Properties in Mayfair.

'I'm sorry Mr Brook,' his secretary, Miriam said, 'but Charles hasn't arrived in the office yet.'

'What time does he normally get in?' Brook knew Landseer was always seated at his desk by eight, rain or shine, and it was now nine-thirty, but didn't say so as he didn't want to alarm Miriam yet.

'By eight most days, but my guess is his train must have been delayed or something. He certainly didn't go straight out to an appointment, as I'm looking at his diary now and he's got nothing on until ten o'clock, and it's a meeting in this office.'

'Could you double-check?'

'One moment.'

Brook looked around him. He realised if Bennett and his son left the shop now, they would probably walk this way, heading for the underground station. He felt a wave of panic, as the shop was less than five minutes away, but relaxed when he remembered that Bennett refused to travel on public transport.

'Hello, Mr Brook. I've had a look in Charles's desk diary and it says the same as my system; he doesn't have any appointments until ten o'clock when he's seeing our lawyer, Mr Rivers, at our offices.'

Landseer would never be late for a meeting, he was too OCD. 'Would he phone you if his train's been delayed?'

'Yes, most certainly, Mr Brook. I must admit, I do find it odd, his phone may have run out of battery or something.'

'Perhaps,' Brook said, but he wasn't convinced. Landseer carried around two phones: a Blackberry he used for work and a Nokia pay-as-you-go which he kept for personal calls. Landseer often described Brook's personal life as 'colourful', but he could think of no better word for Landseer's predilections than 'sleazy'. He'd long suspected he was a regular user of under-age rent boys, and Landseer once let slip while drunk his intention to ditch the Nokia in the nearest dustbin if the police ever came close.

In turn, he would joke that Landseer's removal from his lofty, up-market pedestal would be sudden, a midnight raid on a nightclub and an appearance at Bow Street Magistrates Court, his reputation in tatters and his face and story the toast of the tabloids. In private, he suspected his lifeless body would be found in a skip in East London, the vengeance of an angry pimp or the unbridled anger of a parent. However, the arrival of Jim and Kenny Bennett in his shop and the no-show of Landseer on the same morning was none of these; it had to be something they were involved in together.

'Listen Miriam, if he doesn't show up by ten o'clock can you please send someone around to his house. I fear he may have taken ill or had an accident or something.'

His secretary laughed. 'You know Charles, he's bullet-proof, at least that's what he always tells us. If I can be so bold, aren't you perhaps being a little over dramatic, Mr Brook?'

'Miriam,' Brook said. 'I've tried his mobile, his house phone and now his office, all without success. He's an estate agent for God's sake! Have you ever known him to be out of contact for five minutes, never mind an hour at the start of a business day? What if I was a client planning to sell my eight-million-pound country house. I would think he doesn't want my business and go elsewhere.'

'When you put it like that, Mr Brook, I do have to

agree with you.'

'Thank you. Send someone around to his house soon, please. I'm very concerned.'

'Rest assured, Mr Brook, I will do.'

'Thank you Miriam, goodbye.'

Brook dropped the phone into his jacket pocket, turned around and headed back to the tube station. Bennett and his son were in his shop to do what, exactly? Talk to him, ask his opinion about something connected to the business? Take him away, more like. Kidnap him and subject him to unthinkable tortures until he revealed where all the stolen money was stashed, he suspected. When they got what they wanted, what would happen then? Kill him, murder him in revenge? He shuddered at the thought as he stepped on the train.

Had they got to Landseer already? Could he have spotted the way the wind was blowing and invoked his pre-prepared escape plan, as Brook was doing now? He shook his head. No, Landseer was too dumb to create an escape plan and wouldn't have the balls to carry it through. In any case, how could he see them coming when Brook couldn't? Landseer didn't have the benefit of a paranoid wine shop assistant like Sam whose reading of people and spotting of shoplifters was second to none. Instead, he had the leggy but stupid Miriam, a woman who couldn't spell the word 'crisis' and would be the last to react if someone dropped down dead in front of her.

During the journey home he did his best to assemble the scrambled thoughts racing around his head like a colony of ants. Plan A was to return to the house in Maida Vale, which had a large wine cellar, big enough to keep a small army of drunks in clover for a year. Perry and his people didn't know about Maida Vale and there he could lay low until the heat cooled. It was risky and would create anxiety, as he would be constantly looking over his shoulder in supermarket queues and afraid to go out in case he was spotted.

Plan B was to leave London and never return. This required him to forget about the shop, the ideas he had for its expansion, the ever-busy Hammersmith warehouse and his beautiful house in a lovely part of the Capital. He almost cried at the implications, but no matter how difficult it would be, his mind was made up; Plan B it would be.

In deciding to go away, he added a small proviso. He would keep going until such times as he made contact with Landseer. If he detected nothing wrong, he would return home and call Bennett and try to deal with whatever fuss was bothering him. With Landseer breathing and still at his desk, it couldn't be that serious.

He left the tube station and headed back to his house, the route he had walked in such a chirpy mood an hour or so before. Feeling paranoid, and who wouldn't be in such circumstances, he scanned the faces of all the people he passed and glanced into parked cars, looking for watchers. He reached the front door of his house unmolested, and felt quiet satisfaction for having the presence of mind not to reveal the address of his bolt-hole to anyone.

# TWENTY-FOUR

He turned on the shower and stepped inside, not caring that it ran cold for a spell before heating up. Henderson let the water cascade over his hair and face for several minutes before using soap and then shampoo. He turned off the water and got out and started to rub himself down with a towel, but even then he could still smell and taste the acrid aroma of smoke, and half-expected the towel to be streaked with black marks.

He had done the same thing last night when he returned home from Forest Farm having first slumped down on the settee, and before Rachel had cut his hair to remove all the frizzy bits. He was convinced all the cleansing was to eradicate the last vestiges of the fire, but now he believed it was to erase the picture in his head of Harvey Miller taking his last breaths.

He walked downstairs and into the kitchen. Rachel had left for work some hours before, but she was such a tidy soul there was no record of her ever having been in there. He started up the coffee machine, put a slice of bread in the toaster and stared out of the window while the two machines worked their magic.

It was the middle of June and Brighton was beginning to feel like a holiday resort again, as he could see little groups of tourists ambling past and more cars than usual cruising the street, looking for a parking place. Living so close to Brighton College, his neighbours could tell when something was on in that venerable institution, like prize giving or a speech by a famous former pupil, but he couldn't and ascribed any increased levels of activity outside to tourists.

When going to bed last night, he decided he would only go into work in the morning if he felt fine, as he had no idea what effect the inhalation of fumes and chemicals would have on him. Now that he had eaten and drunk something, he felt good enough to go into work, but then he had a coughing fit that ended with him throwing up in the sink.

In times of illness or injury, the only things that helped him feel better were sleep and exercise, as he couldn't slump down in front of the television and watch an entire series of *Breaking Bad* or *Game of Thrones* as Gerry Hobbs liked to do. Sleep was out of the question as he didn't feel tired and his exercise fall-back, a long run along Brighton seafront, held little appeal for a man with compromised lungs. Instead, he packed his swimming things into a bag and set off at a slower pace than usual to walk to the Prince Regent Swimming Complex.

When he emerged from the changing rooms and stood for a moment to put on his goggles, he was taken aback by the noise level. Early on Sunday mornings when he often came here, the pool was populated by gangs of OAPs either standing and nattering at the shallow end or making their way up and down the pool at a slow, leisurely pace. This was Friday, and instead of a load of white and grey heads, the hair colour of the sixteen and seventeen year-old school kids doing most of the shouting, was blue, red and shades of orange not seen outside of a Pantone colour card.

Henderson walked towards the roped-off lanes and entered the water. Swimming and running to him were automatic exercises, one leg or arm in front of the other while his head went off to a different place, wrestling with whatever problem that was bothering him. Today, it started off in familiar fashion, he trying to make sense of why Harvey Miller was found in the barn at Loxwood and why it had caught fire, while his arms and legs ploughed through the water as if powered by an electric motor. However, by the end of the fifth length, a sharp pain in his lungs flared, breaking his concentration and leaving him gasping for breath.

He resumed swimming and with each length the physical interruptions subsided and as expected, the strong smell of chlorine from the pool water replaced the acerbic taste of chemicals and smoke in his mouth and on his skin. When he touched the end of the pool for the twentieth time, half the distance of his normal workout, he decided he'd done enough.

If he thought the pool area had been noisy, the changing rooms were twice as bad, with kids shouting at the tops of their voices to friends they could talk to in a few minutes time outside. After dressing and drying his hair, he left the swimming complex and walked over to a café nearby. Unlike his experience earlier in the kitchen, he now felt hungry and some of his normal zip and energy had returned, tempered by a not unwelcome dull ache in his muscles from swimming.

He didn't realise, as he didn't come into Brighton at this time of the morning often, but many of the restaurants and cafés in the vicinity offered a breakfast menu and even at this late hour, ten forty-five, several were busy. He entered the café and ordered a 'kill 'em or cure 'em' all day special and settled into his seat to await its delivery.

He made a decision that he now felt well enough after his swim to go back into work and after eating, would return to the house and pick up the car keys and head there. He was watching a young mother outside struggle with a buggy, trying to collapse it while at the same time restraining a toddler from walking off, when his phone rang.

'Morning sir,' DC Sally Graham said, 'how are you feeling?'

Henderson explained about the therapeutic effects of a dip in the pool and the soon to be devoured full English breakfast, and his intention to return to Malling House in the afternoon.

'I'm pleased to hear it,' Graham said, 'when I spoke to DS Walters she said you didn't look at all well last night.'

'I don't suppose I did with my face blackened with smoke and streaked in sweat. How's she?'

'She's fine, sir, no after effects of the fire. She's gone over to Forest Farm to see if the Fire Investigators have found anything and to take a look inside the farmhouse, that is if she can gain access.'

'Not on her own, I trust?'

'No, DC Sunderam is with her.'

'Good, as you never know, the owner of the barn might come back and I have my suspicions they're involved in the wine faking operation in some capacity.'

'I understand. The reason I called was to find out how you were, of course, but also to tell you about something I saw on the serials this morning.'

'What is it?'

'Well, you know in team meetings we've discussed how the wine fakers had to have someone in an upmarket magazine or estate agency who could identify large properties with sizeable wine collections?'

'Yes.'

'An estate agent called Charles Landseer was found murdered in Surrey last night. With half a dozen offices in London and the Home Counties, he specialised in buying and selling large country houses.'

**

She took care guiding the car up the long driveway at Forest Farm in Loxwood, her memory still fresh of the big potholes that she and DI Henderson nearly walked into the previous night. DS Walters could see no trace of the three fire tenders, here tackling the blaze, and the only remains of the magnificent 15th century barn were a few stumps of blackened wood and a foul-smelling expanse of rubble.

A small van with the inscription 'Fire Investigation

Unit' in big letters on the side was parked at the back. DS Walters saw the occupants of the van kneeling inside the barn, their white overalls contrasting sharply with the charred debris all around them.

'Good morning gentlemen. I'm Detective Sergeant Walters from Surrey and Sussex CID and this is Detective Constable Sunderam,' she said displaying her warrant card and jerking a thumb at Deepak standing beside her.

'Good afternoon Detective Walters,' said the older of the two, getting up to shake her hand. 'I'm Bill Danvers and this is my colleague Kingsley Harting.'

'We're here to try and establish if the victim pulled from the fire last night was being held against his will, or if this was a tragic accident; a case of being in the wrong place at the wrong time.'

'What makes you think he was being held prisoner?'

'Why else would he be trying to escape through a locked window?'

'Maybe the fire was burning too fiercely on the other side of the door?' Danvers said.

'Could be, but if it was me in there, I would sooner run through a fire to a known exit, than waste my time attempting to smash a double glazed window.'

He nodded as if in agreement. Their theory about Harvey Miller being held prisoner was also corroborated by DI Henderson, currently at home recuperating from his smoke and fire ordeal, who noticed the office door was shut, seconds before it disappeared in a ball of flame.

'Well, I can't tell you much about the victim, I'm

afraid,' Danvers said. 'Our investigation is concerned with establishing the cause of the fire. I'm trying to find out what created the initial spark and what caused it to burn so ferociously. It's a shame the rain that arrived later and is making this morning a bit of a soggy mess, didn't arrive earlier.'

'What can you tell me about the cause of the fire?'

Danvers gave her a look that she'd seen from suspects and witnesses many times before: will I tell you, or won't I? In the end vanity won over his feeble attempt at proprietary as he wanted to show off to the pretty lady how smart he could be.

'As you can see from all the glass fragments lying here, they are not the more common transparent variety associated with milk and drinks bottles but coloured like that of a wine bottle.' He bent down and picked up a small shard of green glass. 'What's interesting is some pieces are thicker than normal, suggesting a more old-fashioned style of bottle I would say. Kingsley knows more about this than I do.'

The other man stood and walked over. 'I agree with Bill about the 'old-fashioned' angle. Forty to fifty years ago wine, port and brandy bottles were all made out of much thicker glass than in use today. You see, they were transported in the holds of ships and the handling at the dockside was more primitive back then. Those thin, modern bottles you find in supermarkets wouldn't last five minutes in those sorts of conditions.'

'Yes,' Danvers said, taking up the story like the partner in a good double-act, 'this leads us to believe the barn was being used as some sort of wine store.'

'Were the bottles full or empty?' Sunderam asked.

'It's hard to say. We found some evidence of wine over there,' he said, pointing, 'and believe it or not, we found a piece of bottle with some wine still inside. Amazing how it never evaporated in the heat.'

'Do you have any idea how the fire started?'

'Not yet,' Danvers said. 'What we're more sure about is *where* it started, which was about here,' he said pointing. 'If my knowledge of these types of barn is correct, my sister lives in something similar in Ditchling, nothing occupies this space such as a cooker or power point. It's nothing but open space. Therefore, it might have been a lighted rag or inflammable liquid, or the accidental tipping over of a candle or the careless discarding of a lighted cigarette.'

'A dropped cigarette could've caused all this?' Sunderam said.

'Yeah, I'm afraid so. Don't forget a building like this is constructed from varnished, dry wood, and with chairs, curtains, tables and alcohol added to the combustible mix, the barn would have become an uncontrollable blaze in no time. So, before we give you a definite answer as to the cause, we first need to analyse the wood fragments around where we believe the seat of the fire to be, and look for traces of propellants such as petrol or white spirit.'

'Thanks for your time gents,' Walters said, 'you've been very enlightening. Do you know anything about the owners or occupants of the barn? I assume it belongs to the people living in the farmhouse?'

'When we arrived,' Danvers said, 'we met the

housekeeper who I believe is still in the house cleaning, but we didn't see anyone else. If you find the owner, please let me know as I would like a word as well.'

She walked to the back door, the one she had been vainly banging on last night, but this time with Deepak beside her. 'And they say SOCOs are pedantic.'

Deepak laughed, showing a gap in his front teeth. 'Give them time, they're getting there.'

The back door was unlocked and they walked in. 'Hello!' Walters shouted. 'Is anybody there?'

Walters stood leaning against the large table in the kitchen and listened. A minute or two later, she heard footsteps and a small woman walked towards her. She wore green-checked overalls, her hair was tied back in a bun behind her head and in her hand she carried a yellow duster.

'Hello there. I'm Detective Sergeant Walters from Surrey and Sussex Police,' she said holding up her ID. 'This is my colleague Detective Constable Sunderam. The door was open.'

The housekeeper stood at the end of the table, eyeing the younger woman with suspicion written all over her face. 'I'm Janet Grainger, the housekeeper here. How can I help you?' she said, her lips pressed tersely together.

'Janet, I'm here about the fire.' The words tumbled out before she could stop them. Why else would a couple of detectives be visiting this remote farmhouse?

'I thought as much, but I prefer Mrs Grainger, if

you don't mind.'

'Who owns this place?'

'He's not in residence at the moment. He often goes abroad.'

'What's his name?'

'I don't think it's any of your business.'

'Mrs Grainger, need I remind you that I am a police officer and I'm investigating a serious crime. Your lack of cooperation may be hindering the apprehension of a murderer. You can either answer my questions here, or I'll take you back to an interview room at Lewes and you can answer them there; your choice. Do you understand?'

Mrs Grainger pulled out a chair and sat down. 'Murder you said. Who was murdered?'

She was tempted to say, 'I don't think it's any of your business,' but stopped. 'We are conducting an on-going murder enquiry and believe whatever went on in the barn out there is connected to it. Now, let's start with the owner's name.'

'David Frankland. This farm and the barn and the stables are all owned by him.'

She didn't expect to hear his name. David Frankland; Daniel Perry's boot man. The big Australian they'd interviewed in Gosport who came across as another hard, aggressive businessman, but now it appeared he was up to his neck in wine faking.

'Where is Mr Frankland now?'

'I don't know. As I said before, he goes abroad a lot and often at short notice. I haven't seen him for over a week. First I knew anything was wrong was when I saw details of the fire on the local news this morning.'

'Have you been in contact with him these past few days?'

'No, he doesn't talk much to me. I come in two days a week, tidy-up, clean and then I go home to make my Robert's lunch. I've got a key. I don't often see him.'

'Did you notice anything unusual going on in the barn?'

'I know Mr Frankland moved one of his businesses here after the lease ran out on their previous place, but not much more.'

'What does the business do?'

She shrugged. 'I don't know. I didn't ask. All I saw was a bunch of young people coming in here first thing in the morning.'

'I'd like to take a look around the house, if it's ok with you.'

'Be my guest, but there's not much to see, a single man living in a big place like this. It's not natural if you ask me.'

# TWENTY-FIVE

Sally Graham picked Henderson up from outside his house in College Place and they headed north towards Westerham. He preferred using his own car when attending crime scenes as he often stayed longer than many of his officers and had all sorts of equipment and clothes in the boot. He didn't mind this time as he didn't feel much like driving and he knew Sally Graham was a decent driver.

'What do we know about the victim?' he asked.

'As I said on the phone, he's an estate agent and owns six offices in Central London, Surrey, Hertfordshire and Middlesex, all selling large country properties.'

'Do we know if he has any connection with Fraser Brook?'

'Not yet but the detective I spoke to, DI Blake...Do you know him?'

He nodded. 'Aggressive, territorial and ignorant. He won't be pleased when we turn up and start tramping over his patch.'

'He was ok with me. He said he would ask his guys to keep their eyes open for Brook's name.'

'He probably said that to try and keep you in Lewes, but he's a decent cop and if he says he'll do something, he'll do it. Mind you, if we do find a strong connection between our case and his, he'll create a mighty fuss if we try to take it away from him.'

It didn't take long to reach Westerham, a pretty Kent village a few miles south of the M25. Landseer's house was easy to spot as it was large, befitting an up-market estate agent, and replete with incident tape and numerous police vehicles.

It didn't do to blunder into another DI's crime scene and instead he sought out DI Blake. They found him in the living room, watching an ambulance crew zip the inert body of Charles Landseer into a body bag.

'Hello, Eric.'

'Ah, it's you Henderson, and I take it you,' he said turning to DC Graham, 'must be the nice woman who called me.' The smile was snake-like and at any moment, Henderson was expecting to see a forked tongue dart out.

'What happened?' Henderson asked.

'What's it to you?'

'I'm sure DC Graham told you about the case we're working on.'

'I wanna hear it from you.'

The ambulance crew lifted the stretcher and they all stood back and watched as it moved out of the room at a slow, dignified pace.

'We believe Charles Landseer may have been involved in a wine faking fraud case we're investigating.'

'How?'

Henderson explained the role he believed an estate agent would play and how it might be connected to wine dealer, Fraser Brook.

'This is the name my guys have been keeping an eye out for?'

'Yes.'

'Good news. My tech guy out in the study found some stuff on the victim's pc about Brook, but I tell you Henderson, I don't care how much this dovetails with your case, you're not fucking getting it. I've been sitting on my thumbs for the last couple of weeks thanks to that bastard McDowell. If I can solve this, I want to shove the result up his arse.'

'Understood, but I'm not interested in taking your case. I've got enough on my plate as it is.'

'As long as you know.'

'Fine, so what happened?'

He sighed and turned to face him. 'A woman who works for Landseer came round to his door as she was worried when her boss didn't show up for work this morning. A neighbour had a spare key and they found him lying on the carpet. Bullet wound to the knee and one to the head.'

'A bullet to the knee? What's that about?'

'Stop him running away, what the fuck do I know? I'll wait for the post mortem and ballistics before I make any wild assumptions.'

'Any witnesses?'

'It's a quiet street, so no, but a neighbour out walking his dog saw a car drive to the end of the road without its lights on, which he thought odd. I'm not sure I do, but it was around the time we think our victim was hit so maybe I should.'

'What sort of car?'

'Not a bloody clue.' He turned to face the open

lounge door. 'Evans!' Blake shouted. 'In here, now.'

A minute or so later, a red-faced constable entered the room.

'What took you so long, son?' Blake said.

'I was searching the garden for clues like you said.'

'Tell the nice man here about the neighbour who saw the car.'

As Evans reached his notebook, Blake took the opportunity of the diversion to escape. Henderson heard him say something to a colleague before he disappeared out of the room, heading back to the office, no doubt, to start the paperwork and effectively stake his claim on this case.

'A Mr Hadley Youngman was out walking his Labrador, Bruce, at about ten-thirty last night,' PC Evans said, 'when he saw a car travelling along the road outside. He took notice as it was dark and the car wasn't displaying any lights.'

'Where was Mr Youngman when he saw this?' Henderson asked.

'He was walking past Mr Landseer's house.'

'So, if it was the killer or killers in the car, he'd just had a lucky escape.'

'He realises that now, sir. His wife had to give a him a sedative when we told him.'

'So, what did he see?'

'As I said, he saw a car with three occupants inside drive to the end of the road and turn right.'

'Still no lights?'

'The lights came on just as they turned the corner.'

'What sort of car was it?'

'He knows about cars, does our Mr Youngman. It

was blue or black, he wasn't definite about the colour as it was dark, but he was sure about the make: a Range Rover.'

**

Walters walked past the housekeeper of Forest Farm, Janet Grainger and out into a small corridor. DC Sunderam followed behind.

'Deepak, you do downstairs and I'll do up. Look in suitcases, wardrobes and drawers for money, drugs, arms, you name it. Ok?'

'Right sergeant.'

Most of the bedrooms looked unused except for a large one at the end overlooking the front of the house. It offered views out to an expanse of two fields either side of the driveway, the village of Loxwood to the left, and a panorama of fields and trees as far as the eye could see in the centre. The cupboards, drawer units and wardrobe contained the clothes of a tall man who bought with little regard to price. She found cashmere sweaters, linen suits and big name labels, but nothing incriminating.

She heard a car engine and rushed to the window, her heart pounding. It wasn't the return of David Frankland but the red Nissan Micra she saw earlier, the housekeeper off to make her Robert's lunch, or to warn her employer.

The floor was of unpolished floorboards that creaked as she moved, grey in colour, and looking as thick and substantial as railway sleepers. A Chinese-style rug covered part of the floor and she rolled it back and examined the boards underneath. She tried to prise them loose but they didn't budge, and nothing about their shape or colour looked unusual.

Still on her knees, she reached for the rug to replace it when she noticed a small hatch low down in the wall, obscured in part by the bed. She pulled the bed away from the wall and bent down for a closer look.

There was a handle on the hatch, painted the same colour as the wall and making it hard to see at first glance. She turned it and opened the door and could tell from the sudden draught of cold air that it led into a small loft. She looked inside and waited ten to fifteen seconds for her eyes to become accustomed to the gloom before searching around for a light switch.

Expecting it to be chock-full of old suitcases and Christmas decorations, she was surprised to see three boxes, two blue suitcases and an aluminium briefcase. She reached for the briefcase and pulled it towards her. She sat down on the boards and popped both locks. Two neatly pressed shirts and a variety of toiletries met her gaze. She was puzzled as the contents didn't square with the weight of the thing and realised there had to be something underneath.

She removed the clothes and put them to one side and her jaw dropped at what she uncovered: neat bundles of fifty-pound notes and twenties, packed three inches deep. She pushed her hand into the case. Her hand touched something metal. She was about to take out the money and pile it beside the shirts when she heard the noise of a car engine. It was most likely the SOCO team but she couldn't risk the appearance of Frankland, so she closed the case and pushed it back into the loft space before squeezing back through the hatch, switching off the light and closing the hatch.

She ran over to the window and could see the top of a car, parked near the front door, and heard someone stomping around the house. She felt a wave of nausea. If this was David Frankland, a man suspected of kidnapping and murdering Harvey Miller, and a close confidant of Daniel Perry, he was likely to be armed and dangerous.

She brushed her clothes down to remove some of the dust from the loft and as quiet as possible, put the carpet and bedside unit back in their places. She walked into the hallway and was shocked to see David Frankland standing in front of her.

'What's going on here?' he said.

'I'm a police officer, Surrey and Sussex CID. I'm investigating the fire in the barn.' She pulled out her warrant card and showed it to him. 'I would like to ask you some questions.'

'I fucking know who you are. What are you doing in my house? The fire was in the barn.'

'We suspect...' He pushed past her and walked into the bedroom.

'You've been poking around in here haven't you, the bed's been moved.' He strode towards her, his face cold and hard; her hand reached for the pepper spray.

Before she got there, Frankland punched her on the side of the head, and as she recoiled, another fist crashed into her belly. Punches rained down on her head causing her to stumble backwards. She raised her head for a moment and a fist came hurtling towards her, smacking her straight in the face. She blacked out and hit the floorboards with a thump.

Sometime later, she opened her eyes. Blood from her nose had splattered over her blouse, and two football teams were playing a cup match inside her head. Through the fog and the pain, she remembered Frankland, the go-bag with the money and the gun. She tried to tune out the throb-throb of her headache and listened for any movement around the house.

Someone was banging around downstairs, opening and closing cupboards, hurried footsteps across a stone floor. For a minute, there was nothing and she wondered if she'd imagined it, when there was a loud bang, the sound of a door slamming.

With some difficulty, she got to her feet. Her head started spinning and before she could move to the bathroom, she threw up on the floor. She wiped her arm across her mouth, smearing her blouse in blood, but it was already in such a mess she'd decided it was heading for the bin. With heavy slow steps, she made her way back into Frankland's bedroom.

The bed had been left at an odd angle and the hatch door lay ajar. She stood by an open window and gulped down clean, fresh air, a handkerchief held to her nose to catch the dripping blood. Her head was thumping like a big bass drum and even though she knew it wasn't, it felt twice its normal size. Leaning out, she could see the boot of the car below. The tailgate was open but she couldn't see any sign of Frankland.

She moved to the hatch, dropped to her knees and

peered inside. The suitcases and the aluminium briefcase were gone. She returned to the window and seconds later Frankland appeared carrying two suitcases. He loaded them into the boot and snapped the tailgate shut before heading back into the house. She froze. Was he coming back to finish her off? She listened hard but could not hear his footsteps on the stairs. To her relief, he appeared a few seconds later carrying the aluminium briefcase. He opened the back door of the car and placed it behind the front seats.

She retrieved her handbag and pulled out her mobile. 'Control? DS Walters at Forest Farm in Loxwood.' Her voice sounded nasal as if gurgling with a glass of water. 'Suspect David Frankland is about to escape in a black Range Rover reg plate DAF 562. Request assistance.'

'A patrol car is in the vicinity. I'll redirect them to Forest Farm.'

Minutes later, the tall figure of Frankland appeared and walked to the car carrying a small package. He climbed in, placed the package under the passenger seat and started the engine. Glancing up, Walters spotted the welcome sight of a Police Volvo descending the small hill from the village, its indicator light flashing. With a screech of tyres, Frankland reversed and turned down the driveway.

Frankland could see the patrol car blocking his exit but it didn't stop him heading towards it at pace. She watched, holding her breath for a few tense seconds as the Range Rover bore down on the Volvo. She was about to close her eyes at the hideous impact when Frankland swung to the left and bounced into the field. The police driver followed.

Walters couldn't understand Frankland's tactics. The field was surrounded by tall hedges and he appeared to be heading into the corner and certain capture. She suddenly realised the bushes over there were thinner and more sparsely spaced than the rest of the hedge, covering an unused entrance or an emergency escape route.

The police driver spotted Frankland's intentions and tried to cut him off, but arrived too late and could only watch as the Range Rover sailed through the gap. To Walters's astonishment, it didn't hit the road and roar off towards Loxwood, never to be seen again. The car sailed through the air and when it landed, it skidded across the tarmac, made slick by heavy overnight rain, and smacked straight into a telegraph pole.

# TWENTY-SIX

Within ten minutes of arriving back at Maida Vale, Fraser Brook had filled one suitcase with clothes and emptied the bathroom of toiletries. He then called a taxi. He put the suitcase in the hall and took a seat behind the antique writing desk in the sitting room, and removed a piece of lavender-coloured paper from a secret drawer headed, 'Essential Items.' One by one, he extracted the listed articles from various compartments including a large sum of money in Sterling and Euros, an unused credit card, his UK passport, driving licence and European Health Card.

He put everything into the attaché case, first making sure it also included his personal organiser as it contained all the information he needed to access his UK and Swiss bank accounts, not to mention friends all over the world, before zipping it closed.

A few minutes later he heard the familiar clattering of a well-used diesel and walked to the window to confirm it was indeed the taxi. While standing there, he looked up and down the road for idling or double-parked cars or people hanging around and doing nothing. Seeing none, he turned and headed into the hall. He picked up the attaché case in one hand and opened the front door with the other. With one final look around his beautiful house, he lifted the suitcase and walked outside.

The taxi driver took his luggage and placed it in the boot. At the same time, Brook took a look round, at the street, at the parked cars, at the row of houses, his house nestling in the middle as if being hugged on both sides. He shook his head at what he was leaving behind and climbed into the taxi.

He didn't feel vindictive towards Perry and his associates for causing this, he'd known one day it would come to this. He felt scared and apprehensive, of course, but not vindictive. However, his attitude would change if he discovered that Landseer had been murdered. Inside a filing cabinet at his office above the wine shop, he'd compiled a file of incriminating evidence, and all it would take was a simple phone call to Sam or Anders and they would all be put away for life.

Maybe then, he would return and live here, but no, he couldn't kid himself. Daniel Perry was a vicious, devious thug and took offence at the merest sign of betrayal. With several million pounds at stake, it wouldn't matter if Perry, David Frankland and Perry's big Russian ogre, Hal, were all locked away in Belmarsh, Perry knew enough people that could locate him and kill him. He knew he could never return.

Five minutes into his journey to Heathrow, his phone rang. He looked at the display: Jim Bennett. He pressed the red button and ended the call. He would answer it at some point in the day, as he needed to confirm the reason for him being hounded, but not yet.

He had no clear idea where he wanted to go other

than a quick flight to Europe, so he took the advice of the taxi driver and stopped outside Terminal Five. He knew British Airways were the sole user of the terminal, but with their network, they could take him anywhere in the world. Once inside the spacious building, he searched for a sales desk and while waiting his turn in the queue, his phone rang. Again it was Bennett and again he refused to answer it.

'Hello sir, how can I help you?'

'The board says you have a flight to Paris at twelve fifty-five, are there any seats left for little old me?'

'Let me take a look sir,' she said tapping the keyboard with long, red nails. He looked at her face while she waited for the screen to load. A pretty face with neatly trimmed hair, but way too much foundation and mascara, her way of countering the harsh lighting and the skin-drying air-conditioning of this cavernous building, he assumed.

'I am sorry sir,' she said, her ruby lips moving in a way that mesmerised him, 'the flight is full. There's another flight to Paris at fifteen ten, or an earlier one at thirteen-oh-five from Terminal Two.'

'The second flight's too late and I don't want to go to another terminal. Rome, what about Rome? I think there's a flight at one thirty.'

She checked Rome. 'Sorry sir. That flight is full as well.'

Mentally, cracks were beginning to appear. What if he couldn't get away? Stage One of his Big Getaway Plan and he can't go anywhere. Focus Brook, focus.

'Amsterdam? What about there?'

He'd been to Amsterdam many times before, for

business and pleasures of the flesh, and knew the city well. It was low on his preferred list as Bennett knew he liked the place and might be tempted to follow him there, but if he could find a flight an idea was hatching in his mind how he could thwart his pursuers. 'When's the next flight?'

'The next one is at thirteen fifteen, and...let me see. I can give you a seat in Economy or Business. Which would you prefer?'

He felt like leaning over the counter and giving those radiant, red lips a kiss, but he restrained himself and instead handed over his shiny, new, unused credit card.

Clutching his boarding card, Brook stood in a long line of passengers, waiting his turn to be fondled by an acne-scarred man from Security. Once through and standing air-side, doing up his belt and laces, his stress levels took a dip and nudged below the 'anxiety' point for the first time that morning.

Even if Bennett traced him to this airport, he wouldn't know which terminal, and even if he managed to strike lucky and chose Terminal Five, he would be searching the cafés, gift shops and pubs on the landside section of the terminal without any hope of success. If he was on the ball and bought a ticket to anywhere as Brook had done, it was possible they could meet, but Bennett wouldn't be armed as he would have had to pass through security to go airside, and Brook could call the cops if things turned nasty.

On reflection, Amsterdam didn't make such a bad choice, he mused as he sipped a glass of cool, but not cool enough, metallic tasting Chablis in the V-Bar.

Cocaine would be plentiful and the nightlife would be very interesting indeed, plenty of leather and latex from what he remembered. Worth a one or two day stopover at least.

His phone rang. It was Bennett, and again he diverted it to voicemail. At twelve-thirty, he walked to the departure gate and took a seat in an empty row at the back. He took out his phone, and after first checking to see if Bennett had left any messages, which he hadn't, he called Landseer Properties.

'Mr Brook, I'm so glad you called,' Miriam said, her voice tearful and gasping. 'George, our handyman, went round to Mr Landseer's house, as you suggested. When he got no reply, he asked a neighbour to help him. They tried looking in the windows but all the curtains were shut.' She sobbed, big heaves of air suffused with mucus-filled sniffing. 'The neighbour used a spare key to open the door and they found Mr Landseer lying in a pool of blood on the living room floor. He's dead,' she wailed. 'He'd been shot in the head.' She started to wail again and after offering some words of condolence, Brook ended the call.

Landseer was dead! His suspicions were spot-on. Perry somehow had discovered their scam and the bastards had hit Landseer first. He felt vindicated in his decision not to go to the shop this morning; he now knew Bennett was there to kill him. Thank God for the evacuation plan and thank God for clever young Sam; he would send him something in appreciation.

At one time, he used to like Landseer. They'd even been lovers for a short period, but eventually Brook had seen him for what he was: a greedy self-satisfying grub of a man who thought only of himself. He mourned his death not as the passing of a friend, but as the end of a scheme that had made him rich and could have made him even richer if only it had been allowed to continue. It was an impure thought, but he supposed with Landseer dead, all his money would now become Brook's. He tipped an imaginary glass of champagne at the heavens in appreciation.

His flight was called and he joined the queue of backpackers, businessmen and a few lads intent on a riotous couple of days merrymaking. He handed over his passport and boarding card and walked towards the aircraft. His phone rang.

'Hello Jim, how are you?' Brook said.

'I'm fine Fraser,' Bennett replied. 'I've been trying to contact you all day. Where have you been?'

'I had to go and see a customer who wanted their wines valued. It happens from time to time, and I always turn my phone off as I don't want any interruptions while they are talking about their precious collections. What did you want to talk me about that was so urgent?'

'It's not so much me, Perry needs to see you. He wants a chat about a new idea he's got. It's designed to make you both pots of money.'

'What little idea is this?'

'You'll need to speak to him personally to find out. All he's asked me to do is to pick you up and take you over to see him.'

'Is that so?'

'Where are you now? We can come and give you a

lift.'

'That won't be necessary–'

'What's that fucking noise in the background?' Bennett said, his voice raised. 'You're at the bloody airport, you sod.' Brook heard a muffled sound as Bennett put his hand over the mouthpiece to speak to someone. 'He's at an airport, Heathrow probably. Let's go!'

'I suppose the idea that Perry wants to talk to me about is the same idea you spoke to Charles Landseer about, Jim?' Brook said.

'You fucking shit Brook, you and Landseer stole from us and now you're gonna pay, like he did.'

'You won't find me, you animals.'

'We want all the money back, every last penny. You're–'

Brook terminated the call and turned the device off. He walked onto the aircraft and headed into Business Class, locating his large comfortable seat, unfolding the complimentary newspaper and looking forward to the short flight across the North Sea, safe in the knowledge that he would never see Jim Bennett again.

It couldn't have been planned better if he'd tried. The most Landseer knew about the money was that it was held in a Swiss bank account. If they'd tortured him before killing him, which they likely had, they were now aware of this. They would also know the majority of large Swiss banks were located in Zurich and assume that's where the stolen money would be. With luck, they would also assume he was heading there and hop on the next plane to Switzerland.

He'd been to Zurich once before when he set up the accounts, and never needed to go back there as he'd been given electronic access. All he required was the internet, which he could get from any internet cafe or the laptop in his suitcase. In any case, Zurich and the rest of Switzerland closed at ten o'clock, and for a partying night-owl like himself, it was much too sedate.

It helped his cause that a Zurich flight was scheduled to leave twenty-five minutes after the Amsterdam flight. Perry being the selfish and greedy man he was, would expect Brook to head to the place where the money was kept, and wouldn't hesitate to send Bennett there after him.

He stuck his glass out for another top-up of champagne from the handsome steward with the wavy black hair and deep blue eyes. The money, he knew, would not last forever but he would devise a way of selling the house and the business without revealing his whereabouts and that surely would be enough.

If the worst came to the worst, and he managed to spend all the money, he would learn French or Italian and start working in the local wine trade, but what fun he was going to have along the way.

# TWENTY-SEVEN

Henderson arrived at the office at the usual time, seven-thirty, but parked at the back of the car park, sparsely filled on a Saturday. When he woke up that morning, he still felt a bit under the weather and used the walk to his building to gulp in big lungfuls of unsullied air.

Climbing the stairs was slow progress, making him feel like a man twenty years older, and it was relief when he arrived at his office. He couldn't be bothered walking into the Detectives' Room to make a coffee and instead, took a seat behind the desk and started reading a report left there by his boss.

Ten minutes later, DS Walters walked in.

'Morning, Carol. How are you? If I can be indiscreet, you look a bloody mess.'

Most of her face was bruised, with heavier discolouring around one cheek and her nose, which also sported a line of white tape across the bridge, and much puffing around the eyes.

'It looks bad but I'm getting used to it. The only thing that's broken is my nose, thank God, but it hurt like hell at the time. How about you? Are you feeling any better?'

'Forget about me, you shouldn't be here. You

should be at home in your flat in Queen's Park, your feet up and breakfast news on the box.'

'I tried that but I got bored,' she said. 'In any case, we've got a murder case to solve. How are you feeling? You look as bad as I feel.'

'Thanks, and here's me thinking I was getting better.' He ran a hand through his hair. 'I thought I'd start a new fashion trend: singed eyebrows and hair cut to the bone with no frizzy bits. I couldn't face going out to the barbers so Rachel trimmed it.'

'She's done a good job, it suits you. No lung damage from the smoke?'

'Ach, a bout of coughing now and again that makes me sound like a forty-a-day man, but not much. The fire seemed to be burning so fast it didn't really emit much smoke, but I inhaled some foul chemicals. Every so often I can still taste them.'

'Let me get you a coffee. The flavour of that stuff will overpower anything.'

'Hang on a minute. Have you seen Deepak? How is he?'

'He's been a lucky boy, if you ask me. He turned and found Frankland behind him. Before he could react, Frankland smacked him in the face and he fell on the settee, just missing whacking his head on the edge of a metal lamp table.'

'That could have been serious. Is he back on duty?'

'He is, and looking none the worse for his ordeal.'

'Pleased to hear it. How's Frankland? Was he badly injured in the car crash?'

'Not enough for my liking. He has concussion, facial injuries and suffered head injuries from a couple of loose objects that were lying on the seat of the car.'

Henderson leaned over and looked at Walters intently. 'I want Frankland, Perry, Bennett and the rest of that crew locked up and on trial for the kidnap and murder of Harvey Miller. I'm not letting any of them get away with it. Perry can try to be as slippery as he wants, but I'm having him. When can I speak to Frankland?'

'Not yet, maybe in a few days. I'll keep calling the hospital; I'll let you know when they think we'll get some sense out of him.'

'Is he under 24-hour guard?'

She nodded. 'He is.'

'We need to get him out of hospital as soon as possible. There are questions he needs to answer and I'm conscious that time isn't on our side, as Perry has the money and contacts to do a disappearing act.'

'I'm on the case, sir, quit worrying. I'll go and get that coffee.'

The team briefing started at nine prompt. For once a full house; either the ghoulish attraction of seeing a bashed-up Walters and the boss with a homemade haircut, or they believed there was a lot to catch up on.

Henderson coughed to clear his throat. 'We've been working on the scenario that wine merchant Fraser Brook bought large wine collections from country houses. To do this, he needed to have a contact in a country magazine or an estate agent; someone who could identify suitable properties. Yes?' He looked around. Lots of nods and eagerness. His team could see light at the end of the tunnel. If only he shared their enthusiasm.

He handed out an A4 copy of an article printed from the web. 'On Thursday night, an estate agent with six offices in the London area was killed by a bullet to the head at his house in Westerham. His name is Charles Landseer, a mid-fifties seemingly respectable man, but his firm, Landseer Properties, deals with the buying and selling large country houses. A visit to the scene yesterday by Sally Graham and myself confirmed he was a known associate of Fraser Brook, our suspect wine dealer.'

Henderson stopped to take a drink.

'It looks like an assassination to me,' Henderson continued, 'but there's more, Surrey have a witness. A neighbour walking his dog near the property saw a car driving along the road with its lights off around the time of the shooting. In it, he could see three men, and described the car as a dark-coloured Range Rover. You will recall, DS Walters and myself saw a dark-coloured Range Rover leave Forest Farm on the night of the murder, and the car which crashed into a telegraph pole when we captured David Frankland was a black Range Rover.'

Henderson stood at the whiteboard and tapped the picture Harvey Miller had taken of the inside of the wine lab at Uckfield. 'From conversations DS Walters had on-site with the Fire Investigation Team and Phil Bentley's subsequent follow-up, I'm convinced the wine lab moved from Uckfield to Forest Farm. With their business now a pile of blackened wood, why did they kill Charles Landseer?'

'Maybe,' Deepak Sunderam said, 'they decided to pack it in. They set fire to the business and killed all those who knew about it. Landseer first, and, if true, then Brook will be next.'

'Perhaps, but the fire is increasingly looking like an accident.'

'The appearance of Harvey Miller triggered this,' Walters said, 'so when he turned up for a second time, maybe they thought Landseer was the source of his information.'

'Whichever way we look at it,' Henderson said, 'Fraser Brook looks to be next on their list.'

'We must have enough to arrest him,' Phil Bentley said. 'We could kill two birds with one stone, if you excuse my metaphor.'

'It's just what I'm going to do. Carol, prepare a warrant for Brook's arrest and a search warrant for his wine business. I want to turn that place upside down and find some firm evidence of his involvement in passing off fake wine bottles, something this case has been sadly lacking.'

'Yes, gov.'

'Do we have enough to arrest Perry?' Sally Graham asked.

'Not yet,' Henderson said. 'When David Frankland comes out of hospital and we throw charges of assaulting DC Sunderam and DS Walters, possession of a firearm and the deaths of Harvey Miller and Charles Landseer at him, I'll be surprised if he doesn't give up Perry.'

'What about the people who worked at Forest Farm?' Phil Bentley asked. 'Did they turn up for work the day after the fire?'

'I forgot all about them. Carol, did you see anyone when you were over there?'

'Nope. They either saw what was happening from the road and turned back, or one of the gang called them and told them the barn was kaput.'

Henderson wrote something in his notebook. 'We'll talk to Frankland about that as well. This case just keeps getting bigger. Not only are we trying to close a wine-faking business and solve two, possibly three murders, it would be a rich bonus if we could get our hands on the people-traffickers as well.'

'Now, on the subject of Fraser Brook...morning ma'am.'

'Morning everyone,' CI Edwards said walking towards them. 'I see a few bashed faces around the room. How are you both doing?'

'It won't spoil my good looks, ma'am,' Walters said.

'It might give me some,' Sunderam said.

'I'm glad to see you're both back at work. Commendable. Angus, can I have a word with you in private?'

Henderson rose from the chair. 'Dig out what we have on Frankland and Perry while I'm gone,' Henderson said to the team, 'I want to go over it when I come back.'

They walked through double-doors into the corridor. 'We can stop here, Angus.' She turned to face him.

'I'm surprised to see you in today. I read the report on the fire, I think you did a very brave thing at Forest Farm.'

Henderson thought back to the fire as he had done many times since, and sighed. 'It was something anyone in my place would do, but unfortunately, all in vain.'

She touched his arm. 'It must have been hard, especially as it was someone you knew and liked.'

'Aye, he was one plucky investigator.'

'Do we know if he died as a result of the fire, or was he suffering from some other injuries?'

'He died from injuries sustained in the fire, but there's no doubt in my mind he was being held prisoner there. He had bruises on his face and lacerations on his arms and legs from the bindings.'

'So by climbing out of the window he was trying to break his way out?'

'That's what it looks like, although the rope they tied him up with and everything else was destroyed by the fire.'

'What's happening with his body?'

'We're in the process of tracking down a relative through the American Embassy and to inform Robert Wilson, the rich investor he worked for. They need to tell us if they want his body repatriated to the US or buried here. If it's the latter, I'll sort something out.'

'Good. If he's heading stateside, let me know and I'll help you with any clearance as I've done it once before. Now, from the way this enquiry is moving, Daniel Perry is shifting inexorably into the frame.'

He nodded. The mention of Perry's name raised Henderson's hackles. He knew without seeing firm evidence Perry was behind all of this, and his anger would not assuage until he took that man off the streets.

'I'm putting out an arrest warrant for Fraser Brook and once I have him and David Frankland out of East Surrey Hospital and in an interview room, I'm hoping they'll finger Perry.'

'Which means you'll be searching under every brick and stone to find his sticky fingers on anything incriminating?'

'Aye, I know you said we have to have something solid before we can bring Perry in, but we've been working hard on it and I do feel the net is closing.'

She thought for a moment. 'I think you and I need to have a word with the press office. If he gets wind of us coming after him, his lawyers will attack us with everything they've got. We need the public to be on our side from the word go, and not to be seen as the big bad police force pursuing a legitimate businessman with no evidence, as they will try to portray it.'

Henderson didn't feel his usual self, but his senses weren't so dulled he didn't notice the clean and pressed dress uniform, the styled hair, the appliance of more make-up than usual. 'Are you heading off somewhere nice?'

'No. It's a boring meeting with a minister from the Home Office, our lords and masters. He's coming here to talk about the progress we've made towards achieving our fifty million in planned savings, and the Chief wanted a show of strength.'

'Perhaps you should go the other way, ripped jeans and messy t-shirts. Make him think the cuts are starting to bite.'

She clapped him on the shoulder and began to walk away. 'You're obviously feeling better, Angus, the cheeky humour has returned. See you later.'

# TWENTY-EIGHT

The flight to Amsterdam left at the same time as the one carrying Fraser Brook, but twenty-four hours later. Jim Bennett could have busted a gut the night before and caught the late flight, but he suspected Brook was going nowhere for a couple of days at least. Once the coke-loving queer had copped some of Holland's finest nose food and shagged a night club dancer or two, it would take a crowbar to dislodge him. He would be there for the picking.

Brook thought he was being clever jetting off like he did, but Bennett could read him like a book. In his job as a wine dealer, Brook travelled a lot, always with British Airways and always from Terminal 5 at Heathrow. All Bennett had to do was pick the destination in Europe nearest to the time Brook answered his call. It wouldn't be anywhere long-distance, Brook hated long-haul flights, and he couldn't go to many places like the States at short notice without a visa. Bennett then had the choice of Paris, Rome or Amsterdam. It wasn't really a choice, as Brook had visited Amsterdam many times and often called it his favourite city.

Bennett and son, Kenny, were seated in Business Class, being served a complimentary light lunch and a glass of champagne, which he drank despite the acidic and metallic taste it left in his mouth. He couldn't relax. He had fucked up not once, but twice. Once, for not re-setting the alarm at the Uckfield warehouse, and again for Frankland's accusation of supplying drugs to Brook. In fact, he'd fucked up three times if not having Brook's current address was included, as he could think of plenty of opportunities in the past when he might have asked him for it.

He had demonstrated a complete lack of decision-making and initiative-taking, and yet in the Army he would have physically attacked any one of his men and knocked out some of their teeth if they had been guilty of such negligence. Was he losing his touch? Maybe he was just getting too old.

He looked over at Kenny. No point in asking him. The daft bastard thought the sun shone out of his wonderful da's arse. He stared out of the window glumly. Could it be time to get out? He was rich, after all, worth a couple of million, much more than he could have ever have made as a soldier, but it wasn't only money he craved. He loved the buzz of working with people like Perry and Frankland, true professionals who didn't give a stuff about rules, conventions and the law, and took whatever they wanted.

Bennett shut his eyes and talked little to his son throughout the flight. When the plane landed and the 'fasten seat belt' signs were switched off, they collected their bags from the overhead lockers. It pained Bennett to do it, but he allowed Kenny to direct the taxi driver to one of the best hotels in town, Sofitel Amsterdam, a five-star hotel right in the centre.

In his son's simple logic, Brook would be there. They would corner him in his room and wouldn't even need to go outside and get their feet wet to torture the little prick. They could simply pare the wires attached to the radio alarm and attach them to his balls. He would scream out the numbers of his secret Swiss bank account and then Bennett would have the pleasure of sticking a knife in the thieving rat's chest.

Bennett didn't want to burst his son's bubble by telling him that every big tourist city had twenty or thirty top hotels, and the chances of meeting Brook in the same one were pretty slim. He did agree that staying in the city centre made sense, as most of the main hotels were nearby and a man with Brook's refined tastes was bound to be in one of them. In any case, it gave him a chance to splash the cash, as he was a tight bugger at the best of times and needed reminding now and again that he was a millionaire.

They deposited their bags in the Junior Suite and headed downstairs to Bridges Cocktail Bar. Kenny drank Amstel beer while Bennett ordered a double whisky. 'Right, I'm not trudging round every bloody hotel in the place asking to talk to Brook, as my bad knee is starting to play up. So what's the plan you were blabbing about on the plane?'

'We go and find ourselves a computer and print off the details of all the big hotels in Amsterdam. Then we sit in the corner over there and phone them up and ask to speak to Mr Brook. We ask the clerk what room he's in and if he tells us, we go pay him a visit. If he puts us straight through without telling us the number, I say to Brook in a disguised voice that I'm looking for Mr Brown in room 210, ask him which room I've been put through to. Bingo – we're on to him.'

'Good God! It actually sounds plausible. Even if Brook doesn't cough up the room number, at least it'll confirm the hotel he's in. I've been giving this problem some thought myself. If we don't find him your way because he's staying in a cheap hotel or some other place out of town, we'll pay a visit to some of the places he's likely to frequent, like gay bars and nightclubs.'

'You've got to be kiddin' me, Da!' Kenny blurted out. 'I'm not goin' into some fucking place full of queers in tight leather trousers and wi' oily bodies. Not on your life!'

'Ha, ha. You should see your fizzer boy, it's a picture. Don't be so soft. It's no problem around here, everybody's either gay or on drugs. Why else do people come to Amsterdam?'

'I don't care, I think my way's better.'

'Right, smart Alec, let's make a start and see how you get on. We can use one of the computers over there,' he said, pointing to a corner of the foyer with the sign 'Web Access Area.' He slid off the bar stool and headed towards it. 'And order me another whisky on your way over.'

It didn't take long to find a website listing the top twenty hotels in Amsterdam, and one by one, Kenny phoned them. By the time it was dark, he'd called eighteen without success. Next on the list was the Amstel.

'Hello, can I speak to Mr Fraser Brook?' Kenny asked, sounding a cross between Kevin Costner and Inspector Clouseau.

Kenny picked up his beer and took a sip. He said it was better than the stuff he drank at home. The boy was beginning to like Amsterdam

'No thank you, I will call again. Which room is he in? I need to send him some papers.'

'Room 407? Many thanks.'

Kenny thumped down the handset, triumphant. 'Ya beauty. I did it Da!'

'Well done Kenny,' Bennett said beaming as he raised his whisky glass, 'you've cracked it. We'll finish these drinks and get right on it.'

The taxi drove off, leaving Bennett and his son standing outside the entrance to the five-star Intercontinental Amstel Hotel on Professor Tulpplein 1, a tree-lined street on the banks of the Amstel River. They walked up the carpeted staircase towards the main door while Kenny read out its description from a web printout. 'The central location extends to the heart of the financial, cultural and recreational centre of Amsterdam. Restaurant La Rive is renowned for its culinary delights and has a Michelin star.'

He looked at his father. 'Can we eat here Da, I've never eaten in a Michelin-starred restaurant before. Is it them that make the tyres?'

'Don't be soft. You wouldn't know which bloody knife or fork to use. Nice gaff Brook's picked though,' he said, swaggering through its opulent entrance hall.

'It is, and we're bloody paying for it.'

They stopped near reception and dialled Brook's

room on the internal phone. It rang and rang without reply. Bennett walked over to the desk and addressed the pretty, well-manicured receptionist.

'We're trying to contact Mr Brook in room 407 and getting no reply. Can you tell me if you're expecting him back this evening?'

She turned and examined a message in the post box, then keyed something into the computer before turning and speaking to one of her colleagues in Dutch.

She turned to face Bennett. 'I'm sorry sir, but we do not know where Mr Brook is. Maybe he is out shopping or has gone straight to dinner or a show. Would you like me to call you when he returns?'

'No, we'll wait. Thanks anyway.'

He walked back to Kenny who was looking at a display of leaflets highlighting Amsterdam's main attractions. 'I didn't know Anne Frank's House was here, we learnt about her in school. She hid in an attic for years to keep away from the Germans.'

'You learned something in school then,' Bennett said. 'I'm glad to see that all your time there wasn't wasted. Let's find a table and regroup.'

Whisky in hand, Bennett and son sat at a table in the corner, their presence partly-obscured from the entrance to the hotel by a large pot plant. In front of them, a selection of sandwiches and bar snacks, something to absorb the booze and stop them getting pissed. Alcohol make torturing easier, but it left him dull and careless and no way could he afford to make another mistake.

'So what do we do now Da'?' Kenny said, sipping

another Amstel, in his other hand, an Amsterdam information leaflet.

'We wait here in this nice gaff until he shows up. He's bound to, sometime tonight. I mean even if Brook is a party animal, he doesn't know anybody in Amsterdam so he'll be back here when the theatre or cinema or wherever the hell he is, finishes.'

'Don't gays stick together?'

'You mean like some sort of fellowship; like the Scouts?'

'Yeah, so if they come to places like this, they can chum up with the locals.'

'Christ, you really have some daft ideas, son.'

Kenny paused for a moment, thinking. 'What will we do when he does show?'

'When you see him come in, don't shout or let him know we're here, duck out of sight and let him go upstairs. I don't want him to see us or he'll skedaddle back where he came from. Then, after a few minutes we'll go up and knock on his door and give him a new kind of room service.'

'Ha, ha that's good, that is; a new kind of room service.'

'We'll give him such a thumping he'll be begging us to take back the money he stole.'

'How do we get the money? It's not as if he'll be carrying it around in a suitcase, will he?'

'It would be dead easy if he was. Nah, we do it electronically.' Computers were a mystery to Bennett but Frankland had explained what he needed to do and he hoped he would remember it all. 'In a place as swanky as this, Brook will have internet access in his room, so we'll force him to transfer the money from his Swiss bank account to this.' He removed a piece of paper from his jacket pocket and waved it in front of his son.

'What's that?'

'The bank account Perry wants us to use. It's secret; offshore.'

'So,' Kenny said, his facial expressions suggesting the cogs in his simple brain were turning faster than a grandfather clock. 'We're gonna take the money from Brook and give it straight to Perry? Isn't that what we said about Landseer being stupid, letting Brook look after his money? Aren't we letting Perry look after our money?'

'Nah, this is different. Perry's using the offshore account to safeguard the money until he can pass some of it on to me and Frankland. You can't just ship that amount of money back into your Post Office bank account without questions being asked. There's ways the cops can spot large movements of cash.'

They stayed in the Amstel until one thirty in the morning, by which time the lounge and bar area had become deserted, except for Bennett, Kenny and a bored-looking waiter. Every ten minutes or so, a small group of revellers would enter the hotel, on their way to bed or looking forward to some revelry in one of the rooms, and occasionally, a couple of strangely dressed night owls would head out in search of some late-night entertainment. But to the consternation of Jim Bennett and his son, Fraser Brook didn't come into the hotel and he didn't go out.

Jim Bennett was in no fit state to hang around any

longer, or for that matter, deal with Brook effectively; he decided to call it a night. The doorman called them a taxi and Kenny half-carried the drunk and part-comatose Bennett into the cab and they headed back to their hotel.

# TWENTY-NINE

The driver of a non-descript and dirty Volvo estate scoured the lanes of Car Park B searching for a space. It was a big car, and even though the old dear up ahead thought she was doing him a good turn coming out of a tight space in her little Micra, the driver had to drive past with a sigh.

Ten minutes later the car was parked, and after finishing their cigarettes, both men got out and walked towards the sprawl that was East Surrey Hospital.

'Hate hospitals, me,' Steve, the taller of the two men, said. 'Full of sick people. You go in there with a broken ankle and a week after you pick up MRAS and snuff it.'

'MRSA,' Alex said.

'Where?'

'Not where, you dope. The bug that kills people in hospitals is called MRSA.'

'Same difference, and don't call me a dope. I went to the same school you did.'

'This is true, but I didn't spend all my time looking out the window and nipping off for a fag, did I? I listened, and some of it,' he said tapping the side of his head, 'sunk in.'

'Yeah, but look at ye now. Same bloody place as me.'

'You're right there, I can't argue with that one.'

'Christ, look at that pair there,' Steve said, indicating an elderly lady helping her equally elderly partner to reach their car. 'Shoot me before I get that old.'

'I'm tempted to do it now.'

'Ha, bloody ha. I'm only 36, I've got a bit of time to go, but I know I don't wanna end up like that.'

'In our profession, there's a sixty-per cent chance we won't reach 65.'

'Get away, how do you know that?'

'Read it in a magazine. Funnily enough, I read it when I was waiting at a doctor's surgery.'

'What were you in there for?'

'You remember my uncle asked me to collect money from a dealer and then this druggie took a flaky and stabbed me?'

'Yeah.'

'It was for that. Had to get bloody tetanus injections and all sorts, the bastard used his knife for everything; even cutting up his stash.'

'He won't do it again.'

'No, he won't.'

They walked through the entrance to the hospital and after checking the board and making sure they knew where to go, they set off. Unlike many modern hospitals built on multiple floors with fast-moving lifts, East Surrey was low to the ground and to reach anywhere was a long walk.

'There's one good thing about hospitals,' Alex said.

'What's that?'

'The crumpet. Look at these two walking towards us. I'd happily take the one on the right. Is the one on the left ok for you?'

'I suppose so, but as long as I can get a shot of yours afterwards.'

'Afternoon ladies,' Alex said as they walked past.

'At least they smiled,' Steve said. 'It's good to see you've lost none of that boyish charm.'

They were walking down a long corridor, not far from their destination when Steve spotted a changing room.

'In here,' he said.

They reappeared two minutes later, transformed into look-alike junior doctors with pens in the top pocket of their white coats, a lanyard with an ID card around their necks and carrying clipboards.

'I was just saying to Doctor Newman the other day,' Steve said as they passed a small gaggle of visitors.

'You idiot. Doctors have all got posh voices, they don't sound like something out of *Eastenders*.'

'Why the hell not? We've got doctors in Bethnal Green.'

'Yeah, but they all go to the same medical schools don't they? There, they refine their posh accents otherwise the big chief consultant would think they were morons.'

'Get away, he wouldn't think you were a moron just 'cause you came from the East End.'

'Steve, mate, shut up, we're nearly there. Try to look professional.'

The nurse buzzed them through double doors leading into a row of private rooms. The room David Frankland was in couldn't be more obvious, as there was a copper sitting outside the door.

'Now, Steve, keep your trap shut,' Alex said, 'and let me do the talking.'

The copper looked up from his newspaper when he heard their approach, a riveting article in the Sun about a cheating Hollywood heart-throb's love child.

'Afternoon officer,' Alex said in his best posh doctor voice.

'Afternoon doc. Back again? One of your team was here not fifteen minutes ago.'

'We've just received a high reading from his blood pressure monitor. Might be something or nothing.'

Alex reached for the door handle, cool and professional, all the time listening for any movement in the corridor or any sign of the copper reaching for his radio. He walked into the room, Steve at his back.

The patient lay unmoving, all tubes and wires, his eyes closed and no sign he knew they were in the room. Alex looked round and saw the copper had twisted around in his chair looking in. He walked over and closed the door.

'Grab that wheelchair over there,' Alex said, 'and I'll get him ready.' Alex knew some of the connections as he had nursed a terminally ill father with lung cancer for four months, and there was bugger-all to do in places like this if you didn't read books or watch day-time telly.

The saline drip and heart monitor were easy as long as he remembered where the alarm kill button was before he disconnected, but the leg brace was a bit trickier and required a degree in Mechanical Engineering to undo.

Steve pushed the wheelchair closer and with a fair amount of huffing and puffing even managed to get it open.

'Check the wardrobe,' Alex said.

'What for?'

'Kim Kardashian, who else? His fucking clothes. If you think we're taking him out in this hospital gown that opens all the way up the back, you've got another think coming. He'll freeze his bollocks off.'

'Ok, ok. I get the message.'

He turned to the patient. 'David, I'm just going to put you into this wheelchair so I'm gonna have to pull you about a bit. Ok mate?'

'Uh, uh,' came the reply.

'Is he all right?' Steve said as he stood, a strange expression on his face, holding Frankland's clothes. 'Is he gonna die?'

'He's not gonna die, you arse. He hit a telegraph pole at less than fifty miles an hour in a bloody solid car, for Christsakes. A few broken bones and concussion is all. The telegraph pole's in a worse state.'

'Why is he, you know, comatose?'

'He's drugged up to give the nurses an easier time.'

'They do that?'

'Sure they do. Help me get him into his coat.'

They sat him up and laboriously threaded each arm before pulling him to the edge of the bed.

'Listen up, Steve, he'll feel a dead weight so don't

let him fall, ok?'

'What do you take me for?'

'There's no answer to that. After three, ok? One, two, three.'

They got him on his feet and, as expected, it was like holding a six-foot, sixteen-stone rubber doll, as he wasn't helping one bit. With a bit of to-ing and fro-ing they manoeuvred the wheelchair behind him, eased him towards it and pushed him in. Alex buttoned up the coat and made him presentable for a trip outside.

'Let's go,' Steve said. 'I'll push.'

'Not yet. We have to deal with him out there,' Alex said pointing at the door.

'Oh yeah, I forgot about him.'

'Remember our plan?'

'Yep, got it.'

Steve took up position and removed a bottle of isoflurane from his pocket. He tipped some into a clean handkerchief, being careful not to inhale some of the fumes, and nodded to his companion.

Alex walked to the door and opened it. PC 3456 was again reading his newspaper. He had moved to the back pages now, all the latest transfer news.

'Officer, could I ask you to help me for a minute, please?'

He put down his newspaper and followed Alex into the room.

'Hey,' the officer said. 'You can't do this with Mr Frankland, he's not to be–'

Before he could finish his sentence, Steve's arm wrapped around his throat and with his other hand, put the soaked handkerchief over his mouth and nose.

Seconds later Steve let the copper fall to the ground like a sack of spuds.

Steve dragged him into the space between the bed and the wardrobe. 'Is he ok here?'

'I would prefer to tie him up,' Alex said, 'but we forgot to bring a rope. Here, I'll take his legs, you take his head and we'll stuff him in the wardrobe. Do it quick, we gotta go.'

They wheeled David Frankland out of the room and shut the door. Steve pushed and Alex put on his concerned face, rehearsing a story about taking the patient down to the Blood Unit for testing, as he was worried about his BP.

'Piece of cake,' Steve said as he eased the now more compliant figure of David Frankland into the back of the Volvo and strapped him in.

'I'll agree with you when I see my uncle's smiling face as he hands me a thick wad of fifties.'

'What are you gonna spend the dough on, Alex?' Steve asked, as he guided the big car out of the car park before heading north on the Horley Road.

'I'll take the missus on holiday. We haven't been anywhere for about year. Somewhere nice like America.'

'I like Spain, great beaches, fantastic clubs and women out for a good time. You can't beat it.'

'I thought you didn't like flying?'

'I don't, but Spain's only a couple of hours away. I can manage that with a few black rums inside me.'

At Redhill they took the A25 east. Depending on his mood, he might ask Steve to continue along this road through the smart little villages of Sussex and

Kent, or, if needing to get there soonest, head north at Godstone and hit the M25. He hadn't decided yet.

A mile or so after joining the A25 they heard the siren. He didn't need to say anything to Steve as there was nothing wrong with his hearing. Alex didn't turn round and look suspicious to all and sundry, but kept watch in the wing mirror, Steve doing the same in the rear view mirror. This section of the A25 was busy, one carriageway in each direction with few overtaking opportunities, making it hard to put any distance between them and the patrol car, and equally, for it to close the gap on them.

It was a tough call knowing the best thing to do. They could speed up to try and maintain the distance between them and the patrol car, only to find it wasn't them being chased but get pulled over for driving too fast, or they could allow them to close the gap and discover who they were chasing. If the cops were after them, it would be too late to make a getaway.

Alex decided he would try and outrun them, as his philosophy in life was to assume the worst and hope for the best. First, they needed to get off this road. The app on his phone indicated there was a right turn up ahead, but they were travelling so fast he didn't think they would spot it in time.

'You're taking a right in a few secs, Steve,' he said trying to give the driver as much notice as possible. 'It's coming up any minute now, get ready, ready. There!'

The big Volvo had all the aerodynamic quality of a log, great for ramming cars and smashing into shop windows, but it wallowed like a yacht on corners.

Steve was a good driver and well used to the car's unique handling characteristics; he hoped. He jammed on the brakes and carefully picked his time to make the turn, a steel signpost ready to tell him otherwise if he didn't. As soon as the car was facing in the right direction and the violent rocking had subsided, Steve floored the accelerator.

This time Alex did turn round. Seconds later, he saw it through the trees – a fast moving, blue flashing light travelled east along the A25. 'I think we lost them.'

'Thank fuck for that. Where does this road lead?'

Alex consulted his phone app again. 'This is called Outwood Lane and... bloody hell.'

'What?'

'There aren't too many turn-offs that I can see until we get to a place called Smallfield.'

'That's nearly back where we started.'

'I know, I know, but at least we got rid of the cops. You obviously didn't give the copper enough anaesthetic back at the hospital, he must have radioed his mates a few minutes after we left.'

'It usually does the trick. He must have good lungs or something.'

A few minutes later Alex stopped talking and listened. 'I think I spoke too soon.' He eased the window down, and in the distance they could hear the wailing police siren again, growing louder. 'Damn. They must've twigged our move.'

'Shit, what do we do?'

Alex racked his brains. They'd passed no villages, farm tracks or turn-offs, and any tracks he did see led to farms that would take them across a flat, featureless landscape, visible to all. He was out of options.

'Stop the car.'

'What? No way am I handing myself in, think of something else.'

'Stop the fucking car!'

He stopped the car and before the wheels stopped turning, Alex jumped out. 'Help me get him out.'

'What?'

'You heard me, help me get David out. Be quick about it.'

They pulled David Frankland out of the car and laid him down in the road at the back of the Volvo. They'd stopped at the end of a straight section of road; the chasing coppers or another motorist had about a quarter of a mile to see the prostrate figure and stop. If they didn't, they and David Frankland were in for a nasty surprise.

Alex looked down at the unmoving figure, eyes open but with no idea where he was. 'See you, Dave, sorry about this.'

Alex jumped back in the car, seconds before Steve floored the accelerator, and with a puff of dirty exhaust fumes, they disappeared down the road.

# THIRTY

The following morning, without stopping for breakfast, Jim Bennett and his son took a cab back to the Amstel Hotel in Amsterdam. Jim Bennett felt crap, despite enjoying one of the best night's sleep ever in a hotel. Too often the room was cold, the bed hard or the traffic outside noisy, but last night everything clicked; just a shame too much whisky had spoiled the soporific effect.

Kenny, who could enjoy a good night's sleep on the outside step, had tried calling Brook's room several times. On each occasion they put him though and the phone rang but no one answered. This made Brook a night owl and an eager culture vulture, keen to hit the museums before the crowds, two opposing forces that didn't add up. Then again, maybe he was being overly suspicious, as Brook could well be in the john, having a shower or down at breakfast; but in the past, 'suspicious' had served him well.

When they arrived, they enquired once again at Reception and were told they had no idea of Mr Brook's whereabouts, but they both could be assured a message for him had been left at Reception, and another on his room phone. If they were still in the hotel when Mr Brook returned or called, they would be contacted.

He looked over at the lounge where they had spent the previous evening drinking beer and whisky at five-star prices, and headed out to the street. Despite being a millionaire, he balked at the prices for a double scotch, as a couple of those could buy him a bottle of everyday whisky from Asda or Tesco. Bennett felt more despondent now than the previous night, a combination of the amount of time wasted hanging around this hotel and the thump-thump of a monumental hangover.

He didn't have any idea where they were going and, blithely ignoring the trolleybuses, cyclists and a gaggle of tourists taking photographs of the river, they walked across the Hogesluis Bridge and headed towards a small café nearby. Bennett had a light breakfast of coffee and toast as he couldn't face anything more substantial, while Kenny helped himself to copious amounts of bread, ham and cheese and anything his father didn't eat.

By the time Bennett had downed his third coffee, colour had returned to his face and the pounding in his head scaled down from a bass drum to a light snare. In the Army, he could drink his platoon under the table and still appear for parade in the morning, his buttons and shoes shining, but along with creaking knees and a receding hairline, his liver wasn't the fine alcohol processor it used to be.

He put down his cup and looked pensively at his son. Despite necking a good number of Amstels the previous night, the daft bugger looked well and it seemed to have had no impact on his appetite. 'Kenny, if the slippery Brook won't come to us, then we need to go to him.'

He had to wait until Kenny swallowed a large piece of Gouda he'd just popped into his mouth before he regained the power of speech.

'What do ya have in mind Da? How do we get to him if we can't find him?'

'We'll go back into the hotel and without stopping at those useless buggers in Reception, we'll head up to his room. If I can't open the lock with my trusty little lock-pickers, we'll blag our way in.'

'How do we do that?'

He tapped his nose. 'I'll find a way, no worries.'

'Sounds like a good plan. What do you think we'll find in there?'

'What do you mean, what do you think we'll find in there?' he said raising his voice more than intended. 'We're not going there to look through his bloody suitcases and to have a sneaky-peek at his dirty Y-fronts, are we? We'll go into his room and wait for the fucker to come back. He might have been slipping in and out of the hotel without us knowing, did you think of that?'

Kenny's face lit up. 'I see what you mean, maybe he's coming in through the kitchens like they do in the movies, or heading up the back entrance.'

'Ha, ha good one, Kenny, heading up the back entrance,' he said laughing for the first time that morning. 'I think our sleazy wine dealer does a fair amount of that.'

He paid the bill and they walked purposefully back to The Amstel. They breezed past Reception trying to look like residents and, as always, Bennett avoided the double bank of elevators and headed for the stairs. Even with a hotel room on the eighth or ninth floor, he preferred to walk, but even he was thankful Brook's room was on the fourth.

'What, no carpets, and scratches all over the walls? I thought this place called itself a five-star hotel?'

'Nobody uses the stairs in a place like this,' Bennett said, puffing a bit more than normal. 'Everybody takes the lift. Most of the fat fuckers you see out there in the foyer would suffer a bloody heart attack if they came anywhere near a set of stairs.'

They reached the fourth floor and pushed open the door. As Bennett anticipated, a cleaning team were engaged in their morning duties; a cart with towels, coffee and little cartons of milk and sugar was parked not more than twenty yards away. As they approached, Bennett quickly looked round to make sure no one was looking and picked up a door card from a small pile that lay on a shelf inside the cart. They continued walking to the end of the corridor, turned a corner and located Room 407.

'Watch and learn from the master,' he said to his son.

He knocked on the door and listened. No reply. He knocked again, but the same silence returned. He bent over the door lock. 'This is a card somebody left behind in their room when they checked-out, or a spare open-all card used by the cleaners, either way we can use it,' he said. He pushed the card into the door reader but the light obstinately shone red. He tried again, same result.

'No problem. Follow me,' he said. They walked

back the way they had come. 'Take off your jacket,' he said to Kenny, 'and sling it over your shoulder. Make it look like you're just going out for a walk or something.' He did the same.

The service cart was parked outside a room in the process of being cleaned, and through the open bedroom door a chambermaid was busily cleaning the bathroom. He knocked on the door.

'Excuse me, miss.' He held up the door card. 'My card won't work for some reason. Can you let me into my room please? I'd go down to reception for a new one but I just want to pick up my camera.'

She looked at him and smiled. 'Certainly sir,' she said in a thick East European accent, 'just a moment.'

She walked back with them to room 407, and using a card attached to her apron on a long chain, she opened the door. They thanked her and watched as she returned to her cleaning duties and disappeared around the corner without looking back.

Walking into the room, a brief smile flashed across Bennett's face. At last, something was going right. He could be resourceful and clever when the time demanded and Perry would be reminded of that fact when they sat around the coffee table in his Barking mansion dishing out Brook's stolen loot. With a wheeze across the thick pile carpet, the door closed softly behind them.

He walked into the bathroom and was immediately struck by how empty it looked. 'This doesn't look right,' he said out loud. 'I don't see any of his shaving things or shampoo or anything.' He strode into the lounge, his anxiety and anger rising.

'Look, there's no newspapers on the floor or fucking maps and dirty coffee cups on the table.' He walked to the wardrobe and opened the door. Suddenly, he threw his head towards the ceiling and gave out a loud groan that came from deep within his chest, 'AHHHH! He's fucking scarpered. The little bastard's pulled a flanker. This place is completely empty!'

Kenny was standing on the other side of the room near the television, in a small seating area with two small settees, a coffee table and, directly in front of them, a large floor-to-ceiling window. Anyone sitting there could enjoy fine views of the Amstel River and out to the rooftops of old Amsterdam beyond. 'Da take a look at this, it's addressed to you.'

'Whatd'ya mean it's addressed to me? How can something you find in a hotel room in Amsterdam be addressed to me?'

'I dunno but this is.'

'Let me see it,' he said thrusting out a hand.

Kenny handed over a white envelope. Handwritten in capitals on the front of an Amstel Hotel envelope, their distinctive logo embossed in red script at the top, 'TO BE OPENED BY ADDRESSEE ONLY - Mr James Bennett.'

'Where the fuck did you find this?' he said as he ripped it open.

'Propped up beside the telly.'

Bennett pulled out the piece of paper inside and unfolded it. It was written again on Amstel-embossed notepaper. The handwriting looked neat, in black ink.

*Dear Jim,*

*Well done and congratulations! You found me.*

*Oops, sorry, only kidding, no you didn't. When I came to Amsterdam I booked two hotels, this one, where I knew you would look, and a cheaper one elsewhere. For a small fee, the staff were instructed to call me as soon as anyone came looking for me. As a result, I am long gone.*

*Ta, ta, Fraser xx*

*PS I wouldn't like to be the one to tell Daniel Perry that I'd failed.*

Bennett crumpled up the letter in his fist and let out another anguished cry. He turned and punched the wall, cutting his knuckles and putting a large dent in the plasterboard.

Bennett called Perry from the taxi. After checking out of their hotel, they travelled to the airport, the visit to Amsterdam curtailed as their continued presence no longer served a purpose. Perry was furious to hear they'd come close but the thief who'd stolen so much money was heading for destinations unknown. He also reminded Bennett several times that if he had moved faster in the first place and got over to Amsterdam quicker, none of this would have happened.

Bennett was moody and uncommunicative as the Airbus 380 cruised above the North Sea. His eyes were shut but he was not asleep as the occasional transport of his whisky glass from table to mouth testified. Kenny sat in the window seat leafing through the in-flight magazine.

'We could hire a private detective,' he said through pursed lips.

'Sorry Da?'

'You got cloth ears? I said, I think I'll suggest to Perry we engage the services of an international detective agency to track Brook down. There's no way you and me can hunt all over Europe for him. What if it costs fifty or a hundred grand, it'll be worth it in the long run if they find him.'

'Good idea Da, that whisky makes a good job of oiling your brain cogs.'

'You're a cheeky sod son, but this time I think you're right.'

# THIRTY-ONE

The surprise of the day when the team arrived at Fraser Brook's Fine Wines in Chelsea, had to be the non-appearance of Fraser Brook. At first Henderson was led to believe he would be in later or was engaged on some errand, not that he could think of anything to detain him on a Sunday morning unless he was religious. When Brook didn't show up, two hours after the shop opened, he came downstairs to the sales area and talked to Sam, the assistant manager.

'When you said earlier Brook had things to do, did you mean today or generally?' Henderson asked him.

'More generally I suppose.'

Sam Wilson had fair hair, long at the front and short at the back, a round slightly podgy face and looked stocky in build, a school rugby player, perhaps, gone to seed.

'You said he was due in today. Is he coming in today?'

'I dunno—'

'Sam,' Henderson said raising his voice, 'is he or isn't he?'

'No.'

'Does he usually work Sundays?'

'No.'

'Good. I think we're getting somewhere. Where is

he? Did you phone him and tell him there are police swarming all over his business? He's not ill is he?'

'No he's not ill. He's just not–'

'Sam,' Henderson said thumping his fist on the counter, almost pulverising the shop's little credit card authorising terminal. 'You may not realise but we're not here to find Mr Brook's unfiled VAT returns or to see if he's been fiddling Customs.'

'No? Then what are you here for?'

'To find out who murdered three people.'

'What...murder...I...'

'I'm not looking for Mr Brook because I think he's a murderer, I'm concerned he might be the next victim.'

Sam stepped back and slumped on the stool behind him. 'I...I didn't know, I didn't think all this was...so serious.'

'It's serious all right. I believe Mr Brook is in real danger. Where is he?'

Sam went on to tell him about the visit to the shop on Friday of Jim Bennett and his son, Kenny. Sam was a natural storyteller and Henderson could visualise Jim Bennett stomping up and down inside the shop, his face set in a scowl, while Kenny stood quietly at the back, his mind in another place. He explained that when Bennett asked him where Brook lived, he really didn't know as his boss didn't reveal his address to anyone.

'Fraser never talked about his house, the area where he lived, or invited us there. Now I think about it, he probably avoided talking about it as if he didn't want anybody to know where he lived.'

'Maybe he didn't, but we'll get his address from the local council and send someone round to take a look.'

'You can do that?'

Henderson nodded. 'You think he scarpered because of what Bennett wanted to talk to him about?' Henderson asked.

'Yes.'

'Sir?'

He turned and saw DS Carol Walters halfway down the stairs. 'Sorry to interrupt, sir, but you need to come and see this.'

'Ok, Carol. Give me five minutes.'

He turned back to Sam. 'Where would Mr Brook scarper to?'

'I really don't know and that's the truth.'

'Does he have access to an apartment abroad, is there a friend or relative he often visits?'

He shook his head 'I don't know. I wish I did but Fraser said he would contact me when he found somewhere.'

'Do you know what Bennett wanted to talk to him about?'

'I have no idea, but it didn't look like a friendly chat.'

Henderson climbed the stairs at the rear of Brook's Fine Wines. In many ways, Brook's behaviour didn't surprise him, any sane man would do the same after hearing that a close associate had been murdered, most likely by the gang they both worked for. It didn't stop him wanting to grab Sam by the neck for not telling him sooner, but he could also understand why he wanted to protect his employer.

Upstairs, a wide open area had seven desks, filing cabinets, photocopier; all the accoutrements of a small office. This room was the financial and administrative hub of Brook's wine business, a busy wine shop here in Chelsea and a growing web-based business operated from a large warehouse in Hammersmith.

Walters and the team of four were taking the place apart, paper by paper, invoice by invoice, and so far they had bagged a sizeable amount of information about the wine collections Brook bought from large country houses and the auctions he frequented to sell the wines. Walter sat behind one of the desks, a small file opened in front of her.

He took the seat opposite. 'What have you got there?'

She looked up. 'Ah, hello sir.' She flipped over the front of the folder. 'It says insurance on the cover but what's inside didn't look like cover notes and certificates to me when I first spotted it. It's full of emails between Brook and that estate agent who was murdered, Landseer, and our old friend, Daniel Perry.'

'Let me take a look.'

He skimmed through an email between Brook and Landseer, looking not only at the content but also the language. Yes, it was about all the money they had made at auction, and yes, it was clear they were close business associates, and so one line on the whiteboard back at the office could be changed from dotted to thick black, but it was also about thieving. He grabbed another couple for comparison and it was obvious that

Brook and Landseer were using the wine auctions to steal money from Daniel Perry. He sat back, amazed at their audacity, or perhaps naivety; Perry was a dangerous man to cross.

The pennies dropped in his head like counters on a Battleship board. Perry had obviously discovered what was going on, and here was the reason why Landseer was killed and Brook bolted.

'Why is the file called Insurance?' he asked the sergeant.

'I think Brook compiled it as his insurance in case they were on to him and he had to run.'

'Like now.'

'Yes, like now. I suppose a call to Sam or Anders and they would hand the file to us; he's included enough in here to bring Perry and his team down.'

**\*\***

The trip to Brook's shop in Chelsea this morning had interrupted a fine sleep, much required after a late night boozing with his sociable neighbours. Taking advantage of the recent dry weather, drinks had been served out on the patio before they all sat down to an equally liquid 'supper.' They didn't get home until after two.

Henderson picked up the thickening wine-faking file and stretched. With a sigh, he walked out of his office and headed into the Detectives' Room.

He could see pleased looks on the faces of DS Walters and DS Wallop, their morning's activities had been most productive, but he decided to keep their powder dry for a few minutes.

'What's the latest on PC Quinlan?' he said when everyone in the room had quietened down.

'He took a bang on the head when woke up inside the wardrobe and tried to stand, and still feels off-colour from the anaesthetic,' DC Sunderam said, 'but there is no lasting injuries.'

'At least he didn't need to go far to receive treatment,' Walters said.

'I'm pleased to hear that he wasn't badly hurt. Is he back on duty?'

'No sir. He'll be off for the next few days.'

A few officers, including Walters, groaned and no wonder, looking at the bruises on her face.

'What about our patient, David Frankland, the reluctant escapee?'

'He's none the worse for his ordeal,' Sunderam said. 'He was heavily sedated to aid his recovery before being kidnapped, and doesn't have a clear recollection of what went on afterwards.'

'Just as well,' Walters said. 'I'd have nightmares about lying down on a busy road with lorries thundering by.'

'Just think if the sedative had worn off,' Phil Bentley said. 'A confused half-dressed man wandering around the countryside; doesn't bear thinking about.'

'It couldn't happen to a better person,' Harry Wallop said.

'What about our hospital abductors. Any news there?'

Sunderam shook his head. The young man could do a sad face better than anyone in the room. There had to be a good use for such a talent, but at the moment he couldn't think what it might be. 'I'm afraid not, sir. None of the cameras could give us a clear shot of their faces.' He looked around for Phil Bentley. 'Phil, do you want to talk about the hunt for the car?'

'Sure. They were driving a dark green Volvo estate. We picked the reg up from the hospital car park CCTV.'

'Good work,' Henderson said.

'Thank you sir. We traced it to a Graham Sullivan and to cut a long story short, he's the admin guy at Daniel Perry's company. All the cars and vans used by the business are managed by him. He reported the Volvo stolen on the day of the abduction.'

'No doubt he reported the theft some time after they realised the rescue mission had gone pear-shaped.'

'You're probably right, sir.'

'Sometime soon,' Henderson said, 'Essex Police will be called out to a burned out shell in Epping Forest.'

'They need to check there isn't a couple of bodies inside,' Walters said. 'Daniel Perry doesn't tolerate failure. Either that, or two frightened guys will have made their way to Spain or Morocco.'

'Harry, what news from Landseer Properties?'

'The search of their offices didn't reveal anything to move this case forward, but that was before I found out this little gem. I called one of the detectives on the Landseer murder team and he'd just received the ballistics report on the bullets removed from the victim's body. If you remember, DS Walters saw a gun in an attaché case first seen in the attic of David Frankland's house and subsequently recovered from his crashed car. We sent the details of our gun to Surrey and as suspected, their bullets match our gun.'

'Whoa!' was all Henderson could say as everyone began to talk at once.

'Frankland's bad week just got worse,' Sally Graham said.

'Yeah,' Phil Bentley said, 'he might be getting out of hospital, but he won't be out of jail for a very long time.'

'Brilliant work, Harry, well done,' Henderson said. 'Are they sending down confirmation?'

'Yep. They'll send it and the guy I spoke to, DS Stevenson, would like a word with you. He'll call you in the morning.'

Henderson tried to suppress his delight at this excellent bit of news. It was the first piece of real, solid, tangible evidence in this case; everything else, their assumptions about relationships and actions, the perpetrators and their presumed guilt or innocence, mere supposition based on whatever facts they had to hand.

'That will make our conversation with David Frankland flow a bit easier,' Henderson said. 'When do you think we can interview him, Deepak?'

'Today is Sunday.' He paused for a moment, thinking. 'I would say the hospital will release him about Wednesday.'

Henderson could rely on Sunderam's assessments of patient recovery times, as he didn't use his experience and gut feel as many officers did, but his own medical knowledge. His father was a heart surgeon and his son at one time was heading for a career in medicine before finally opting to join the police.

'This is better, I feel at last we're making progress. Put out an all-ports alert to find Fraser Brook before he ends up like Landseer. I want a warrant prepared for the arrest of James Bennett, Kenny Bennett and, I never thought I'd get to say this, Daniel Perry.'

# THIRTY-TWO

The plane landed on time and the passengers arriving into Heathrow on the Amsterdam flight made their way into the airport terminal. Some rushed to make important meetings, others sauntered with the air of people who had little idea of what they would do next.

The queues at Passport Control were light and they passed through quickly. Despite the lax drugs policy of the Netherlands, Customs focussed their main resources on targeting big players, and Jim Bennett and his son reached the Arrivals Hall without molestation. In spite of the obvious temptation, Bennett didn't bring back any dope.

Bennett saw Hal as the automatic doors opened and the weary travellers were faced with a large crowd of friends, business colleagues and taxi drivers, as if they were celebrities and these were their fans. Hal nodded. It wasn't hard for the Russian to spot them, not that Bennett's ever-present black leather jacket and Kenny in his Red Sox gear were so distinctive among bright tracksuits and garish jumpers and jackets, but Hal was six-foot-six and occupied the standing space of two ordinary men.

'I know Perry wanted an update,' Bennett said to Hal when they approached him, 'but I thought he'd wait until I'd been home for a shit, a shower and something to eat.'

'Boss wants to see you now,' Hal said.

Hal strode out to the car park, the two sullen travellers walking some way behind. They couldn't keep pace with the Russian's big legs while pulling their small cases, made heavier with the whisky Bennett bought in Amsterdam. Hal climbed into a Mercedes 4x4 and by the time he found his shades and put the exit ticket in a place where he could easily find it, Jim Bennett and Kenny had clambered in to join him.

'This is a better class of transport than the old Volvo you usually drive, Hal,' Bennett said.

'I agree. The big Volvo car is lying low for the moment.'

'Why?'

'You need to ask boss.'

Little conversation flowed between them as they made their way east. Bennett didn't feel sociable after the debacle in Amsterdam, and Hal didn't know much English. Traffic around London and the M25, was busy even for a Sunday evening, when he imagined most people would be at home sleeping off a big Sunday lunch. It didn't surprise him as everywhere he went in London these days was busier than he ever remembered.

An hour and a bit later, they drove into the car park at DP Building Supplies in Barking, closed at this time of the day. The only other car there, beside two of the company's vans, was Perry's light blue Aston Martin.

Bennett and Kenny walked into the shop. The

lighting was dim with only the security lights burning. They headed towards the little office Perry often used when he visited the branch, but a shout from the Manager's office redirected them.

Perry was sitting behind the scratched wooden desk where Kevin, the manager, usually sat, biting his nails; never a good sign. There was no smart suit today but a yellow Pringle sweater and snazzy blue shirt and the lightly greyed hair, cut every three weeks, coiffured to perfection.

'The intrepid travellers return. Take the weight off, the pair of you.'

They took the two seats opposite the desk.

'I'll come straight to the point: you couple of tossers have fucked-up big style. Brook jetted off with over three mill of my money and you don't have a clue where the fuck he is.'

'We nearly nabbed him.'

'Nearly doesn't cut shit in my business. Show me the letter he left.'

'I binned it.'

'Tell me what it said.'

Bennett did as he was told while Perry sat back in the chair listening. 'So, what do you propose we do next?'

They both started talking at once, trying to tell him about the private investigator idea they had come up with on the plane.

'Hal, take Kenny out to the drinks machine and get him a drink while I have this conversation with his pa.'

Hal went out with Kenny and shut the door. Perry

leaned over the desk and pointed a finger at him.

'If you'd gone out to Amsterdam when I said you should go, none of this would have happened.'

'Of course it bloody would. Brook's been planning this for a long time. I mean, he's been nicking money for years, he needed to have some idea how he was going to get away with it if the bubble burst.'

'It doesn't matter if Brook had a plan or not. We were right on his tail and you let him go. Makes me think you deliberately let him go. Maybe you're in the scam with him; I remember times when the two of you would go into a huddle, thick as thieves.'

He remembered too, but it was about cocaine, not money.

'Why the fuck would I let him go?' Bennett said. 'He and Landseer nicked my money, same as yours.'

'Maybe you wanted a bigger share.'

'Don't be daft. Are you doubting my loyalty?'

'I don't doubt you've got it, but you're loyal only to one person, Jim Bennett. You don't give a toss about the organisation or what I'm trying to build here.'

Hal came back into the room and closed the door.

'Where's Kenny,' Bennett asked.

'He's watching TV,' Hal said.

'So what is your great plan to find Brook?' Perry said. 'I'd like to hear it.'

He explained the idea of the PI and why he believed the cost would be irrelevant, given the amount of money they would gain in return. 'Hang on a sec,' Bennett said. 'This place doesn't have a TV. What have you done with Kenny?'

He smelled a rat and rose from his seat,

automatically reaching for his piece in the shoulder holster, but it wasn't there. They didn't give him time to go home and get tooled up.

Bennett leaned over the desk, his face red with anger. He pointed an accusing finger at Perry. 'If you think I'm taking the fall for–'

Hal wrapped something around his neck and pulled tight. Oh no, not his fucking trademark cheese wire. Perry's face flitted in and out of focus as he pulled at his neck, desperately gasping for air.

**

Some time later, Jim Bennett woke up. The fog in his brain worse than the nastiest hangover and the thump in his head like the crappiest 'flu symptoms. A spasm shot through him and in an involuntary action he opened his eyes and without warning, a bucket of water was thrown over him. Water dripped into his eyes making it hard to see, but when he did manage to focus, his clothing was ripped and electrodes were attached to his skin.

He screamed and shook in panic. He could take beatings, water boarding, be deprived of water and food, but he hated the thought of being electrocuted. He feared electricity with all the rationale of an agoraphobic or a hydrophobic; there was no childhood incident to recall, no recurring nightmare that nagged at his subconscious, no scary *Doctor Who* adventure to spook him. It just did.

'Ah, I see you're with us again, Bennett,' Perry said. 'You will see Hal has attached some wires to your chest and balls. They are connected to the alternator and battery from a forty-four-tonne DAF truck. You think he's just some thick Russian, only good for bashing people's heads in, but let me tell you, he's a genius with car engines. If I turn this little handle here...'

Bennett screamed as an electric jolt surged through his body. He shook and shivered, fear gripping his senses like a vice.

'What do you want from me?'

'I want to find out if you're working with Brook.'

'No, no I'm fucking not,' he bellowed.

Perry reached for the handle and turned it, causing Bennett to spasm and shake.

'I'm not working with Brook,' he said but it came out more like a wail as his voice sounded cracked and thin. 'It was him and that crooked estate agent, Landseer. I swear.'

'I believe you. I was just testing.'

'Me or the kit?'

'You.'

'I passed, yeah? Let me go.'

'No way. You fucked up more than once and I don't tolerate fuck-ups. This is payback time and you must know by now, as I've heard you say it about me more than once, what a sadistic bastard I can be.'

'I never did–'

'Don't lie to me, Bennett. It was never 'Daniel', 'Mr Perry', or 'boss', it was always 'Perry'. You're an insolent bastard. How you ever progressed to Colour Sergeant in the Army I will never know.'

He began to turn the handle with a determined

look on his face, but this time the rotating handle didn't stop. 'This is for switching off the alarm at Uckfield and letting that PI into our warehouse,' Perry said, 'this is for selling coke to Brook when I expressly banned drugs; this is for allowing Brook to go to Amsterdam when you could have caught him sooner; this is for your insolent attitude to me...'

It turned and turned and turned until he could take no more; he blacked out.

He woke up some time later, with no idea of how much time had passed as it was dull in this place and it didn't look much different from before. He was still attached to electrodes and the infernal device was still there, ready and willing to torture him, but with no sign of Perry or Hal.

He moved, trying to get more comfortable when he realised the ropes holding him didn't feel as tight as they once were. He twisted his wrist and gradually could touch the end of the cord wrapped around his hands. Gripping the end through two fingers he pulled as hard as his constraints allowed, but the tension in his fingers caused unbelievable agony in his damaged muscles and tendons and he had to stop and restart a few minutes later.

He tugged the cords for what felt like half an hour and pulled out about four inches, but still it wouldn't give. Sweat poured down his face hampering his concentration and he was as thirsty as a camel in the desert; he should have kept his mouth open when they threw the water at him, he thought bitterly.

He steeled himself for one final effort and pulled through the pain. Sweat dripped down his face and neck as he pushed himself harder and harder until finally the cord slackened and his hands fell free. He slumped forward, exhausted.

For a few minutes, he massaged life back into his wrists and then untied his feet. Light was coming in from a pair of open double doors. With no other exits visible in this, an abandoned factory, he walked towards the doors, staggering unsteadily with all the finesse of a Friday night drunk. Outside and away from the putrid odours of his own body fluids and oil, he gulped down air like a drowning man and a few several seconds later, tried to orientate himself.

Across from where he stood, he could see in the dim light a row of workshops, and rising up behind them in the distance, two tower blocks, but still nothing looked familiar. There was only one way out of this place as there was a wall to his left, so with uncertainty blunted by pain and exhaustion, he started walking.

From the shadows a voice said, 'You made it, Bennett, well done. Hal you owe me fifty big ones.'

Bennett began to run, but his movement felt stuttered, as if the ground was smeared in treacle. He heard the noise of a suppressed shot and he fell headlong into concrete. His left leg had been hit but he knew the bullet came from a handgun and not a limb-damaging SA80 or Armalite, it could be patched up. He tried to get to his feet but a boot caught him in the back of the neck forcing him face down.

'We've toyed with you long enough,' Perry said. 'This is what happens to useless fuck-ups like you.' He heard the metallic squeak of a trigger being pulled.

# THIRTY-THREE

Henderson took a seat in the interview room beside DS Walters. Facing them was David Frankland and his brief, Dominic Shearer. Frankland didn't look too bad for being in a car smash and then being left lying on a country road, except for a few marks and bruises on his face and walking with a crutch.

'Good morning Mr Frankland; Mr Shearer.'

He went over various items of housekeeping as Walters started the recording machine.

'I'm glad to see your move from hospital to Lewes nick went without a hitch,' Henderson said, 'or the reappearance of your two escape buddies.'

'For all they say about NHS food, it was ten times better than the slop they serve in Lewes, and those two men weren't my buddies. I don't know who they were.'

'Two men you didn't know tried to kidnap you from hospital? Give me a break. If they were your enemies, they would have left you in the middle of the M25, not on a quiet country road.'

'My client has said he didn't know the men, Inspector, that should be the end of it.'

'I'm not bothered one way or the other, Mr Shearer. I can hardly charge Mr Frankland with trying to escape from custody while being sedated, can I?'

'Quite so.'

'No, I'm not concerned, there are plenty of other items down here on this charge sheet that will give Mr Frankland loads of time to get used to the food in the prison service.'

'I do not agree with your analysis of the current situation. Unless you can show more evidence than you currently have, I insist you release my client without further delay.'

Henderson looked him straight in the eye. 'In case you haven't read the charge sheet, item three is the assault of two police officers at Forest Farm, or didn't you see it? I don't think even Mr Frankland would have the gall to try and deny it.'

Shearer opened and closed his mouth but no words escaped.

Henderson turned to Frankland. 'Mr Frankland, at the heart of this investigation is the wine-faking business operated by you, Daniel Perry and James Bennett from premises in Uckfield and, later, the barn at the side of your house in Loxwood. I'd like to know how it all worked.'

'What wine-faking operation?'

'DS Walters, let Mr Frankland see the pictures.'

'For the record,' Walters said, 'I am placing a series of photographs in front of Mr Frankland that show the inside of a warehouse on the Bell Lane Industrial Estate, Uckfield.'

She laid out the pictures taken by Harvey Miller of the Uckfield warehouse and Henderson watched as the colour drained from Frankland's cheeks.

'Where the hell did you get these?'

'A source. How did it work, what was your involvement?'

He took a final look and pushed the pictures back towards Walters. 'All very interesting, I'm sure, but bugger-all to do with me.'

'So, you are denying any participation in this wine-faking business, and also denying you received financial benefits from its operation?'

'I told you, mate I know nothing about it.'

'Mr Frankland–.'

'Inspector, I think my client has made it perfectly clear. He is innocent of these charges.'

Henderson reached for another file and placed two pages in front of Frankland, at the same time saying what he was doing for the tape. It was a list of bank transactions with several highlighted in yellow.

'This is a print-out of one of Fraser Brook's bank accounts where he deposited the money he made from selling wine collections, including fakes from this business that you deny knowing anything about. The items in yellow are marked 'Frankland.' When we took a look at your bank account, Mr Frankland, you know what we found?'

He shook his head.

Henderson passed another couple of sheets of paper over to the lawyer and his client.

'There, sitting in your bank account, are the exact amounts Brook transferred. There's two hundred thousand in the first sheet alone. Now isn't that an amazing coincidence?'

'Bloody hell,' Frankland exploded.

'I'm sure there is an innocent explanation for all –'

Shearer said but a hand clamped on his arm from Frankland stopped him.

'Where the hell did you get this?' Frankland asked.

'We found it when we searched Brook's shop in Chelsea,' Henderson said almost casually, wanting to make its discovery appear accidental. Brook was in enough danger already without alerting the gang to the 'Insurance' file's existence.

Lawyer and client talked in low voices. Shearer said something to him and Frankland looked up to the sky and sighed. He turned to Henderson. 'You got me there mate, I can't explain it.'

'So, people you don't know come and try and rescue you, and other unknown people deposit large sums of money into your bank account? As a plot for a book it belongs in *Alice in Wonderland*, not a crime novel or thriller.' Henderson slapped his hand on the statements, exasperated at Frankland's continued obstruction. 'This money came from the wine-faking business, didn't it?'

Frankland smiled. 'When you put it like that, it does sound a bit flaky.'

'Flaky? It's bloody preposterous,' Henderson said. 'Look mate, we've got enough evidence here to take this thing to trial and get a conviction, and make no mistake, we will. If you tell us how the process worked, it will work in your favour when the case comes to trial.'

Frankland leaned over to Shearer and said something. Lawyer and client had a quiet discussion for a few minutes before Frankland turned to face the detectives.

'Ask away.'

'How did it start?'

He stopped to take a drink of coffee. 'It was my idea. I come from New South Wales, an area full of vineyards and I saw how rich folks fawned over bottles with old labels and were willing to pay fancy prices for them. I quit the Army and came over here and started working for Daniel. When I found out he owned a couple of vineyards, the idea just grew from there.'

'Daniel Perry did what, financed it?'

'No, I did.'

'C'mon, you don't expect me to believe that? In some of the other financial records we recovered from Brook's shop, we can prove large payments came from Perry to Brook, presumably to finance purchase of the wine collections, and later, a larger payment going back the other way. We'll need more time to match them to specific auctions but we'll get there in the end.'

Frankland whispered something to his brief that had Shearer shaking his head.

Frankland said, 'Perry financed it.'

'The main beneficiaries are who: you, Jim Bennett, Daniel Perry, Fraser Brook and Charles Landseer?'

'Nah, it was me, Jim Bennett and Daniel Perry. Brook and Landseer got twenty grand each for every sale.'

'Sounds a bit mean when you guys were sharing a couple of hundred grand.'

'In hindsight you might be right. The slimy bastards started stealing.'

'Who? Brook and Landseer?' Henderson said, feigning innocence as he already knew.

'Nicked about three mill, the bastards.'

Henderson whistled. 'Three million pounds and you didn't notice?'

'When you say it like that it does sound a bit careless, I suppose, but we had other things to worry about.'

'That may be so, Mr Frankland but we cannot ignore how you dealt with one of the thieves, Charles Landseer.'

'Before we cover the final charge, Inspector, I would like ten minutes with my client.'

He looked at Walters, who nodded. 'I fancy a coffee.'

'Me too,' Henderson said. 'Fair enough Mr Shearer. We'll stop for ten minutes. Interview terminated at 16:34.'

Henderson instructed the PC standing outside the interview room door, additional security in case Frankland's break-out boys tried their luck here, to bring some refreshments for Shearer and Frankland. The two detectives climbed the stairs up to the second floor and walked into the Detectives' Room where they knew they could find a decent coffee machine.

'In the space of thirty minutes,' Walters said, 'he moved from looking like a gangster, confident of being released, to a convicted murderer waiting to be hanged. I couldn't believe his faked innocence over money hitting his bank account, and even his aborted hospital rescue.'

'Frankland was probably pressuring his brief to get

him out of here, and, scared of facing Perry and telling him bad news, the brief told him what he wanted to hear.'

'I don't understand why, he would know that assaulting a copper would give him a couple of years at least. How did he expect to get off? Was he going to suggest that me and Deepak beat up one another? You can still see the bruises on my face, the bastard.'

'His brief knew about the ballistics report and our intention to charge his client with Landseer's murder. Even to prove possession of the weapon would give him four or five years. He should have come into that interview aiming to strike a bargain, not deny everything and make us lay out the case, sheet by sheet. If he'd given me Perry on a plate, I'd maybe go easy on one of the charges.'

'You're right, he should have.'

'Go and talk to Phil Bentley. Find out the latest about the hunt for Perry and Bennett.'

Henderson returned to his office and without waking up his pc, pushed back the chair and put his feet on the desk. Where was Daniel Perry? Henderson was pleased to have Frankland in custody and, in time, Bennett and Brook would be added, but they were consolations, a couple of trout when what he really wanted was salmon. This case hinged on Perry and Henderson wouldn't stop until the man was in custody.

Perry was a savvy, street smart operator and would know that the net was closing. It was probably he who had put together the break-out team at the hospital and chances are, he would also know about the death of Harvey Miller. It was therefore no surprise when they discovered no one at home in Perry's large house in Barking when the boys from the Met called around that morning. It was a similar story when Spanish police turned up at his villa near Estepona. With all the CCTV, ANPR cameras and passport controls at their disposal, how could he just disappear?

Walters walked into his office shaking her head. 'We've checked out all the business addresses, it looks like Perry and Bennett have done a runner.'

# THIRTY-FOUR

Fraser Brook woke early and was surprised to find that after consuming copious amounts of wine the previous night, he had a clear head. This was a trait, no doubt, of working in the wine business where the ability to drink every day and still function was inherent in the job description. In addition to the obvious drinking opportunities available in the shop, with breakages and free samples, he was often invited to wine tastings, product launches and innumerable social functions.

He cycled into town and breakfasted in the same café as he did the day before. Today, he didn't linger over the food as he was keen to get started. He spent the rest of the morning in as many up-market agenzia immobiliare as he could, which in an expensive town like Lucca were not difficult to find.

He put the brochures and papers into a small carrier bag given to him by one of the estate agents, and after securing it on the rack on the back of the bike, he headed back to the villa. He crossed the River Serchio on Lucca's north side on the Via Per Camaiore. Traffic was heavy and he knew from experience how inattentive Italian drivers could be, easily distracted by mobiles, music and mouthy girlfriends, and he made sure he kept to the cycle lane.

A few kilometres later, he turned off the Camairore and joined the Via Della Maulina towards San Concordio di Moriano and, on his side of the road at least, the traffic was lighter than before, everyone heading the other way and into the market at Lucca.

He rolled past large fields of maize, bordered by tall cypress trees swaying gently in the breeze. Houses were dotted across the landscape, smallholdings, each with their own vineyard and olive grove, and in the distance, beautiful villas up on the hillside, hidden by trees, away from the prying eyes of tourists.

Turning up a driveway, one he missed the first time in the hire car, he reached Villa Arsina and propped the bike up against the wall. He removed the bag from the rack, unlocked the back door and walked into the house. He passed the lounge en route to the kitchen, and something there caught his eye. Someone was there, but it didn't look like Signori Belcapo, the man he rented the villa from.

'Hello,' Brook said.

'Ah, there you are. Hello Fraser, nice to see you again. How are you?'

Brook stood in the doorway, his mouth agape and heart pounding. He recognised the voice but not the face or the clothes. What the hell was he doing here! He looked for the phone, he was going to call the Politzia and have him arrested.

'You're being very rude Fraser, not greeting your guest. Cat got your tongue?'

That voice, the sneering expression, the almost feline features. Oh My God! No! Not him! It *is* him!

'I didn't recognise you, Daniel.'

'Amazing what a change of hair, clothes and not shaving for a week or two can do for a man. Well, don't just stand there hovering like a bloody waiter, come into the room and join me.'

Brook moved into the room and as he got closer to Perry, he could see the pistol beside him. He was dressed in long khaki shorts, Nike trainers and a plain purple t-shirt. The baseball cap lying on the floor with the words 'Lucca' across the top completed the tourist uniform. It was an amazing transformation from the well-dressed businessman he purported to be.

'What...what are you doing here?'

'You make it sound like I shouldn't be here,' he said, his tone harsher. 'You're the one who stole *our* money. I am here to get it back.' He paused. 'Before we get down to the serious stuff, is there any chance of a cold beer? I'm parched?'

'Yes. There's some in the fridge,' Brook said. Almost in a trance, he turned and walked into the kitchen.

'Don't try anything stupid like running away. You know I can always find you. I tracked you down here, don't forget.'

Brook stood in the kitchen, his mind buzzing. Perry was here to kill him, he knew it. He opened the fridge and removed two bottles of Nastro Azzuro. When he turned to remove the bottle opener from the drawer, he looked around for a weapon, but all he could see was a rolling pin and pizza cutter. A tougher man than him would get close enough to Perry to use something like that, but he wasn't so brave. He lifted the bottles and walked back into the lounge.

He handed a bottle to Perry and took a seat on the other side of the room on the small settee.

'Cheers mate,' Perry said, swigging the Nastro Azzurro. 'Not bad, Italian beers, but not a patch on London Bitter. Although I suppose it's all Greek to you as I imagine you stick to wine.'

'Eh?' he replied, thrown at the banality of the question. 'Oh, yes I do prefer wine. How did you track me down?'

'It's not so difficult. I have a friend at a mobile phone company.'

Brook's face reddened. He had considered throwing away his trusty iPhone and buying a new pre-paid, but all his friends in London, San Francisco and Los Angeles had his number and he was loath to lose contact with any of them. He instantly realised his vanity was about to cost him millions, if not something more.

'I called in a little favour and asked him to monitor your phone. Hey presto, all the calls you've been making to the shop were logged and through a process they call triangulation, the readings from the three nearest mobile phone masts were used to tell me exactly where you were. How I got past all those border checks and controls, you've got to love the good old EC for the Schengen Agreement. I drove from France to Italy without seeing one customs official.'

'What happens now?'

'It's a good question, mate, and depends on you.' He paused to take a swig. 'I want you to give me back all the money you stole. Then, depending on how cooperative you are, I may or may not let you live.'

Brook shifted uncomfortably in his seat. He could still come out of this in one piece, and rich, as he had only told Landseer about one Swiss account. As their haul mushroomed, he had moved money to other accounts in several other Swiss banks. If he could persuade Perry there was only one account, which as of last Wednesday was showing a balance of two and half million, it might be enough to send him away happy and still leave him enough funds to enjoy a good life.

'The money's in an account with UBS in Switzerland.'

'Does it allow internet access?'

'Yes.'

'Good, saves us a trip to Florence or bloody Milan or wherever the fuck UBS have a branch in Italy. Do you have a laptop and online access here?'

'Yes.'

'Bring it in here and you can make the transfer.'

Brook walked into the bedroom where he'd been up late the previous night emailing some of his boyfriends around the world, and picked up the laptop. He returned to the lounge and placed the laptop on the coffee table and switched it on. While he waited for it to boot up, he looked over at Perry who was staring back with a wicked grin on his face.

'It might not have occurred to you, Brook, but we could have had every gangster in London out looking for you if we wanted. I bet you didn't know you were so popular?'

'What?'

'Yes. If I'd put word out that a snivelling little creep called Fraser Brook ran off with three million smackers, every psycho would be bursting their balls to get you and grab a piece of the pie. Isn't that a pleasant thought?'

Brook felt the colour drain from his face. He had never considered himself to be important, or the theft of the money to be serious. After all, it was earned by duping rich wine buyers in the first place. The thought of several fifteen stone, bald-headed, tattooed thugs combing the streets of Lucca searching for him filled him with dread.

What *was* a pleasant thought though, was Perry's admission that he was only looking for three million. He would see two and a half in the UBS account and take the lot, and if pushed at the point of a gun, Brook would admit to another half million in Credit Suisse. The rest would be his. A half a million in BNP Paribas was enough, it would have to be enough. The computer was ready.

'A lot of the money in this account is my own money, money not taken from you but built up through my own wine business.'

'I don't give a shit if I leave you penniless and begging on the street for your next meal, I want it all, every last penny. If some of it didn't come from us, well bad luck, call it a bonus for all the trouble you've caused.' Perry walked across the room and sat beside Brook on the settee. 'I want no fancy stuff Brook, just transfer all the money to this account number.' He handed Brook a piece of paper.

Perry watched as Brook logged onto the UBS

website from his 'favourites' file, and gave him a playful nudge when he spotted Gay Times, Pink Paper News and Boys Toys on the same list. When the UBS website loaded, he clicked on 'e-banking'. They waited while the UBS computers silently shifted his enquiry to a secure bank of servers using some of the world's finest firewall software, encryption algorithms and anti-hacking detectors.

Brook keyed in his username and password and after a small delay, one account number was shown. Thank God he hadn't opened another account with UBS. He highlighted the number and clicked on the left wheel of the laptop touch pad. A few seconds later a short statement appeared. At the top, opposite the words 'Account Balance' and written in large, coloured type, it stated '£2,624,879.98 sterling.'

'Who's been a greedy boy then,' Perry said looking at the total, his eyes wide and a small smile playing on his lips. 'It's not three mill but what the hell, that was just a ballpark figure Bennett came up with.'

'I told you before, some of that money is mine, earned by me in my business.'

'I don't give a toss, it's all ours now. Do the transfer.'

Brook keyed in the details. He was about to press 'go', when Perry stopped him.

'Let me check,' he said, looking at the account number and comparing it to what was on the screen. 'Yep, looks fine. Go ahead.'

Brook moved the curser over 'Transfer Funds' and pressed it. They waited twenty seconds or so before a flashing message popped up.

'*Funds Frozen On Orders of the District Judge.*'

Perry pulled the laptop towards him. 'What the fuck's going on? What are you trying to pull, Brook?'

'I don't know anything about this, I swear. Look at the account,' he pressed the 'back' button and again selected the statement of account, 'I transferred money five days ago, see.' He pointed at the last transaction where four thousand Euros had been moved to his Barclays current account. 'Something must have happened since then.'

Perry stood and began pacing around the room. A few minutes later, he stood over Brook and said, 'give me your phone.' Brook handed it over and Perry dialled a number from memory. He waited but after receiving no reply, ended it and called another number.

'Hi Sarah, it's Daniel. Is Dave around?'

He listened for a few moments. 'What?' he said raising his voice. 'When did this happen?' He kept quiet for a few minutes more before uttering a loud expletive.

Perry brought the call to an end and slumped on the settee beside Brook. 'David's in jail awaiting trial on five charges including murder. That fucking lawyer told me the cops had nothing on him and he would be out in 24 hours. I've been out of the loop for so long I didn't hear what had happened.'

'The cops have found out,' Brook said, 'and put a stop on the account; the devious bastards.'

'Shit!' Perry said, chewing his nails. 'I'll bet that bastard Henderson is behind it. Hal should have done him in when he had the chance. Right,' he said as if suddenly coming to a decision. 'Move, Brook. Outside.'

'What about the money?'

'I'll get my hands on it some other way. Hang on, write down how you got into that account, passwords and all that stuff.'

Brook did as he was told and handed the paper to him.

'Good,' he said, before stuffing it into his pocket. 'Let's go. Out to the pool.'

Brook put the laptop down and opened the French windows leading out to the pool. Perry walked behind him, the gun pointing into his back.

'Don't kill me Daniel. We're colleagues.'

'Shut the fuck up, Brook and keep walking.'

Brook walked down the side of the pool towards the deep end. As he edged nearer the side to avoid a chair, the gun fired and he felt a searing, fiery pain in his shoulder. He crumpled to the ground, screaming in agony. Seconds later, Perry's foot pushed him into the pool.

'I want to make you suffer, Brook. Shame I don't have a phone with me otherwise I'd film it.'

Brook tried to swim but couldn't as the shock had numbed his senses and frozen any movement in his shoulder. He bobbed up and down in three metres of water, desperately trying to keep his head from going under. The bullet had passed clean through his body, but the large exit wound leaked a continuous stream of blood, marking the deep blue water with long streaks of red.

'This is slow even for my tastes.' Perry raised the

gun. Brook struggled to get away and only succeeded in turning his back. The gun fired again and hit him with the force of a hammer in his thigh.

The pain was indescribable and it took a huge effort to say, 'you bastard Perry...I've left stuff...paperwork...they'll hunt you down.'

'Is that the best you can do? I'm a wanted man already.'

Brook bobbed up and tried to open his mouth and gulp some air, but each time he did so, he swallowed more water. He surfaced three more times, his body sinking lower and lower into the water until finally, he did not surface again.

Perry tucked the gun into the waistband of his shorts and turned to go. His gaze was met by the shocked face of Signora Belcapo, the wife of the villa owner, there to deliver her homemade zabaglione to the nice Englishman, Signori Brook.

Perry had no idea how long she had been watching but the look on her face said it all. He lifted the weapon and shot her twice in the head.

The zabaglione flew into the air and came down on the edge of the pool in a cascade of cream and egg yolk. It leached slowly into the pool where it drifted in the breeze, and soon became indistinguishable from the remnants of Fraser Brook's blood.

# THIRTY-FIVE

'Why didn't we sail to Scotland?' Rachel said putting down her in-flight magazine. 'It would be lovely on the water at this time of year.'

'Why do you ask?'

'There's an article in here about sailing holidays and it got me thinking.'

'Firstly, I didn't consider it at all as it would take too long.'

'How long is too long?'

'Maybe a week or more, depending on how strong the wind blows. Plus the same to get back.'

'Ah, right. Bang goes all my holidays. There's more?'

'Yep. Once you clear the Lizard at the southern tip of Cornwall, you hit the North Atlantic and let me tell you, the water there's not so forgiving as the English Channel.'

'What, even in summer?'

'It's often worse in summer as at least in winter you know that storms are coming, but at this time of year, they can happen so fast and when people are least expecting it. As much as I dislike flying and security procedures at airports, I think this is the fastest and safest way.'

The plane landed in Inverness on time and once

they collected their bags, they picked up a hire car. Outside the sprawl of the city, the road soon followed the contours of the River Ness, intermittently visible through the trees, and at the aptly named village of Loch End, they reached the river's source, Loch Ness.

'Isn't this the longest lake in Scotland?' Rachel asked.

'Loch, Rachel. We call them lochs in Scotland, but no, Loch Awe is longer.'

'It must be the deepest then.'

'It holds the most water, but the deepest accolade belongs to Loch Morar and before you ask, there's a monster in there too.'

'What's that one called? Moggie?'

'No, Morag.'

'Ha. I take it by the tone of your voice that you're a sceptic, so I imagine we're not stopping at the Nessie Visitor Centre, a place I've seen advertised every mile along this road?'

'Why, do you want to?'

'No, not really.'

'I will if you want to, but I warn you, it's full of grainy old photos that don't look like a dinosaur, more like lumps of wood. Don't you think if there was a large animal living down there, someone in this modern day of digital cameras, Nessie hunters and smartphones, would have taken a decent picture of the thing?'

'Yep. As a clear-headed journalist, I would be forced to agree with you, but wouldn't it be such a great story if it was true?'

'I don't think it matters if it's true or not. It's a bit

like the Queen and the royal palaces. Tourists often come to Britain and say they're here to see the Queen but how many people actually see her? Very few, I suspect. Instead, they stand outside Buckingham Palace and take pictures or wander around Windsor Castle, but they go home happy all the same.'

Henderson's parents lived on Alma Road in Fort William, in a large whitewashed semi-detached house, with stunning views over Loch Linnhe.

'It looks a big house,' Rachel said.

'It's larger than our place in College Place with a much better view, but it's not worth half as much.'

'If a stat like that is supposed to make me feel richer, it doesn't. I just think of the high mortgage we've taken on and all the money going out every month.'

'You're on holiday, forget such things and enjoy being away from the grind for a while.'

'Good advice from a cop who never switches off. I'll try.'

He lifted the suitcases out from the boot of the car and followed Rachel up the steep stairs that bordered the garden, already a problem for his father as his knees weren't as reliable as they used to be.

The door opened before he got to it and for a moment, the smells of his childhood washed over him like a bow wave: Vick's Vapour Rub, Rive Gauche perfume and farmhouse scones, toasting on the griddle.

'Hello, love,' his mother said, grabbing him in a bear hug, a strong grip for such a small woman. 'It's lovely to see you, son.'

'It's great to see you too, Mum.'

She released him slowly.

'This is Rachel.'

His mother gave her a hug too, a sign of mellowing in old age perhaps, as previous girlfriends had to make do with a cool handshake and a steely glare.

'Come away in,' Mary, his mother said, 'and take the weight off your feet.'

He walked into the lounge, a place where he used to play Scalextric on the carpet and dreamed of being the captain of a large ship. Not a big leap in imagination for a small boy, as he could see from the front window several boats a day making their way up Loch Linnhe to the Caledonian Canal.

His father was ensconced in his favourite chair, his concentration fixed on the newspaper in front of him. In the morning and afternoon it would be *The Scotsman*, and later in the day, *The Press and Journal*. Once a week he bought *The Oban Times*.

His father looked up as he came into the room. 'Hello Dad,' he said.

His father stuck out his hand without rising from his chair. 'Good to see you, son,' he said shaking his hand vigorously and slapping him on the back as he leaned down for a hug. 'Sorry I can't get up, I'm feeling a bit out of sorts today.'

Henderson introduced him to Rachel and after enquiring about his health, he walked into the kitchen to see what was causing the delicious smells. He lifted a tea towel covering something and underneath saw fruit scones, farmhouse scones and pancakes.

'Don't you go pinching anything, Angus

Henderson. Go away into the living room and talk to your father and that pretty girlfriend of yours. I'll bring you all a cup of tea in a jiffy.'

Ten minutes later, he introduced Rachel to his mother's baking and to the delights of home-made strawberry jam. The tea tasted better too. People often said it was due to the homecoming effect, but as a man less prone to sentimentality than some, he suspected it was down to a higher level of water quality. Sussex water wasn't bad, but whether as a result of high levels of chalk or something else, it couldn't match this.

'What's been happening on the crime scene down there in Sussex?' his father said. 'I look for things in the newspaper every day but bad things only happen in big cities like Glasgow and London. Sussex seems to be a bit of a backwater where criminals are concerned.'

'Maybe it's just as well you don't read about all the cases I'm working on, it can be hard to maintain a sense of perspective from up here.'

'You think we don't get crime up here in the Fort? Only last week a woman ran over a sheep and a man accidentally discharged his shotgun into his neighbour's hut.'

'Your dodgy knees haven't affected your sense of humour I see,' Henderson said.

'Are you popping into see old Archie and wee Eric? They're always asking after you whenever I see them.'

'I intend to,' Henderson said. He turned to Rachel beside him. 'In case you're wondering, they're a couple of bobbies from the local cop shop. Archie is about fifty, old for a cop but not to anyone else and wee Eric is six-four.'

'How do you know them if you never worked for the police up here?' Rachel said.

'I came up for the weekend from Glasgow one time and went into the police station to report a crashed car I spotted on the A82. They say criminals can spot cops but cops can recognise their own kind. I told them what I did and they told me about their job. We've kept in contact ever since.'

After a hearty dinner that he doubted even Rachel, with her library of Jamie Oliver and Nigella Lawson cookbooks, could match, he needed some exercise to burn some of it off. He said goodbye to his parents and took Rachel for a walk into town.

'Your dad's got a wicked sense of humour,' Rachel said, 'the way he baits your mother makes me cringe and giggle at the same time.'

'It's like she's not bothered but she's taking it all in. She'll have it out with him when we're not there.'

They walked the steep hill of Alma Road, a bugger to walk up after a night in the pub, after a long shift at the sawmill or on the beat, and headed down Belford Road past the hospital.

'This hospital isn't like the Royal Sussex, only catering for Brighton and surrounding area, they take in patients from all over the West of Scotland, some coming by ambulance and the more serious by helicopter.'

'I suppose as this part of the country is so rural they have to do that, as Fort William isn't big enough to support such a large facility on its own.'

'Aye you're right, and it's the same for schools. In the place I went to, Lochaber High, we had people in there from little villages out west, the names of which we'd never heard of, and others were from far-flung islands, only accessible in fine weather.'

'That must create its own problems.'

'How do you mean?'

'Well if you live in a place like this, it's not a big city like Brighton for sure, more like an oversized town, but the people here would be more switched on than some farm boys from a Gaelic speaking island.'

'Some of them were a bit strange right enough, but once we got used to their odd sayings and habits they settled in fine.'

'You didn't bully them?'

'Nothing I would care to admit.'

They took a walk along the shores of Loch Linnhe, the water as flat as glass, and stood for a moment looking over at Caol and Corpach and down towards Loch Eil, the lights in the distance twinkling like mini-stars in the fading light.

They turned back and headed over to the Crofter Bar and walked inside. After the calm of the lochside the bar fizzed with heat, noise and the strong aromas of food, sweat and beer. He looked around while waiting to order but didn't see anyone he recognised. By the look of the bright North Face jackets and trendy haircuts, most of the people there weren't locals.

He had just taken a seat, looking forward to a pint of John Smith's in front of him, now that the food groan in his stomach had subsided, when his phone rang. He stepped outside to take it as he couldn't hear a word inside the pub.

'How are you enjoying your holiday, Angus?' Carol Walters asked.

'I've only just arrived but so far it's shaping up.' He looked at his watch: 21:45. 'Are you still in the office? Don't you have a home to go to?'

'I have and I'll soon be returning, but I'm calling to say there's been a development.'

Henderson sighed. 'This only happens to detectives and prime ministers; just when we go on holiday, all hell breaks loose.'

'It's not so bad, unless you're Fraser Brook, of course. Italian police found him today, dead and fully-clothed in the pool at the villa where he was staying in Italy. He had gunshot wounds.'

'In Italy?'

'Yep, in a villa near Lucca, and beside him the villa owner's wife. Brook had a bullet wound in his shoulder and one in his leg but the cause of death is thought to be drowning.'

'Before or after being shot?'

'After.'

'So, someone shot him and threw him in the pool, or they threw him in the pool and then shot him. Either way, he couldn't swim and drowned.'

'Yep. The owner's wife received two bullets to the head.'

'She saw something she shouldn't have?'

'It's what the Italian police think.'

'Hang on a sec. Landseer had a similar, non fatal injury as Brook, but in his leg. It makes me think the killer is torturing them before killing them; Landseer to give up Brook, and Brook to give up the stolen money.'

'Could be.'

'Do the Italian police have any suspects?'

'No, but we think it was Perry. Bennett is an old-fashioned kind of guy. He would just shoot Brook where he stood; forget throwing him in the pool.'

'Damn. We asked Interpol to keep a look-out for Perry, Bennett and his son.'

'Europe's a big place.'

'It is and thanks to the lack of border controls, a suspect can shift between EC countries without cameras and border checks picking them up.'

'If Perry did it, I'd like to know how as his name didn't pop up in any of the systems as having left the UK. We've got them monitored.'

'Probably on a fishing boat out of Harwich or on someone's yacht. Thanks for the heads up, Carol. I assume I can depend on you to liaise with our European colleagues.'

'I'm not getting off the phone yet, there's more.'

'There is?'

'CI Edwards has warned everyone to be on their guard until Perry is caught.'

'He's been missing for weeks, hence I'm up here taking some overdue leave. Why the caution now?'

'The Italian Police looked through Brook's laptop and believe he was trying to transfer funds from a UBS bank account. This is the account where, according to documents found in his office, Brook kept the money stolen from Perry and his gang.'

'The funds I ordered to be blocked.'

'Yes.'

'So, the Chief thinks what? He'll come after me or you in revenge for blocking his money?'

'She's just being careful, Angus. He's a dangerous man and who knows how he'll react when he realises his source of easy pickings has dried up.'

He thought for a moment. 'It's you that needs to watch your step. An internet search will tell him where you're based, but I'd like to see him try and find me up here. Even tourists with maps and sat-nav systems get lost.'

'Where are you going after Fort William? Are you still going touring?'

'We'll stay here a couple of days to catch up with a few friends and look up some old colleagues. Then, we're heading out west to Kilchoan, a place I've visited a few times before and really liked. We've rented a cottage there.'

'Well, I hope you both have a great time.'

'Don't worry we will. Talk to you later.'

# THIRTY-SIX

On Monday, two days after arriving in Fort William, Henderson and Rachel packed the car, said goodbye to his parents and drove south towards Corran. He often felt melancholy about leaving Fort William and his family, but not today as he wasn't heading straight back to the office and would still be in the area if anything happened. Not something he could say when down in Sussex, over 500 miles away.

'I didn't know your dad had served in the Navy. It wasn't until I looked at some of the pictures dotted around the living room that I noticed him in uniform.'

'He keeps it quiet for some reason. A lot of men who served in the Falklands saw the true horror of war at first hand. When they returned home, I think they found it hard to talk with people doing everyday jobs like repairing roads or looking after their sheep. War is so alien to what they know or what they're used to.'

'All the same, we should make more of war veterans than we do. They often get a bad press but they're just following the orders of their political masters. It's the politicians we should criticise not the armed forces.'

'I agree, and not just because my brother was once in the Army.'

'As that how got his dodgy knees?'

'No, that was playing bowls and golf in all weathers.'

The previous day they'd behaved like tourists. In the morning, they drove to the Glenfinnan Monument, the place where 'The Young Pretender,' Bonnie Prince Charlie, raised his standard in 1745. In the afternoon, they took a chairlift up the Nevis Range to admire Scotland's tallest mountain and to breathe in air blowing all the way from Scandinavia. It was a warm summer's day at ground level in Fort William, but bitter and chilling at 2,000 feet, and colder than anything he had ever experienced in Sussex in the middle of winter.

'When you said we were going on a car ferry,' Rachel said as the Corran Ferry approached, 'I imagined one of those big ships sailing between Portsmouth and the Isle of Wight.'

He laughed. 'How could you fit one of those monsters into this little crossing? We could just moor it across the loch and walk over the deck to Ardgour.'

He drove down the steep landing and bumped on to the ferry, the ruddy-faced worker in a high-vis jacket with a heavy woollen sweater underneath coaxing him closer and closer to the bumper in front. Thankfully a tap on the bonnet stopped him from having a shunt as he didn't take out Collision Damage Waiver insurance when he hired the car. He pulled on the handbrake as instructed by the sign on the side of the ferry, and got out of the car.

Some tourists were adept at driving into tight spots like this, while others made a complete pig's breakfast of it, making him wonder how the staff maintained their happy demeanour. Rachel joined him as the boat dropped its mooring and headed towards Ardgour on the Ardnamurchan peninsula. There wasn't much to see as the chilly start to the day had deterred many sailing boats, and only a few hardy line fishermen had ventured out. It was a short crossing but it saved them over an hour of driving as the alternative route was to round Loch Eil and then to drive down the west side of Loch Linnhe.

'I remember someone telling me,' Henderson said as he steered the car up the steep ramp while waving farewell to the ferryboat crew, 'about a local man who drove up here from Glasgow with a faulty car battery. It meant if he switched the engine off, the car wouldn't restart, so if he had to stop, he kept the car running, even in the long queue for the ferry at Corran. When he finally got on the ferry, he must have felt so relieved to be almost at his destination, he switched off the engine.'

'Oh no, what a place to be stuck. How did he get off? Or did the ferry go back and forward all day with his car on it?'

'You saw how steep the Ardgour ramp was?'

'Yes.'

'A couple of crew members pushed him up to the top and then gave him a bump start.'

'I call that real customer service.'

Close to the start of Loch Sunart, a body of water that would accompany them all the way down to Kilchoan, they stopped at a tea room in Strontian. It was a lovely old fashioned place offering cream teas and slices of various cakes, but surprisingly owned by two young women who looked like escapees from Hampstead.

He plumped for a slice of the coffee and walnut cake while Rachel confirmed her growing fondness for farm scones by having another.

'This is delicious,' she said as she tucked in, 'I must get the recipe.'

He sighed. 'Another piece of kit to clutter up our smart but small kitchen.'

'Why?'

'I'm no expert, so you'll need to ask Shona behind the counter, but I believe farmhouse scones are made on a thing called a griddle. If so, it's the only piece of equipment our new kitchen doesn't possess.'

\*\*

She fell to the floor and before she knew what she was doing, blurted everything out. 'He's in Scotland. Fort William first and then to a small village called Kilchoan today.'

'How long is he there for?'

'Until the end of the week.'

'Very good, Detective Sergeant Walters. See, it wasn't so hard, was it?' Daniel Perry said, his smile like that of a cartoon snake. 'Maybe now I'll only let Hal rape you.'

She'd left the office at eight. When she'd entered her apartment, Perry was waiting. Brighton had been experiencing a warm spell and a few windows were open to air the rooms, but mindful of a recent spate of burglaries around the Queen's Park area, she didn't think a child could squeeze through the tiny gap she'd left, never mind a full-grown man.

Perry didn't muck about, he knew Sussex Police had instructed the Union Bank of Switzerland to block the funds Brook stole from him, and now he wanted them unblocked. She told him she didn't have the authority to do so, but that didn't seem to hinder him from punching and kicking her and threatening to pick her nostrils apart with his sharp knife.

When it finally got through to him that she couldn't unblock the funds, he stopped hitting her and demanded to know Henderson's whereabouts, because for some reason, he knew the DI wasn't in his office right now. When she refused, the beating started once again. Her thoughts were now on how she could warn Henderson that Perry was coming to get him.

Perry pulled out his phone.

'Hal, where the fuck are you? You're supposed to be down here in Brighton helping me.'

She could hear part of Hal's garbled, high volume response. She couldn't make out what he was saying but it sounded like he was in trouble.

'There's police at your house and you're being arrested?' Perry said. 'What are they doing there?'

Perry listened again.

'What are the charges? I'll get Danny the solicitor to come down there as soon as.'

She tuned out and looked around for something to hit Perry with, or a way to escape, but to her dismay, he seemed to have all the bases covered. She was sitting on the couch, opposite the door and within touching distance of Perry who sat on the chair. If she made a run for it, he could get to the door before she could, and then there was the issue of the Sig Sauer pistol lying on his lap.

In any case, she didn't think she could run anywhere as an earlier thump on the face felt like it had fractured her jaw, her kicked ribs were aching and making movement difficult, one of her eyes was closing up and a kick she received to her knee had left it swollen.

'The good news is,' Perry said, dropping his phone back into his pocket, 'Hal can't make it as he's been picked up by your lot in London, the bastards. The bad news is Alex is available. Alex is a horny bastard and who knows what will happen when I leave you two lovebirds and head up to Scotland to find your boss?'

'Why are you telling me this? I thought you said you weren't going to kill me.'

He shrugged. 'A man can change his mind can't he?'

'You'll never get away with it. You killed Brook and now Interpol are hunting for you. If you kill me, every copper in Britain will know your face, if they don't know already.'

'Don't I get credit for all the others?'

'What others?'

'There's a few I could mention, but don't go looking for Jim Bennett and his dopey son Kenny, if you know what I mean.'

'Jim Bennett and his son? What did you kill them

for?'

'They cocked up once too often for my liking, that's what.'

'Does that list include Chris Fletcher?'

'Who's he?'

'The lad who was killed on a cross-Channel ferry.'

'Ah yes, Chris Fletcher. Now I think about it, another cock-up by Bennett. I should have cut off his balls for that one.'

'What happened to Harvey Miller?'

'Stop it Walters, I'm bored with this. Go into the kitchen and make me a coffee and don't fuck around. You come at me with a knife, I'll put a bullet through your head without hesitation. Understand?'

'Yes.'

'Good. Milk and two sugars. Go get.'

She rose from the settee with some difficulty and headed into the kitchen. She owned a smart coffee machine that made a lovely cup, but she didn't want to waste good coffee on a man like Perry. She reached for the kettle, filled it and switched it on.

If Perry thought she would lie back and be raped by Alex and then shot without putting up a fight, he had another think coming. She often went out to work in a skirt but last week she'd taken several to the dry cleaners so today she wore trousers. Thank the Lord she did as this particular pair had a side pocket and there she could hide her expensive but ultra-sharp three-inch paring knife.

She carried a cup of coffee through to the lounge, but tempting as it might be, she didn't spit in it, or if the kitchen was more secluded, her preferred choice would be to piss in it. She could always chuck it over him, but knowing Perry in the short time she did, the cold bastard would ignore the pain and still manage to shoot her.

'Ta,' he said when she handed it to him. 'Are you not partaking?'

'No.'

You don't like coffee? There's not something wrong with it, I hope.'

'No, there's nothing wrong with it. I like coffee well enough, I just don't fancy one right now.' She wanted to say her bashed up jaw would make it difficult to take a drink, but she didn't want to provoke him.

'Fair enough.'

He started to chit-chat about meaningless trivia: how long she'd lived there, what the neighbours were like, what sort of people used the park which could be seen from the front window; like an old pal who just dropped by for a coffee and a catch-up.

The door buzzer sounded, sending her spirits soaring, as it might be her friend Michael who was a big lad, or Sally Graham from work dropping round to borrow something for her new but sparsely furnished flat. However, her spirits sank fast when she looked at Perry. He was holding the gun in a tight grip and would have no hesitation in killing them too.

# THIRTY-SEVEN

Henderson and Rachel arrived in Kilchoan, a village on the western end of the Ardnamurchan peninsula, a few minutes before three in the afternoon. They had intended being earlier but he insisted on stopping at various places along the way, evoking memories of the times he'd been there before.

He'd almost forgotten how quiet and peaceful this part of the UK could be after the bustle of Sussex with its tourist filled towns, rowdy weekend nights and flights leaving and arriving at Gatwick Airport every couple of minutes. Any time they stopped for a break, they could hear water lapping on the shore of Loch Sunart, the rustle of small animals in the heather and the light flap of a buzzard's wing in the air above them.

Bay Cottage sounded like something with panoramic views over the Golden Gate Bridge and Alcatraz, and not a double-fronted house with two large windows on a raised position overlooking Kilchoan Bay. Such views to him were the equal of anything on the Californian coast, but while Kilchoan couldn't boast 24-hour coffee shops or waterfront bars, it didn't have a morning fog to chill the bones or noisy cable cars, a fatal hazard for the deaf or unwary.

They got out of the car and stretched. Although it

hadn't been an arduous journey as there had been so many stops, it felt good to get out in the fresh air and walk around at the end of a trip. They heard a door close and saw, walking towards them, a tall, stout man with a mop of curly black hair and trotting alongside, a lively collie dog.

'Mr Henderson,' he said when he got closer, 'and Ms Jones. Pleased to meet you. I'm Donnie McLean the owner of the house you see behind me here, and Bay Cottage where you will be staying.'

They shook hands.

'Did you have a pleasant journey?'

'I certainly did, remembering places I'd been to be before but I guess it might not have been so interesting for my passenger.'

'I had my heart in my mouth a few times on those single track roads,' Rachel said.

'Aye, I admit they can be a bit tricky until you get used to them. By the sound of your accent, you're from these parts, Mr Henderson.'

'Call me Angus, Donnie. I grew up in Fort William and moved away in my early twenties, first to Glasgow and then to Brighton.'

'You couldn't get further away.'

'It wasn't deliberate, but there may have been something in my subconscious about getting far away.'

They had been talking for nearly ten minutes, when he noticed Rachel fidgeting, something she did when out of her comfort zone. He imagined it would be something that could happen often up here, as people had a different view of time from those scurrying about in the city; they were interested in other people, where they came from, where they were going, and didn't feel the need to be constantly checking their phones.

Donnie showed them around the house and even though he knew that villages in this area were only connected to mains electricity and received colour television broadcasts within living memory, this place had the lot. In truth, neither of them came to watch television and it was doubtful they would need to put on the heating, as the air felt warm and in any case, after a day out hill walking it would take all his energy to climb the stairs and fall into a bath or bed.

'Well, I'll leave you both to it,' Donnie said at the door.

'Thanks for all your help.'

'No problem. If you need anything at all, Ferry Stores will have it or they can get it for you. If you want to go fishing or shooting, and it's really good around here, I know the best places and I can either take you myself or show you where to go and lend you the equipment if you need it.'

They thanked Donnie and went inside. Rachel put the kettle on while he carried their bags upstairs. He dumped them into the largest room and walked to the window. Thanks to a bright, sunny sky with little cloud, he could see across to the island of Mull and down the Sound of Mull, past Morvern towards Oban.

He was so engrossed in the majesty of it all, he didn't realise Rachel had come up the stairs and jumped when she wrapped her arms around his waist and nuzzled into his neck.

'The views up here are terrific, don't you think?' he said.

'The views down here are pretty terrific too. Close the curtains, all this fresh air is making me frisky.'

He turned to face her and kissed her passionately on the lips. 'No need for such niceties around here, we're not overlooked.'

**

Daniel Perry walked out into the hall where the video unit in Carol Walters's flat was hooked on a wall. He talked briefly to the caller before pressing the 'Open' button, and stood waiting while someone walked up the stairs.

A young guy came into the flat, early thirties, handsome in a rough way, wearing a polo shirt, chinos and a light jacket. Perry hugged him like a long-lost relative.

'How are you doing, Alex?' Perry said. 'Thanks for coming.'

'No problem. I was just having a few drinks with a couple of mates in Crawley.'

'Good. She's in there,' he said jerking a thumb towards Walters. He lowered his voice but she could still make out what they were saying. 'Look after her until you get my call and then get rid of her.'

'But she's a cop.'

'So what? You know the score, Alex, these are tough times, we need to make tough choices.'

'Yeah, you're right. Why not now?'

'I need her for insurance, in case her boss refuses

to cooperate.'

'Got it. I've to wait for your call. When should I expect to hear from you, approx?'

'Let me think. Late tomorrow afternoon should do it. Sound ok to you?'

'Count on it.'

'Good man,' Perry said, clapping him on the back. 'Got to go and catch some transport to Scotland. See you later, Alex.'

The door slammed, Perry exited and Alex walked into the room.

'Christ,' he said looking at her for the first time, 'he's made a bloody mess of you.'

She was about to say, 'I'll live,' but thought better of it and said nothing.

'You shouldn't have held out. You should just have given him what he wanted at the start and saved all the aggravation. He always gets what he wants.'

'Hindsight's a wonderful thing.'

'I suppose you're right. Now what am I going to do with you? I'm here all night and most of tomorrow, I reckon.'

'Let me go.'

'Ha, I couldn't do that. You wouldn't want to put me in your shoes, would you?'

'Chance would be a fine thing.'

He pulled out a gun from the back of his waistband and pointed it at her. 'Into the bedroom.'

She laboriously got up, her hand brushing against the knife in her trouser pocket. No way would she let him have his way with her. As soon as the opportunity presented itself, she would reach for it and even though he was armed, she would take her chance and make it count.

'On the bed, flat on your back.'

She did as she was told. He walked around the bed and fiddled with his clothing, mercifully not unbuttoning his trousers but trying to remove a rope from his jacket. He reached out and grabbed her wrist in a tight grip and quickly wrapped a section of rope around it before securing it to the metal headboard.

He walked around to the other side of the bed and did the same to her right wrist. When he'd finished, she steeled herself to kick him with all her might if he reached for her trouser buttons, but instead, he grabbed her ankle. Taken by surprise, her first instinct was to pull away.

'Don't even think about trying to kick me or I'll shoot you, contrary to my boss's instructions. If you did manage to do something, and say you knocked me out, you'd never get out of this place. How are you going to get off the bed with both hands tied? Think on sister, behave if you don't want to starve to death.'

He pulled her leg and tied one ankle and then did the same with the other. He could try and rape her, helpless as she was, but it would be much more difficult now as he would need to cut her trousers off. If that didn't serve to curb a rapist's ardour, she didn't know what would.

'If you start shouting or bang the bed against the wall or something, I'll tie the ropes tighter and stick this rag in your mouth. You don't want me to that, do you?'

She shook her head.

'I thought not. Right, catch you later. Don't do anything I wouldn't.'

'Fat chance.'

He made to walk out when she called him back.

'What if I need to go to the loo?'

He laughed. 'It's your bed, sister, piss in it all you like.'

# THIRTY-EIGHT

Henderson woke early as he often did, and seeing Rachel still in a deep slumber, headed downstairs. It was a few minutes before seven, and looking out of the window while filling the kettle, he imagined he was the only one awake, but he could see Donnie with his collie, Jet, herding a small herd of cows in for milking.

He had spotted a bottle of milk in the fridge when they first arrived, in what didn't look like a shop-bought container. He now knew Donnie had put it there and according to an information sheet left on the kitchen table, a fresh pint would be delivered every day. He looked forward to pouring it over his bowl of granola later, or perhaps now he was in Scotland, porridge.

There were maps in the house, better than the ones they'd brought with them. He pulled them all out, selected one and spread it out over the kitchen table. This area, like much of the West Coast of Scotland, was a hill walker's dream with dozens or even hundreds of places to explore. Yesterday, the day after they arrived, they'd gone to Ardnamurchan Lighthouse and afterwards walked along the fine, white sands of Sanna Bay, Rachel amazed at the amount of driftwood and flotsam thrown in by the strong Atlantic tide. Today would be their first serious hill walk.

By the time Rachel surfaced, he'd narrowed today's walk down to a shortlist of three, and as it was her holiday too, she could have her choice. After he poured her a cup of tea, they both sat down and she began to look at his suggestions.

'First off,' he said, 'we could tackle the hill above the Ferry Stores. It leads into a volcano-like crater and at one end we'll see the remains of a crashed German bomber from World War Two, according to Donnie. It's a short walk and I suggest we carry on a bit further over the tops of the hills where we should get a good view of the lighthouse and out to some of the islands.'

'Ok, sounds promising. What's number two on your list?'

'We climb the hill you can see behind the cottage, called Glasbhein. At the top, we'll get great views of this whole area down there,' he said pointing out the window at the front of the house, 'towards Mull and down the Sound of Mull, eventually to Oban. When we're up there, we can walk for miles into the hills if we've a mind to. We should see deer, pine martins, foxes; you name it.'

'An equally interesting option. We're spoiled for choice around here. What's the third?'

'Route number three is we climb the mountain you can see out the window to our left, the one we noticed on the way here called Ben Hiant. It's about two thousand feet high, and as I understand it, we'll be walking not climbing. We should see buzzards and maybe a Golden Eagle. So, what's your choice?'

'I think number three sounds the best bet. I've

never seen a Golden Eagle in the wild.'

'Donnie says it's not definite we'll see one, but we might be lucky.'

'Great, that's settled. Hang on though, it sounds like we'll be doing a lot of walking, but we didn't buy anything for a packed lunch when we were in the shop yesterday. We'll need some sustenance if we're out in the hills all day. You know what you're like, twenty minutes in and you're looking for something to eat.'

'You're right. Give me a list of what you want and I'll nip down to the Ferry Stores and buy it.'

'While you're doing that I can crack on and make a hearty breakfast. What do you fancy: bacon, eggs, and some of that black pudding the woman in the shop said was delicious?'

'I'll have the lot; I'll look forward to it after my walk. See you later.'

**

The plan forming in Carol Walters's head before she fell asleep was still fresh in her mind; today was decision day, double or twist. She had to try and force her way out of captivity or die in the attempt. Not only did she not want to be around when Daniel Perry phoned Alex and told him he no longer needed her, Henderson was in real danger and she had to warn him.

Yesterday was her first full day in captivity. Alex periodically let her loose from her bindings, allowing her to go to the loo and have something to eat, but at all other times he trussed her up to the bed. It was bloody uncomfortable as she couldn't scratch an itch, go to the toilet when she wanted, and the tight bindings were playing merry hell with her circulation.

He spent all day watching television or talking to fellow criminals on the phone. On occasion, he would leave the apartment and she dreaded to think what he told neighbours if he bumped into them. She had heard of the Stockholm Syndrome, when kidnapped victims gradually sided with their kidnapper, and in some cases, eventually joined their gangs. With confidence, she thought it wouldn't happen here.

One conversation made her smile. She knew now Alex and a bloke called Steve were the people who tried to hijack David Frankland from hospital. Steve was now on the run to Spain, fearing the wrath of Perry while Alex stayed put to tough it out, having less to fear as Perry was his uncle. On the phone, Steve was pleading with Alex to speak to Perry as he wanted to come home, but Alex was telling him it was too early and to stay put. At one time, he quoted the phrase Perry said when referring to her: 'These are tough times, Steve, we need to make tough choices.'

Like all good foot soldiers doing a repetitive task, Alex was starting to get sloppy. She could see gaps opening up in the way he treated her, and in one lapsed moment, her chance would present itself, but could she take advantage of it? Ordinarily, the answer would be 'yes' as she was resilient and tenacious but after being beaten and tied up for such a long time, it would take a while for her muscles and joints to get back to full capacity and she worried something would fail right at the crucial moment.

She whiled away her time thinking about the case, piecing together everything said by Daniel Perry and adding bits of information offered by Alex, often at his most talkative when she was on the loo. He had the decency to push the door over but he said he would come in if he heard sounds not consistent with toilet duties.

She was certain now that Perry and a Russian bloke called Hal, now in Met Police custody, killed Jim Bennett and his son Kenny. It seemed Perry considered them responsible for a number of failings, from the botched murder of Chris Fletcher, to the photographs Harvey Miller took inside the Uckfield warehouse.

Alex told her that Perry now recognised the murder of Chris Fletcher was the trigger that brought his lucrative wine-faking operation to a halt, as DI Henderson would never have taken an interest in the case without it. Perhaps Perry expected Bennett to abduct Chris in France and bury his body in woods where it would never be found. Whatever their failings, Jim Bennett and his son could now be taken off Interpol's hunted list.

Walters was surprised no one from the office had tried to contact her. It was now Wednesday and she had been tied up since Monday night, so she'd missed a full day in the office without telling anyone where she was; a big no-no in their line of work. Detectives often disappeared unexpectedly to speak to narks or watch the movements of a suspect, but they were required to tell someone. It didn't need to be the exact location or the name of the person they were seeing, but enough information to call in back-up if the operation went pear-shaped.

If Alex was smart, he wouldn't try to kill her in her apartment. He'd been here a day and a half and a casual wipe down with an old hanky would not erase his prints as he'd been in every room and touched just about every surface. In all likelihood he would take her out to his car under the cover of darkness and off to Beachy Head or any number of wooded areas in Sussex. If this was his plan, it would present her with the best opportunity to overpower him. She needed to be ready.

To make sure she didn't struggle, he might drug her and take her out to his car rolled up inside an old carpet or wrapped in a sheet. If that seemed too much like hard work, he could kill her here and set fire to the place, a reasonably effective method of covering up his presence, but bad news for her neighbours. Mrs Severs, in the flat below, was disabled with MS and moved around with the use of two sticks. In the floor above in a flat bought for him by his father, Henry James was a regular drug user and at most times of the day was out of his head. Alex didn't come across as the smartest sailor on the ship, but in selecting the most judicious method to do the dirty deed, she was sure he was top drawer.

Her morbid musings came to halt when she heard the front door opening and the sound of Alex dumping his purchases in the kitchen. He was on the plump side and obviously didn't like anything in her cupboards, because the first chance he had, yesterday morning, he nipped out to a supermarket and stocked up on his favourites.

He was whistling his favourite song, *Kiss it Better* by Rihanna, a tune she used to like, but he whistled it all the time and forever it would remind her of this. What he did now was make himself a brew of something, and wander into the living room and play on his laptop and soon she would hear the tap-tap of his fingers on the keys. Sometime later, he would remember about his captive and let her loose for her first ablutions of the day, and allow her to have something to eat, before tying her up until late in the afternoon.

She dozed for a spell, when she heard him enter the room.

'Morning Carol, how are we today?' he said.

'Why are you so chirpy, did your Lotto numbers come up or something?'

'That would be amazing if they did, as I don't do it. No, this is the day.'

'Eh? Oh, I see.'

'Yeah, today is the day my boss does what he went to Scotland for. When the job's done, I'm out of here. It's not a bad place to be, your little flat, but it's not a patch on mine.'

Yesterday, she plotted Perry's route north in her head. She didn't know if he could catch a direct flight to Fort William, but if not, he would've flown to Glasgow the previous morning. Then, in a hired car, he would drive to Kilchoan which she knew was somewhere west of Fort William, arriving late afternoon.

After locating the house where Henderson and his

girlfriend were staying, he would spend time reconnoitring the site. Alex didn't receive a phone call from Perry last night, so he didn't confront the DI yesterday, but by the whistle in Alex's pipe and her own estimates, everything was due to happen today. She then realised Perry would try to make contact with Henderson this morning and felt a wave of panic; she couldn't wait until nightfall to warn him. If she was going to something, she had to do it now.

# THIRTY-NINE

Donnie McLean, the owner of Bay Cottage, had left a couple of mountain bikes in a shed for visitors to use, but Henderson hadn't ridden a bike in years, impossible even to own one when living in a top-floor flat in Seven Dials. When he lived in Glasgow and was still married to Laura, they often went out cycling, and when his two children, Hannah and Lewis were old enough, with them too. When they could ride longer distances, they would take their bikes to Loch Lomond and the Trossachs, careering down forest tracks in the Queen Elizabeth Forest Park, or marvelling at the mirrored sheen on Loch Katrine when the wind dropped.

Not willing to risk the ignominy of falling off at his first attempt, he walked to the shop. It was a cloudy, overcast day, ideal for hill walking as it was warm without being too hot, and dry without the threat of rain. Kilchoan was a well spread-out village, probably only a couple of hundred inhabitants, but it would take hours to walk the three roads that the houses were scattered over.

Village amenities consisted of one pub, part of the village's only hotel, The Kilchoan Hotel; Ferry Stores, which was not only a general supplies and a grocery shop, but a petrol station too; a village hall; a pier and two churches. To him, there didn't seem to be much difference between The Free Church of Scotland and the Parish Church, but living in multi-racial Brighton had taught him to be more tolerant of different beliefs.

The last time he was in Kilchoan was with Laura and the kids, and they took the ferry from Mingary Pier across Loch Sunart to the picturesque town of Tobermory on the island of Mull. Even though Hannah and Lewis were beyond the reach of children's television, and now more interested in music videos than Peppa Pig, they were thrilled to be in the same place where one of their favourite childhood television programmes, *Balamory,* had been filmed.

In the Ferry Stores, he soon found everything on Rachel's list but had to wait to pay while old Mrs McPherson gave the shop assistant a blow-by-blow account of a recent visit to the Isle of Lewis. He was tempted to tap her on the shoulder and suggest she start a blog where she could post all the details of her trip and save her telling everyone the same long story. In response, she would probably say it was too late for her to learn anything about computers and tell him to be more patient.

He walked outside and bumped into Donnie's wife, Ellen. He'd chatted to her once before and knew she didn't come from the area. Not only did she speak with a Geordie accent, tempered by seven years in the Highlands, she didn't have the ruddy, country complexion of many of the local girls and looked pale, as if she didn't get out much or she suffered from anaemia. He'd found a leaflet in the house with pictures of the beautiful range of pottery that Ellen made and sold on the web, and her pallid skin was more likely due to spending too much time in her studio.

'Are you and Rachel settling into the cottage, Angus?'

'Yes we are. We've got everything we need.'

'If you don't have it or you've forgotten something, you can always get it here, from lights bulbs to bottles of Calor gas as the locals say. Donnie tells me you're both keen hill walkers. If you are, you're spoiled for choice around here.'

'So I'm beginning to realise. Today, we've decided to tackle Ben Hiant.'

'Good luck with that, it's a long climb. I did it last summer with a crowd of girls from the village to raise money for a new kitchen in the village hall, and my legs hurt for days afterwards. It shouldn't trouble you two though, you both look fitter than me.'

'I'm not so sure, not if you're walking down to the shop every day.'

'I sometimes take the car, but don't tell Donnie. I don't know if he told you, but it's easier to approach your climb of Ben Hiant from Camas Nan Geall.'

'Where's that?'

'You might remember when you were driving here, about ten miles back there's a long stretch of road where it seems to have been cut out of the rock. You can see a beach far down below and there's often a herd of Highland Cattle grazing near the shoreline.'

He smiled at the memory 'I know it. Rachel kept

telling me to slow down and keep my eyes on the road and not the scenery.'

'Ha. Go back there and you'll find a place to park on the Glenborrodale side. It's a short distance to the mountain from there and it'll save you the long trek over moorland that you'd need to do if you approach it from the Kilchoan side.'

'Thanks Ellen. It's good to get the benefit of some local knowledge.'

'Even if I'm not one myself.'

'Don't you qualify by being resident for as long as you have?'

'Only if I was born here and my father and mother had been as well.'

'I've heard a few non-local voices around the place so I guess you're not the only incomer here.'

'True enough, and places like this do need an injection of new blood now and again to keep them alive or they grow stale. I just wish they wouldn't keep reminding me of it, you know, 'maybe that's how they do it in Newcastle', or 'but you're from England, aren't you?' whenever they see my knitting or baking.'

Henderson laughed.

'Oh, I can talk when I get going, can't I? I mustn't hold you back, Angus, you'll want to make the most of the fine weather. Donnie or myself will be around for the morning, so if you need any more information before you set out, you just need to ask.'

'I will, Ellen. Thanks again for your advice. Bye.'

Henderson headed back to Bay Cottage. He was thankful he didn't know anyone else in the village as he passed a few locals on the way back and if he stopped to speak to them all, he wouldn't reach the house by lunchtime. He walked up the drive towards the house and saw Donnie doing something out in the field and gave him a wave.

Henderson pushed open the door and closed it. 'I'm back,' he shouted as he walked into the kitchen. He deposited the bag of groceries on the table and wandered off in search of Rachel.

He found her in the lounge. Daniel Perry was by her side, a gun pointing at her head.

**

She massaged her wrists and ankles and slowly forced herself awake. Alex was there on the other side of the bed, watching. He liked to keep a safe distance between them to allow enough time and space to draw his weapon. Sleepily Carol Walters walked into the bathroom, pushed the door closed and sat on the toilet. She hadn't woken up desperate for the loo, even though it was after eleven o'clock, because she wasn't drinking as much coffee as she did at work, and didn't have the usual glass of white wine in the evening. Nevertheless, it was a welcome break from lying being tied to the bed.

'Brighton's such a great place to live,' he said, trying to drown out her tinkling. 'There's local shops to buy whatever you need and loads of young mothers walking around to say hello to. If I lived here I would...'

She tuned out and loosened the button on the pocket shielding the knife to check it. She did this whenever she was set loose but couldn't yet find the chance to use it, Alex was being too careful. She turned on the tap and washed her hands and face, and stood looking at the reflection in the mirror. Her complexion had taken on a pasty appearance, lack of sunlight and eating whatever junk food Alex decided to buy.

Reluctantly she walked out of the bathroom as she liked its coolness and perfumed smells, unlike the sweaty pall of her bedroom, and longed for a long soak in the bath. She was moving towards the kitchen to fix some breakfast when the brmm-brmm, brmm-brmm of the video entry phone sounded.

It was directly behind her in the hall and as she turned to look, Alex did the same. She reached down for the knife and before he turned back, swung her arm around in a smooth arc and plunged the blade deep into his belly, up to the handle. Shock creased his face and two hands shot down to cover the wound. She pulled out the knife with one hand and with the other, whipped the gun out from the back of his trousers.

He collapsed, blood leaking out over the beautiful parquet floor, laid only last year. Holding the weapon in two hands she covered the prostrate figure, as she glanced at the video; it was DC Sally Graham and DC Phil Bentley. She pressed the 'Talk' button. 'Guys! Up here now! We have a situation!'

She opened the door, still covering Alex with the weapon in case he was feigning, and listened for the heavy clumping of two sets of feet on the uncarpeted staircase.

Phil Bentley arrived first. 'We just came to...what the hell's going on here?'

'Phil, I'm so glad to see you. Cover him with this,' she said handing him the gun. 'Sally, call an ambulance.'

She looked around for her own phone and found it beside the television but it was switched off. She couldn't wait for it to boot up so she went back to the hall. When Sally finished talking to the ambulance controller, she took the phone from her and immediately called Henderson's mobile. To her utter dismay, it came back with the 'no service' tone.

'Is Henderson in a rural part of the Highlands? I can't get through.'

Graham gave her the look of one who knows. 'Are you getting 'no service'?'

'Yeah.'

'Most of the Highlands is rural. A lot of places don't get any mobile reception at all.'

'Damn!' She rushed back into the lounge and picked up Alex's MacBook. She ignored the porn site he had been looking at and opened Google. She then keyed in 'Fort William' and switched the screen to Google Maps.

She expanded the map to look over the Fort William area, all the way down to the sea and the west coast and began searching for a village called Kilchoan.

'Ambulance is on its way,' Sally Graham said. 'What are you looking for Sarg, and what the hell happened here?'

'I'll tell you later. I'm trying to find the village

where Henderson went. I don't where it is. He's in danger.'

'It's called Kilchoan.'

'I know that but I'm not sure how to spell it. I was trying to find it on the map first.'

'I know how to spell it; K-i-l-c-h-o-a-n. He told me all about it, said it's a great place for seeing Golden Eagles.'

She went back to Google and keyed in the name of the village and after some searching found a phone number for the village shop.

She reached for DC Graham's phone and dialled the number on the laptop screen.

'I can hear sirens,' Graham said. 'I better go outside and direct the ambulance.'

'Hello, this is Ferry Stores, Fiona speaking. How can I help you?'

'Hello Fiona, this is Detective Sergeant Walters from the Major Crime Team at Surrey and Sussex Police.'

'How exciting. How can I help you?'

'This is a long shot, now I think of it, but I'm looking for my boss. His name is Angus Henderson and he's been staying in your village for the last few days.'

'Let me ask.'

She heard voices and a loud shriek of laughter.

'Hello Sergeant Walters. Old Mrs Geddes, who is 87, said isn't he the tall and very handsome man who's here with his girlfriend to do a bit of hill walking?'

'Yes, it sounds like him.'

'They are staying at a place called Bay Cottage if

that's any help.'

'It is, I assure you. Do you have their telephone number?'

'But of course.'

Walters dialled the number and a gruff Highland voice came on the line. She introduced herself as she had done to Fiona in Ferry Stores. The voice on the other end of the line said his name was Donnie McLean, owner of Bay Cottage.

'Mr McLean, please listen carefully. Your tenant, Detective Inspector Angus Henderson is in serious danger. A gangster called Daniel Perry is close by and he is there to kill him. If you see no suspicious activity or people around Henderson's house, go over there and tell him what I have just told you; I will alert the local police. If you see suspicious activity, stay indoors, lock your doors and wait for the police to arrive. On no account must anyone approach this man. He is armed and extremely dangerous.'

# FORTY

'What the hell are you doing here, Perry?' Henderson said.

'Nice to see you too, Inspector. Quit pissing about. Get in here and sit down.'

Henderson walked in and took a seat on the settee beside Rachel who immediately grabbed his hand and held it tight. 'Who is this man?' she hissed. 'What does he want?'

She was scared but not turning to jelly as many other people who found themselves in this situation would be. Good. If they were to get out of this unscathed, they both needed clear heads.

'This is a nice place,' Perry said, 'very rustic.'

'What do you want Perry?'

'Thought I'd look you up, Henderson. See how you were enjoying your holiday in this beautiful part of Scotland.'

'I was enjoying it fine until you came along.'

'Tsk, tsk, tetchy ain't he? Now listen up both of you. I'm here because you, Mr Police Inspector, put a stop on my money. To be more precise, the money the late Fraser Brook stole and squirrelled away in a Swiss bank account.'

'You seem very well informed. Did Brook tell you this? Did you force it out of him before you killed him?'

Perry got up, turned a simple wooden chair around to face them and sat down, leaning on the back. 'I didn't need to torture him. He told me all I needed to know.'

Perry was no longer wearing the snappy suit and shiny shoes, although the bouffant of thick, grey hair was much in evidence. For his foray into the Highlands, Perry wore jeans, walking boots and a North Face sweatshirt and looked like any other tourist here to walk the glens and see the sights. His beard hid part of his face but not the cold stare of his eyes.

'What do you want the money for, you must be rolling in the stuff? The wine-faking operation went on for years and must have made you millions.'

'You're missing the point. Those bastards stole from me and I want it back. If someone steals from me, I make sure they pay me back, in spades.'

'Is this why Landseer and Brook were both murdered?'

'What do you think?'

Henderson knew the story well enough, but he wanted to hear it direct from Perry's lips to confirm that he was as deeply involved in all the murky business dealings as Frankland and Bennett.

'I understand you've got David Frankland,' Perry said. 'How is he?'

'He's fine after his car crash, but he'll be with us for some time to come with all the charges we've got against him.'

Perry shook his head. 'No way. That lawyer of mine

is good. He'll do his homework and get him out.'

It was Henderson's turn to shake his head. 'Not with a charge of murdering Charles Landseer and Chris Fletcher against him he won't.'

Frankland hadn't been charged with Chris's murder, only Charles Landseer's, but they'd got enough evidence to hang a conspiracy charge around his neck. If Frankland didn't kill Chris with Jim Bennett standing beside him, he knew all about it.

'Don't be fucking dense,' Perry shouted. 'It was nothing to do with him. It was that prick Bennett and his stupid son. It was Bennett's idea and he cocked it up. He said he made it look like suicide, but he should have picked him up in France like I told him to. David didn't do a bloody thing.'

'Where is he now, Jim Bennett? He wasn't back at the parcel business the last time we checked. Is he one of yours as well as Fraser Brook?'

'With David inside, someone has to tidy up the loose ends.'

'What did you do–'

'I could chat to you about this all day, but enough of your questions, Henderson, I'm here for my money not a bloody confessional. What I want you to do, is make a call and undo whatever court order or what the hell you set up to hold on to my money. Then, with this,' he said pointing at the laptop beside him, 'I'll get back what's rightfully mine and then I'll leave you two lovers in peace.'

'I can't do it, I don't have the authority.'

'You put it on, you can take it off.'

'I didn't.'

'Don't lie to me Henderson, Detective Sergeant Carol Walters told me all about it.'

'What...Walters? How?'

Perry fished out his phone. He looked through it for something and when he found it, held it out for him to see. The bloody and battered face of Carol Walters looked back at him.

'What the hell, Perry? What have you done with her?'

'She's in a safe place where your pals won't find her, but she won't be safe much longer if you don't do what I ask. One phone call from me and she's toast.'

Safe place, what rubbish. The picture was of Walters's flat in Queen's Park, he recognised the black and white settee. He'd sat on it enough times waiting for her to get ready. She looked battered but alive, although he had no way of knowing how old the image was. She could be dead now.

Perry took the phone back and, as he put it back into his pocket, the gun wavered and for a moment, it pointed at the wall. Henderson, his anger stoked at seeing the photograph, leapt at him. Perry reacted quicker than expected and smacked him in the face with his fist before whacking him in the side of his head with the gun.

Rachel screamed.

'Shut the fuck up, woman, he'll live. Henderson get up on your feet and pull out your phone.'

Using the chair for leverage, Henderson stood and reached for his phone. His head hurt like hell and the room looked hazy.

'Call your office. Feel free to tell them you've got a

gun pointing at your head as the nearest cops are at least an hour away; I checked. When I pass your colleague's little panda car on the road on my way back to civilisation, I'll give him a friendly wave.'

Perry was right. The nearest cop was based in Strontian police station, only thirty miles away but over an hour on slow, single track roads. While many of the residents of Kilchoan owned a shotgun, and perhaps a rifle for shooting deer, the local bobby would be unarmed.

Henderson nursed his injured jaw; it didn't feel broken. Such irony if Perry had broken his jaw and he couldn't speak. His first instinct was to tell Perry to go to hell, but at the end of the day, it was only money, a replaceable commodity against the lives of Rachel and himself, and now added to that list, Carol.

'I'll do it.'

'Good, I knew you would see sense.'

Henderson looked at his phone. 'There's no signal in here due to the thick stone walls, I'll need to move outside.'

'Fine. You first, Henderson. Me and your missus will follow behind. No fancy tricks, or I'll shoot her. You know I will. If that doesn't convince you, if you do something stupid and anything happens to me, Walters will get it.'

'You've thought of everything, Perry.'

'I try to.'

Henderson reached for the handle of the front door.

'No way I'm falling for that one, Henderson. We'll go out the back door. I've taken a good look around this place and no one will see us out back.'

Henderson walked into the kitchen, Rachel then Perry walking closely behind.

'Put down the gun!' shouted an unfamiliar voice.

Henderson turned. Christ! Donnie McLean was standing at the end of the kitchen table, a single barrelled shotgun in his hand. The barrel was held in a steady grip with no sign of waver.

Henderson turned to look at Perry. He spotted a twitch in his gun hand and could see a steely, cold look in his eye.

'Shoot him, Donnie, shoot him!' Henderson shouted as he pulled Rachel towards him.

The deafening boom of the shotgun and the sharp crack of Perry's handgun filled the air. Almost simultaneously, Rachel collapsed limply into his arms.

# FORTY-ONE

The King Air 200c helicopter rose with a thunderous roar that shook the windows of Bay Cottage and set Jet the collie off into a barking frenzy. Inside the fast moving machine, medics were frantically trying to keep Daniel Perry alive on the thirty-plus minute journey to Glasgow, where he was due to be treated by a Trauma Team at The Queen Elizabeth University Hospital. The prognosis wasn't good as he'd lost too much blood while waiting for the arrival of help, much of it on the kitchen floor of Bay Cottage and left in situ for crime scene detectives to mull over.

'Coffee, Angus.'

It wasn't a question, as when he opened his eyes, Rachel was handing a steaming mug to him. Her hand shook with the vigour of a Parkinson's sufferer but no bloody wonder. She placed it on the small table beside him and as she bent down, he leaned over and kissed her.

'Donnie's got the water back on, has he?'

'No,' she said. 'Ach, how can you joke at a time like this? I made these in their house, well Ellen did. You told Donnie that no one was to go into our kitchen until we got the all-clear from the police.'

'That's right, so I did.'

'Before anyone goes back in there, someone will

need to mop and disinfect the floor and the cupboards first. There's so much blood, it's like the set for the Texas Chain Saw Massacre.'

'Don't worry, it won't be you. When we get the all-clear, we're moving to the Kilchoan Hotel for the night and then we'll drive back to Fort William in the morning. Donnie's sorted everything out.'

'That's a relief. I don't think I can go back into the cottage again.'

She sat down on the seat beside him. He put his arm around her shoulders and she leaned back and closed her eyes, allowing the warm afternoon sun to play on her face. They were sitting on a bench outside the kitchen window of Bay Cottage. It was beautiful view from a vantage point at the top of the steep driveway, where at the moment, a ferry was slowly making its way up Loch Sunart on a journey back to Oban from the Outer Hebrides.

'Donnie's patched up the bullet hole for now to stop the place flooding,' she said. 'He'll fit a replacement pipe when he can pick one up from some guy in the village.'

'We were lucky Perry's bullet went into a water pipe and not into you or me, but it was close.'

'I don't know how I could cope with being in a wheelchair.'

He squeezed her tighter. 'Let's not go there. Look forward not back. It's the best way to handle situations like this.'

'Will anything happen to Donnie? Will he face trial or go to prison?'

'Unfortunately, it's not up to me, but the

Procurator Fiscal in Fort William who will decide if he has a case to answer. In my opinion, it will almost certainly be 'no' as Donnie acted in self defence against a dangerous man, armed with a gun. With you and I as witnesses, I think there's no way he'll be prosecuted.'

'When will we find out for sure?'

He shrugged his shoulders. 'Detectives are on their way from Inverness, but who knows when they'll get here.' He slumped down in the seat and pulled his hat lower over his eyes. 'Everything moves at a slower pace around here, Rachel. You should know that by now.'

# About the Author

Iain Cameron was born in Glasgow and moved to Brighton in the early eighties. He has worked as a management accountant, business consultant and a nursery goods retailer. He is now a full-time writer and lives in a village outside Horsham in West Sussex with his wife, two daughters and a lively Collie dog.

Red, Red Wine is the fifth book to feature DI Angus Henderson, the Scottish cop at Sussex Police.

For more information about books and the author:
Visit the website at: www.iain-cameron.com
Follow him on Twitter: @IainsBooks
Follow him on Facebook: @IaincameronAuthor

# By Iain Cameron

*One Last Lesson*
*Driving into Darkness*
*Fear the Silence*
*Hunting for Crows*
*Red Red Wine*

*All books are available from Amazon*

Printed in Great Britain
by Amazon